# Charleston

# Tides

BOOK THREE, TORN ASUNDER SERIES

## TARA COWAN

*Charleston Tides*

Copyright © 2020 by Tara Cowan

ISBN-13: 978-1-7332922-4-5 (paperback)

ISBN-13: 978-1-7332922-5-2 (ebook)

Book cover and interior design by TeaBerryCreative.com

CHARLESTON, SOUTH CAROLINA

# Chapter One

October in Charleston was not as crisp and colorful as it was in the mountains of North Carolina where Adeline Miller-Ravenel had grown up. The city instead retained the charm of summer long past the change of seasons. But there was a slight relief from the heat, thank heavens. Tourism was down, too, so it made it easier to move and do things in the city—not that Adeline ever got out.

The completion date for the Ravenel-Thompson House project was closing in fast. With renovations complete for the house's red bedroom, Adeline moved onto the next, which happened to be Jude's room. She asked the crew to move the storage boxes out of the room that would be the nursery for the newest Ravenel. Then she paid the cleaning service extra to clean it from top to bottom and moved Jude's things into the nursery temporarily while she worked. She'd discussed the transition with Adrian first, worrying it would upset Jude's routine with school back in session. But the little guy seemed to take the renovations in his stride.

Adeline had read old letters in which Ravenels past had discussed painting a room in the house a dark green. Adeline decided to incorporate that color in Jude's room, a decision of which he approved. The crew set to work on the almost one-foot-high baseboards first. They sanded them, restored any problem areas, painted the wood a pristine white, and aired the room before Adeline came in to start on her part. The doors for this house, with magnificent panels and original hardware, were one of its best features. Each knob alone took a half day to restore. This was where she started.

As Adeline stood in Jude's room next to the fantastic window which overlooked The Battery, she wondered whose room this would've been during their target era. She had speculated before that it was Frederick Ravenel's. She turned, looking at the coal-burning fireplace, and pictured an enslaved person stoking it before Mrs. Frederick Ravenel even awoke. A disturbing image. It was easy to forget at this distance, surrounded by such beauty, but slavery had been a reality in this house.

She conjured a vision of the past, closing her eyes. Real history had happened here, right where she stood. There had been hoop skirts here, probably babies had been born here, and people had died here. People had been held in bondage here. And someone had left a necklace across the hall for safe-keeping, and another just like it out on Santarella Island. Was it strange that it sometimes felt like all of it, all of *them*, were rather closer than a glance at history's timeline would indicate? Adeline had always felt connected to the past, to those who had gone before, and she felt it strongly in this room.

She turned around in the room, her TOMS discordant against the, admittedly battered, original floors. The old boards would take probably two weeks and several thousand dollars to restore. Was it worth it? That was Adrian's call, luckily, and not hers. She would drop the money in a heartbeat.

Adeline headed down to talk to Adrian around 7:30 that night. She looked cute, if she did say so, in a black swing dress, black tights, and booties.

She turned the corner to pass through the living room when she heard Jude crying in the kitchen. He seemed to be having a meltdown while Adrian helped him with his homework. The poor kid grew more and more upset by the moment. Adeline stopped in the hall, wincing, feeling for them both. Jude was exhausted and readjusting to his school schedule. He had been assigned, it seemed to her, a lot of homework for such a little guy. But she, admittedly, knew little about it.

He was pretty much throwing a fit. This was normal, she knew, for most six-year-olds, but not for Jude. At least, not in her experience; Adrian didn't seem to be too shocked. The more hysterical Jude got, the softer Adrian spoke until she could barely hear his quiet voice. At some point, Jude began to feel foolish for his volume and toned it back until he was just whimpering softly. In ten more minutes, Jude was pretty much calmed and leaving the kitchen tasked with preparing for his shower.

Adeline waited another minute before going into the kitchen. Adrian glanced up from the table with a long-suffering look. "I guess you heard that," he said, sighing. He looked extremely tired. He was, she noticed as she neared, circling correct numbers and filling in blanks in a passable impression of Jude's hand. Her eyes twinkled because he was usually one to stick with all the rules. Occasionally, though, some battles just weren't worth fighting.

"Yeah. Poor little guy. You're great with him, though," she said, putting her hands on the back of a chair.

Adrian finished one worksheet and flipped to the next. "He's worn out."

Adeline winced. "Do you think he's not sleeping well in the other room?"

He looked up. "No, he's sleeping fine. I check on him. It's just school starting back."

"And changes?" she suggested.

He held her eyes for a second before going back to the worksheets, finishing them soon and putting them in a folder in Jude's blue backpack. He got up and went to the sink to wash his hands. "Want tea or something?" he asked.

She followed him over there. As she lay her hands on the tall counter, her ring caught the light, distracting her, as it always did. "Um, yeah, that would be good!"

He got two glasses and went to the fridge. When he handed hers over, he looked at her as if actually seeing her for the first time that night. "You look pretty," he said.

She smiled. "Thanks. I'm going to be needing lots of compliments to keep up my body image."

He smiled. "You look great."

"Thanks," she said again, suddenly unable to make eye contact, as if a cute guy had complimented her at the lockers. She needed to pull it together. She tucked a curl behind her ear. "Um, so I was thinking maybe we could talk about the flooring in Jude's room. You need to make the call whether to restore it or put down a passable imitation."

"How much?" he asked, knowing the game by now.

She told him, hoping her face didn't show how much she wanted to restore the old flooring. She didn't want the fact that she was his wife to influence this renovation. They might not have begun their marriage in usual circumstances, but the relationship could still complicate things. "That's fine, Adeline. I knew it wouldn't be cheap."

But she worried about the money for his sake. As far as she had tallied, they'd spent about three times her annual earnings to date. He had a good job. She didn't know what he made, and it was likely a lot. But...

"Don't worry about the money, Adeline," he said. "I saved a long time for this."

She looked up, meeting his eyes. "Yeah, but..." She never would've questioned it before they were married, before her life had taken this crazy turn and forever linked their paths. She needed to be professional, treat this like any other job, and get super excited when the owner gave her the thumbs up. "You have a lot of other expenses; Jude is clearly going to Yale…"

He hesitated, eyes holding hers in that disconcerting way. "Don't worry about Jude," he said. He crossed his arms, shifting before clearing his throat. After a long pause, he said, "Not that it was the only cause by any means, but the brakes malfunctioned on Lauren's car. We settled out of court. I collected the settlement on Jude's behalf, so it's his. It was a lot, since it was for his injuries and her death."

"Oh," Adeline said. "Well, that's only fair, I think. It's not as though any amount of money could repay what the two of you lost that day."

He wasn't making eye contact. He was silent for a moment. "Well, like I said, it wasn't the only cause."

Adeline didn't know what to say or how to touch that kind of anger. He looked up at her, seeming to come back to the present. She took a step forward, holding his eyes, and got close, tentatively laying her hand on his chest. She wanted to soothe away the cloud from his expression, yes, but she also liked him near. He touched her waist. "Can I lift some of my hands-off policy?" she whispered. "I mean, I don't want you not to…you know… And really—"

His lips were on hers before she could even finish the thought. He pulled back slightly. "Is that—"

"Yeah, that's fine," she assured him, getting closer, bringing him back to her.

His hand slid down her back to bring her closer, his kiss all-encompassing. What was that line from *Gone with the Wind*?

"*The sinking, the yielding, the surging tide of warmth that left her limp. And the quiet face of Ashley Wilkes was blurred and drowned to nothingness.*" She'd always loved that line, and it was applicable here. It wasn't like any other man would ever measure up. She wasn't sure about anything else in this relationship, but she knew she wanted Adrian like she wanted her next breath.

"Adrian," she breathed.

His hand came up to touch her face and then to cup her neck. She was pretty sure her hair was a mess by now. It was almost as though he would break away, but then he brought her back, hungrier than ever. She was pretty much attacking him at this point. However, she knocked something off the counter, the clatter making them jolt.

He broke off, breathing heavily, looking at the floor where her nearly-empty cup lay. "Glad that wasn't glass," he whispered as he rested his forehead against hers.

She laughed softly, liking his casual touch, his nearness. She flickered her eyes up to him. Poor man. He was starved. She wondered if he could actually hear her traitorous heart, which wouldn't listen to her brain. Oh, gosh, she shouldn't have done that. She should have kept that boundary up. Now her brain was in a tangle of confusion. And Adrian was going to end up a victim of insanity.

He kissed her forehead and then stepped back. And, of

course, he read all of this in her eyes. "I should go check on Jude," he said, clearing his throat.

"Yeah," she agreed, nodding. "I'll clean this up."

He bent down and picked up the cup, handing it up to her and reaching for a towel to wipe the tea. "Thanks," she said, taking the cup.

"Mm hmm," he said, leaving without another word.

# Chapter Two

There was the briefest silence, deafening. John Thomas stared in shock.

"Why?" he whispered. "I thought..."

Shannon stood across from him in his quarters, in the very same room with him. He blinked as he tried to comprehend that fact, as he tried to grasp what she had said. His every nerve stirred to life from her nearness. *"Will you have me back for your wife?"*

He took her in as his blood whirled and his ears hummed. She stood here in the flesh. Shannon. His Shannon. Graceful form, all-seeing eyes, sloping, unusual nose. Beautiful. Exquisite.

His throat expanded and tightened. Had he spoken? He couldn't remember.

He must have. She shook her head, her face pale. "I'm sorry," she whispered. "There are no words to convey how much…" She bit her lip. She wouldn't have known that she was looking vulnerable and even beseeching. Every protective instinct within him assaulted him, but he stayed as he was.

"You want to stay?" he heard himself asking as though from afar.

She looked frightened but brave. *Ah, Shannon!* His heart leapt in recognition as though it had remembered an old acquaintance. He clenched his jaw tightly.

"If you will have me," she whispered.

He blinked, recovering from his stupor but still shaken. Then he nodded as he held her eyes. "Yes," he said. "Yes."

Her lips pressed together as she looked at the floor, and she appeared possibly on the brink of collapse. Her trembling hand gripped the post nearest to her. Relief? *What is it, Shannon? Why have you come back to me?* Whatever her feelings, she did not appear to be quite steady on her feet, and heaven help him, neither was he.

She looked up again, appearing to measure whether she ought to speak. "You should know that I have fallen out with my father," she said, shoulders straight. "I am now estranged from my family."

He absorbed this news. After a moment to clear his head, he said distractedly, turning this over in his mind, "He did not wish you to return."

"He ordered me to do so."

John Thomas looked up quickly, and she rushed to say, "It was my decision to…to return." She swallowed, holding his eyes. "But as I was attempting to tell him this, he informed me that I would no longer be welcome in his home. I didn't want you to hear that and think it was the reason I have come." She shook her head. "It isn't."

He nodded once. Running his hand over his mouth, he said, "I have no wish for you to be at odds with your father. Why not let it pass?"

Her chin tilted up. "You cannot understand what it is to be a woman."

He studied her. After a beat of silence, he said softly, "No. I cannot."

A quiet grew, which neither seemed to know how to break. At length, she cleared her throat and said, not quite meeting his eyes, "You...will have heard that Marie..."

His mind cleared, earnest sadness overtaking him. "Yes," he whispered. He did not mention that when one of his fellow officers had said off-handedly that Ravenel would be out of commission for a few days, having lost his wife in childbed, he had been entirely unmanned. "I cannot imagine your grief. She was a sister to me. I hope you know that."

She nodded as her eyes filled, although tears didn't fall.

"The child as well?" he rasped. "That is what we heard."

She nodded again, her head lowered. "It was...very difficult, though I don't mean to compare our grief to Frederick's. Yet, he knew he must go on for Rose. You knew, of course, that he later married Elizabeth Middleton." She lifted her head, meeting his eyes.

He was still looking at her, not taking his eyes from her. He couldn't do so if he tried. "Yes—that is, not until the reports began to emerge from…Santarella. They called her Elizabeth Ravenel, but I knew how it must be."

His eyes flickered up to her hair, but it was concealed by her hat. Shannon met his eyes. Holding them, she put down the valise and reached up to dislodge the pin. Then she removed the hat and let him see her hair.

His lips slowly parted as he took a step forward, surveying her. He remembered the first time he had seen her long tresses, falling nearly to her waist, on their wedding night. He had watched her in the candlelight, standing transfixed, as she had unbound it. Now, the length was not much different from his own, startling proof of what she had endured. He said, "You and your sister-in-law have a claim for war crimes."

"A married woman may not bring her own case," she said.

"Her husband might."

"Yes. But who would bring mine?" she asked, folding the ribbons of her hat.

"I would."

Shannon looked up quickly. His tone had been sure, and the look in his eyes was rather deadly. She inwardly trembled, knowing that to prosecute against or sue his own military would damage him. And so, she shook her head. "No," she said softly, giving another little shake. "It is in the past."

With a beleaguered face, he took another step forward as he continued to study her. He was still looking the same as when she had walked through the door: nervous and unbelieving. He stopped just a foot from her, meeting her eyes. "What...changed?" he whispered, looking almost afraid to do ask. "You wrote...that..."

As she swallowed, she felt her throat tightening. What to say to him? What could she possibly say to convey what she truly meant? Oh good heavens, it was going to happen, just as it had the first time she had come aboard the ship a few days ago. She could feel the emotion rising, her heart pounding, her eyes flooding. She tried to speak, but tears spilled over, flowing down her cheeks like rivers. And then she was in his arms.

The solid warmth of him was her undoing. He was here. He was alive. What else could possibly matter? "Shannon," he whispered over and over with an unsteady voice. "Shannon."

She lifted her face to him, and they kissed. They grew more and more passionate, and she wondered vaguely whether the salt she tasted were only her own tears. As the intensity grew, images, long buried in a place she hadn't touched for years, returned to her. His hands glided over her skin, and his kisses seared holes into her. Would it be the same, she wondered, eyes closed as pleasure coursed through her.

He was feeling for her hooks. He had grown adept, once upon a time, at finding them. It seemed he had not forgotten: one by one they gently were undone. She found herself uncharacteristically timid. Admiral Haley was a far cry from Lieutenant Haley, and it had been so long. She was uncertain of herself, more now even than on their wedding night. She was frightened that she didn't know him, that there were boundaries she must not cross.

As her dress fell to the floor, she whispered, barely breaking the kiss, "The door."

"Yes," he whispered, reaching for the key and turning it. She could feel him trembling as she sensed his passion. Still, he was gentle and even reverent. He always had been, but never with such utter poignancy. "Shannon," he whispered again, as though the word were torn from him.

She reached for her own corset, but, looking at her, he gently took her hands and redirected them to his coat. She needed no further invitation. And when they were on the narrow bed, his body above hers, his fingers threaded through hers above her head, he halted, breaking the kiss. He whispered, "You're certain?"

"Yes," she breathed. "Yes."

# Chapter Three

John Thomas stood in the anteroom which was part of his quarters. He leaned over, fingers curled around the washstand, breathing quietly but quickly as though he had been running. Morning had come, its soft light breaking through the small window, and Shannon still slept. He could scarcely believe she was on his ship, let alone in his bed. Never in his wildest imaginings had he believed she would come back to him.

But just now he struggled to steady himself, with only one thought in his head: *love is stronger than death.* Last night had proven the truth of that declaration a hundred times over.

Shannon began to gain consciousness and was aware of an inner glow, a sated and content feeling that was scarcely remembered. Her eyes flickered open, and she saw John Thomas's mussed sheets. Her hand trailed them as she searched for him. But she shouldn't have to seek far; the bed was barely large enough for the two of them.

She turned and discovered that the other side was empty. Her eyes scanned the room almost frantically only to find that she was alone. She sat up, biting her lip. Just as she was despairing, a door she hadn't noticed the night before opened, and John Thomas stepped through. He appeared hesitant, as though unsure whether she would wish him to come to her. The buttons of his white shirt were undone at his neck. She watched him swallow and then looked back up to his eyes.

She smiled tentatively. His shoulders easing, he came forward, sitting on the bed beside her. He whispered, "Good morning." He leaned to touch his lips to hers, just a gentle press, but it was long and poignant. They stayed as they were for a long moment, his eyes closed. His thumb stroked her cheek. "I did not hurt you?" he whispered softly.

Her eyes slipped closed as they hovered, her face close to his. The thought that he still remembered her ailments warmed her from her veins to her skin. "No. I told you last night," she said sweetly, reaching up, shyly stroking a hand down his chest.

He nodded. His eyes trailed to her rusty, shorn hair. Slowly, his hand lifted to it.

She whispered, "Do you dislike it very much?"

"No," he answered, voice cracking. "It is becoming, as

you know perfectly well." There was a loving smile in his voice, and her lips lifted. His smile soon fell, though, and something dreadful took its place. "Tell me what was done to you," he said, leaning his forehead against hers briefly before looking at her again.

She drew a sustaining breath, clutching for her necklace, which wasn't there, of course. It had been lost during the fall of Santarella. She closed her eyes, remembering giving it to Phoebe to hide, remembering *Phoebe*. Gathering herself, she recited the story as briefly as possible, finding it difficult to relive the horrors. And yet, she found herself recalling details and revealing to him things she had told to no one else. He listened intently, his hand tightly clutching the sheet at intervals.

When she was finished, he sat a long while in silence. She bit her lip, hesitantly covering his hand. "We are alive."

It took him a moment to respond, but he nodded. He simply held her gaze, and she watched as anger warred with grief and anguish in his features. He seemed to remember that his sorrow was difficult for her, though. At length, a ghost of a smile appeared in his eyes, even if there was lingering pain in them. "Did you truly start ranting about Babylon and Jerusalem, and dashing infants against rocks?" he asked.

Her eyes lit. "No, *not* dashing infants against rocks," she pleaded. "I didn't know that followed, or naturally I would have chosen a different verse! And it's quite your own fault, you know. Shannon *Ravenel* never would have remembered scripture." She studied him, still smiling faintly. "How on earth did you know that?"

"I read the transcripts from the court-martial," he said. Her lips parted in surprise.

He paused. "I don't know if it was because you were my wife, or... Perhaps they knew the Copperheads would cast the war in the worst light possible if they didn't hold a trial. But eventually Captain Connor was drummed out of the Army, and..." He hesitated, seeming to gauge her preparedness. "And the other officer—a lieutenant—took his own life."

"Good heavens," she breathed. She swallowed. "Was that his name? Connor? I suppose I never imagined a man like that *had* a name."

"Shannon," he whispered, as though unable to bear it. "When I heard, I..."

"It is in the past. Finished," she said softly. She wanted to touch him, to comfort him, but something held her back. She looked down, smoothing a hand over her middle. "It is in the past."

He continued to give the appearance as though it were, to him, anything but. Yet, he said finally, nodding once, "Yes." His eyes roved her features thirstily like he had believed he would never see them again. He lifted his hand, touching her cheek as one would something precious. The silence grew and time lapsed, but he seemed unconscious of this.

"Won't you be looked for?" Shannon whispered, likewise lingering on his countenance. She had remembered the general construction of his face, of course, but she had forgotten how handsome he was. Just hearing his breathing was extraordinary. "I fear you have stayed too long with me. Won't your superiors reprimand you?"

When he didn't answer, she saw that he was flushing faintly and that there was the slightest smile in his eyes.

"Oh," she said, aghast. "You have no superiors."

"We all have superiors," he answered softly. "Of course I have superiors."

"Who, President...Johnson?" she demanded in awe.

"He is one of them, yes."

"You are famous," she added. "That is... We hear you are a much-beloved war hero."

His cheeks tinged a darker red. "I daresay the reports were exaggerated. There were many of us thrust into some degree of fame. Poor Grant—yes, there is nothing like his fame, poor man. He can scarcely stir out of doors without throngs of people rushing to greet him. My prominence is nothing to his, of course."

She searched him seriously. "Is it just as you make it seem, John Thomas? Can *you* go about as you please without being accosted by admirers?"

He didn't answer, merely looked at her reticently.

"Have you been out in society?"

"A little," he answered gently.

"Well, then?"

"There was some degree of notice," he allowed, "but while we were still at war—"

"John Thomas, if what we have heard is true, your life is forever altered," she said emphatically.

He hesitated, meeting her eyes and then looking contrite. "Shannon, I will try, with everything in my power, to ensure that you lead a life as normal as possible. That you aren't hounded or... You have already been thrust into the public eye far too much given the terrible things that happened to you in November."

She let a silence grow. "Not to mention my desertion," she whispered finally, bringing up the topic which hovered thickly. She risked looking up. "I daresay that was blazoned across every newspaper in print."

He didn't answer. He merely studied her, seemingly weighing his options, perhaps afraid to hurt her. "You can tell me," she said, lowering her head. "I...ask that you tell me."

There was a long silence during which she felt his deep study of her. Finally, she heard his voice softly, a little scratchy in the beginning, say, "At first, it was just Washington. And then... Once Memphis fell—yes. It was very much publicized." A muscle flinched in his neck; that was the only indication she had that he was in discomfort.

She shook her head, pressing her eyes shut. "I'm sorry," she said. "I cannot imagine—that is, I always knew it must have been that way, but..."

"Shannon..." He touched her face. "Do you think I cared for one moment what anyone else thought?" he asked fervently. "Or that I would willingly upset you now? I could wish them all to the devil happily—"

"What anyone else thought—no, I know you too well to believe that. But you were forced to suffer a great deal, and *I* care what *you* thought. And you *must* want an explanation."

He shook his head.

"You *must*," she demanded, eyes glistening with tears.

He turned his face away, his jaw tightening. He said nothing, and a silence developed. She sat looking at him in profile, at his unreadable countenance. Fear clutching her heart, she reached to cover his hand quickly. "I'm sorry! I didn't mean to... I oughtn't to have brought it up."

He looked back at her, his face tender and strained. He cupped her cheek. "No!" he said earnestly, eyes still roving her features in that wonder-filled way. "I am not angry." He drew a breath. "I do want an explanation," he allowed, careful not to touch her gaze. "But not now. Not after what you have been through. Nothing must be allowed to upset you," he said gently. "And discussing it can only do that."

"Oh, John Thomas," she whispered. "*You* have been through a war."

"And so have you," he responded.

She swallowed, her throat tightening. Then she lifted her head to see his blue eyes upon her. To be in proximity to him at all was disconcerting, inconceivable, wondrous. Tears welled in her eyes at the nearness.

"Shannon." His voice scraped as he stroked her hair. "Don't cry; I can't bear it." He leaned forward, kissing her forehead, lingering there in a kiss which could not erase the past three years, but in which every painful moment of them was felt. She reached tentatively to touch his face, and he kissed her lips, the desire and love unmistakable in his touch. And she was lost again.

John Thomas escorted her to dinner. Shannon held his arm as they traversed the narrow corridor. He led her into the dining hall, where the men in blue stopped talking, some holding their utensils mid-air. Then they stood. Their chairs scraped the floor loudly, followed by a deafening silence.

John Thomas had told her that it was not at all unusual for an admiral's wife to come aboard a ship, but she had no delusions: she was a fish out of water, an anomaly at which to gape. These men had not seen a woman in weeks or months.

John Thomas presented her to them and told them she would be staying aboard the ship. He asked that they treat her with the utmost respect and courtesy. It was said pleasantly enough, yet with an undercurrent of warning. He then took her to the captain's table where they sat alone. She looked at him several times to find him glancing at her until finally he flushed, smiling a bit before returning to his food.

She asked him how he had become an admiral, and he answered modestly. All he would talk of were the deaths of superior officers and the timing of things. But she knew deaths alone were not enough to cause the promotion of a man of only twenty-nine years to that rank.

She longed to ask about his family, about every moment of his life. He was very kind, almost reverently so. However, some slight distance, barely discernable, kept her from enquiring. He seemed to answer her questions reservedly. But perhaps it was only in her mind.

She was hoping that was the case when she noticed someone walking toward their table. The officer was a dark-haired man who looked at her hesitatingly, waiting, it seemed, for her to speak. Finally, it struck her, and she said, standing, "Captain Jay! Richard!" She leaned forward to embrace him warmly. "I am not used to seeing you with a beard: *that* was my undoing!"

He returned her embrace, glancing a little guiltily at John Thomas. Shannon blushed, just now realizing that John Thomas might not want her to be familiar with another man, a junior officer at that. Or that Richard Jay might wish to distance himself from her or feel disloyal to his friend by association with her. She looked down, unsure that she had ever been so mortified in her life. She could only wait for the moment to pass now.

John Thomas had stood, and he reached to touch the small of her back. He looked at her in concern. He knew all which had passed through her head, that much was plain. Giving her a small, encouraging smile, he said, "I'm unsure anyone could recognize Jay, frontiersman that he appears now." He smiled at his friend, conveying something with his eyes that Shannon couldn't quite read.

Jay looked back at Shannon, smiling genuinely and reaching for her hand. "It is good to see you, Mrs. Haley, in good health." He kissed the air above her hand.

Recovering for John Thomas's sake since he had tried desperately to rescue her, she said a little breathlessly, "And in a shabby dress!"

"Never," he returned with false earnestness, which made them all laugh.

Shannon rested her hand against her bodice, feeling as though there were as many mines in her path as the Rebels had lain in the Charleston Harbor.

*"You cannot possibly mean what you say."*

*John Thomas, in full uniform, sat in the parlor of his father's Boston home. It was a bleak time, January of 1864. Death tolls were rising, spirits flagging, hopes waning. Exhaustion didn't begin to encompass what the Union was experiencing, or what he felt. And his father's funeral had taken place two hours previously.*

*John Thomas leaned with his arms on his knees, his hands clasped. It was foolish, but it almost seemed as though he* could *feel* the weight of the black crepe mourning band which wrapped his left arm. The house was crowded with his siblings and relatives, but it felt empty.

*Or was that his imagination? He had grown accustomed to emptiness, for desperation faded, and then anger, and once the pain had dulled, he simply felt hollow. And then he* missed *her. A kind of missing that even in a crowded room brought a prick of tears to his eyes for no reason at all, or maybe a very small one. He no longer wished to bury himself and die, and yet... Somehow this was lonelier.*

*He had no cause to be thinking of this loss when comrades were falling, while a war was in miserable progression. And the truth was, he didn't think of it very often, save a general awareness of it always, as one was aware of one's limbs. But here, amongst his family, who had consciousness of the situation written in their eyes from dawn until dusk, it was difficult to think of anything else.*

*John Thomas looked across the patterned carpet to his mother, who was sitting in her widow's weeds on the matching settee.* "I do mean what I say," *he said gently. She was tired, her nerves frayed in a manner he had rarely seen. She was not herself. She had loved his father more, perhaps, than she had ever realized and now contemplated a life without him. Possibly a long life, for she had been much younger than her husband.*

"You would take *that* female *back under your roof?*"

*He blinked, never having heard her speak so unguardedly. He couldn't tell her that living without Shannon was like living without the sun. He couldn't say he had caused it—she wouldn't believe him.* "No. I said that, if she came back to me," *he repeated softly,* "I would at least listen to what she wished to say. But all of this is to no purpose. She couldn't, and the last word I had from her is that she won't."

*She watched him, mouth slowly opening in awe. She was generally mistress of her emotions, but today they were on full display.* "You intend to ask her at the first opportunity. You intend to beg. My son, the nation's war hero, intends to go on his hands and knees to a hussy," *she hissed.*

"That is quite enough," he said quietly, his jaw tensing.

"What do you imagine she has done with her time in South Carolina? Do you think women in her position—separated from their husbands—very often live like virgins, John Thomas?" she asked, tears in her blue eyes. "I know the world, as do you, for that matter. I never liked her, never thought she was good enough for you. To...To come flouncing in, in all of her Southern pride... I...I was amazed you turned her head, let alone held her attention for two years. She was born to a different world, John Thomas, bred in a different nursery. They're not like us. And then to humiliate you utterly, to do something so unthinkable! To rush headlong into flight from her husband. Do you know that I am fifty-three years old, and I have never, in all my living, known a woman to commit such an act with such flagrance, so utterly in the face of all which is accepted?"

He sat silently, calculating his words, even as emotions quivered within him. Finally, he said in a quiet tone, "I couldn't help falling in love with Shannon, Mother. It happened, not against my will, but without any conscious effort on my part. And I didn't want to help it. I know you believe her society was different from ours, and that is true, or perhaps it once was. We were from opposing worlds, Shannon and I, and we knew that. But that is to no purpose. There was something more to her than what is immediately tangible. Something even you saw—"

"I was mistaken. There was nothing, there could be nothing to a woman who would leave you." He saw tears trembling on her lashes and realized that she was hurt, too. Shannon had deserted more than just her husband. It was the first time *he had considered it, and it caused a wave of pain to pulse through his chest and limbs. And, surprisingly, anger. He had thought he had bested it.*

*He bit his lip. "Shannon...did something—yes, unthinkable. I won't speak of my feelings upon the matter; they must be obvious. I do not deny that it would be hard to forgive her. I merely say that I would hear her if she wished to speak to me, someday, if this war is ever through."*

*His mother stared at him and, instead of looking appeased, anger hardened her face. She stood. "I will tell you what you will do, John Thomas Haley. You will maneuver your way to Charleston as soon as is militarily possible."*

*He had stood as she had, and he watched her as she strode to the door. He called, his eyes pinched at the corners, "Are you suggesting that I divorce her?" He stood astonished. "I, a Haley, Mother?"*

*She stopped, her profile toward him, her hand on the door. Her lip trembled, and she shook her head. "No," she whispered. "No, forgive me. I cannot suggest that." And she fled the room in tears.*

Shannon had nothing remotely resembling a parasol to take with her on deck, but she cared far less for her complexion than once she would have. In any event, she hoped the gentle April sun would be merciful. She climbed the steps and scanned the large deck and beyond it to the bay. She was able to see Charleston, but just barely. What remained of the

Holy City's many church spires and steeples towered above the rest of its buildings.

When she had left, there had been festivals of freedom taking place in the streets of Charleston. The freedmen were celebrating their emancipation with great joy. Of course, she couldn't see at this distance if the festivities continued. It felt odd to be so close to the city yet cut off from it entirely.

She passed several men who inclined their heads respectfully. As she passed them, she said, "Good morning," but nothing more. It was her third day aboard the ship, and she couldn't afford a reputation for being too friendly with the sailors. Not when she imagined her character was in tatters and shreds in the North. And after her most recent decision, she imagined the same was true in the South. If she had been highly regarded in Charleston for leaving John Thomas, she couldn't imagine she would be loved for returning to him.

Still on rather uncertain ground with him, she stood back at a distance. He seemed to be conferring with his officers, deeply concentrated on the subject at hand. They looked handsome in their blue; she couldn't deny it.

Afraid she would be in the way and sensitive to suspicions of spying, she started to leave. Oh, good heavens, why hadn't she *thought* of that? She had made her choice to spend the war in the South, and everyone knew it.

But just then, John Thomas spotted her. "Shan... Mrs. Haley," he said, touching the arm of the nearest man as he made room to walk between the officers and started toward her.

He came to her and, looking anxious, touched her arm and said, "Forgive me, I didn't see you. Had you been standing there long?"

"Oh, no, only a minute," she answered, looking up at him a bit shyly.

His mouth hinted at a shy smile, too. His thumb stroked her sleeve. She felt her blush deepening. He flushed also but cleared his throat, reaching to take her hands and pressing them. "What are you doing up here?" he asked softly. "You'll burn to a crisp."

"Coming to find you," she said, looking at him.

"You needed something?" he asked, searching her face.

"No, and you mustn't hold my hands," she whispered. "The men will see, and—"

"I don't care for that," he said. His eyes roved her countenance, as though still in awe of her presence. "I do think you will be too warm up here, though."

"I'll go soon. Only, I wanted to see the sunshine for a bit—"

"Of course." He reached up, brushing back one of the ribbons of her bonnet. His brows pinched. "The situation is less than ideal. I must think what is to be done."

"Time enough for that, as long as it is not improper for me to be here."

"Oh, no."

"Well, then," she said, smiling. He seemed to look at her strangely, as though he could not quite fathom her willingness to stay aboard a ship with few clothes and no comforts, not even a maid. Or perhaps it was her calm acceptance of the situation which surprised him.

"You're sure?" he asked softly, uncertainly.

"Yes, for the time being, I am quite content if my husband will allow me to see the sunlight—just from time to time!"

She had been gently teasing him, but he looked penitent. "Of *course*. But we must find you some shade," he said. He took her to a partially covered area where a table had been set up, perhaps for them to strategize. He helped her to one of the chairs and asked if she were thirsty.

She smiled. "No, I am quite well and won't melt, I hope. I mustn't distract you and incur the dislike of your men. Do go back to your meeting."

He made a study of her as he leaned over her. Then he nodded, straightening and going back to them. But he looked over his shoulder at her once.

Perhaps she imagined it, but the next time she saw John Thomas, his reserve had grown. This was while they had dined together amongst some of the other officers. He had made sure she was seated and then mostly ignored her, though perhaps that was because the men were in deep discussion about supplies. She certainly understood that he was under great strain just now.

Since she was the only woman, she supped quietly until Lieutenant Simmons said bashfully, "I hope you have been able to hear from your family, ma'am?"

She smiled at him a little sadly. "No. But they know where I am, so they won't be worried."

"It seems a shame, them being so close. But I don't suppose it would be quite possible just now for you to see them."

He didn't know about her estrangement, but indeed, it would be quite unseemly for her to socialize with her Charleston loved ones. The thought made a blanket of despondency spread across her.

Shannon attempted a smile, saying, "No, not just yet," and turned the conversation away from herself. She asked Lieutenant Simmons from whence he hailed and learned that he was from Ohio. They chatted amiably throughout the meal about his home and family.

And when she later arose, saying that she would retire to bed, John Thomas merely inclined his head, saying, "Goodnight"—and nothing more.

Shannon sat on her bed, wondering what she ought to do. John Thomas had begun to distance himself; she was certain of it now. His days were filled almost to the brim with military duties, but when they were, on rare occasions, together, his reticence seemed to grow by day.

He was gentle, and he treated her with respect. He still slept in the bed with her, but he did not touch her beyond what was necessary given the small quarters. He was generally gone before she awoke and returned long after she had fallen asleep. When they did awake in a compromising position, his arm around her or her head on his chest, he did not toss her off. He merely smiled kindly and extricated himself.

During meals in which they were alone, he talked agreeably to her. But that there was a certain aloofness in his manner and expression she could no longer deny. Not a word passed of their time apart, of the war, of the agony of their separate existences, or of their families. She had thought that it was only in her imagination, or perhaps that he was merely distracted due to his heavy duties or the war itself.

Until one night when she had been late to dinner and had seen him talking to Richard. John Thomas liked him very much, and they had been through a war together. He would never be what Frederick had been to John Thomas, but the affection between them was deep. It was only with such people that John Thomas truly released his reserve. She had witnessed the open laugh, the twinkling eyes, the gentle, bantering conversation. And that was when she realized she had been relegated to the ranks of those with whom he was either unacquainted or uncomfortable.

Shannon sighed. Another woman might have had the situation in hand weeks ago, but she did not, despite possessing what she had always felt to be expert handling of men. That he was afraid of her she knew perfectly well. And yet she had no idea how to convince him of the sincerity of her commitment that she would never leave him again. She was unsure even how to become reacquainted with him.

She considered seducing him. That she could do this, she had little doubt. But as his remoteness grew, she put the matter to deep consideration, thinking in a way that would have chilled Elizabeth. Who was to say there would be anything to be gained from it? She sometimes thought that the closer they drew, the more reserved he became. She had pained him deeply, hurt him to his very core. Of that, there could be no question. He would never say it because he was a gentleman, but his friends' cool reception of her told her what he would not.

She scarcely saw him over the next few weeks. All of his days and most of his nights were spent in Charleston handling military matters and, she assumed, keeping his distance from her.

The only thing of note to happen during that time was that while Shannon was walking on deck with her guard, a chain had loosened in the wind and struck her in the face. It caused a cut and some bruising on her cheekbone which hurt very much, but she had restrained her reaction. John Thomas, when he had been sent for, had been shaken. He seemed to think that it had happened because he had not been with her. She deduced that he was feeling guilty for avoiding her, since he couldn't have been with her in that moment.

He was excessively kind over that, doctoring her himself, treating her like a delicate flower then, and later during their dinner. But then she had felt him withdrawing quite soon after.

She tried not to be disturbed and attempted to occupy herself. She sent away the orderly who cleaned his quarters and cleaned them herself. There wasn't much tidying to be done, but she did wipe the dust from the battened-down furniture.

She alternatingly hung up the two dresses she had brought from Ravenel House. She tried to keep them in good care, unable to bear the thought that Phoebe would be ashamed of her. She didn't have half of what she needed, and her dresses were four years out of fashion, but at least she was clean and neat. She thanked Providence that she was the only woman on board. The men scarcely knew these defects.

Noting one day that there was a musty scent which must be common to ships, she remembered some lavender pouches in her valise and went to find them. She reached into the bottom of the bag and felt a scrap of paper. Frowning, she unfolded it.

*'Tis not to make me jealous*
*to say my wife is fair, feeds well, loves company,*
*Is free of speech, sings, plays, and dances.*
*Where virtue is, these are more virtuous.*
*Nor from mine own weak merits will I draw*
*The smallest fear or doubt of her revolt,*
*For she had eyes and chose me.*

Her hand shook. She hastily put the paper back into the bag and reached for the pouches. Opening them, she blinked away tears as she distributed the lavender about the room, pushing memories vigorously away.

# Chapter Four

New resolution: stay away from Adrian at all costs. Adeline wasn't sure exactly what it was about him that scared the living daylights out of her. You'd think he'd be the one afraid after his life experiences, but nope. She was the one wanting to put on that pair of running shoes she never used and flee. It was the situation, she knew, the out-of-order way they'd done everything, the feelings he evoked, the way she was afraid to trust herself, to share her life.

She avoided him as October progressed, except for meals, and, of course, when he slept next to her. It was easy because they were both putting in a lot of hours, but she knew he was aware by the way he sometimes looked at her.

Adeline, putting that aside, filled her days with restoration and shopping for the house. She found some great pieces at the massive Charleston City Market downtown, and of course, at some fabulous antique stores.

It was there that she received a call from Annie, her sister, who wanted to know why Adeline hadn't told her about the baby earlier. Adeline wavered uncomfortably but decided that her sister could take it. "Because I was pregnant before we married, Annie, and I didn't want to upset Mom and Dad."

A long silence. "How far along are you?"

"Six months."

This had led to more shocked expressions, tears, and demands for explanations. She couldn't pinpoint the reason because her sister wasn't usually petty, but Adeline almost heard irritation that Annie wouldn't have the first baby. Sometimes her perfectionism took her a bit too far. "I mean, are you going to keep the baby from us and only let it see its Charleston family?"

"Adrian's family lives in Georgia. And of course not, Annie. Does that sound like me?"

"No," She sniffed through her tears. "Addy...do you love this guy?"

A question that stopped her cold. She swallowed. "I... I'm sorry, Annie. I don't want to talk about that. But he's a good man. I wouldn't have married him otherwise, under any circumstances. You don't need to worry."

"But that *is* what worries me. What about your heart? What if it's not right?"

"Anns... Not everybody wants to date for nine years."

A silence. "Point taken." She seemed to sense that further questioning would be fruitless. "Well, he *is* really cute."

Adeline smiled and turned the conversation into safer waters.

Over the next few days, she spent a lot of time at the local plantations, researching the South Carolinian style and special architectural techniques. She was surprised at how many colonial touches there were but knew she needed to tone those back at Ravenel-Thompson, since it had been built in the 1830s.

And she avoided the house some more, eating lunch out with Jane occasionally and researching at the library. She also took a lot of calls from Virginia Ravenel about the baby shower which the women in her Sunday School class were hosting for Adeline in November. Apparently, there were a lot of details to be decided, and that alone could have kept her occupied for a week.

She climbed the stairs at Poogan's Porch to meet Jane and Jude during Jude's fall break, entering its elegant upper dining room and smelling the unique Charleston fare. Jane had set it up so that Adeline would eat beside Jude, which she appreciated. They ordered and then let Jude carry the conversation—all about his teacher and his friends. Adeline asked him what he was going to get Mira for Christmas and learned that he and Mira were no longer an item. She had sat next to George at lunch, and he'd broken up with her. He and her brother Brynlyn remained friends, however.

"When are you going to start a nursery for this little one?" Jane asked in that direct way of hers, ready to move on from first-grade drama and romance.

Adeline took a sip of her water. "I was planning to get the rest of the house finished hopefully by the first of November and leave that room. That'll give me something to do over the next couple of months. I won't really need help on it since they've already done the baseboards and painting." It was a light gray, perfect for a boy or girl.

"You'll be sorry if it comes early," Jane said.

Adeline kept from widening her eyes by focusing on the appetizer. Gah, pressure. "Well, we're still on target for the beginning of January," she said. "And I want to wait until the baby shower at least."

Jane then became very lovely, asking how Adeline was feeling, if she'd been thinking of names, and telling her she looked great. Adeline hadn't gained much weight, except for her bump, of course, and her friend Candace had told her she had the cutest bump ever, so that was something.

As they ate dessert and Jude colored, Jane said pointedly, "Adrian seems to be working a lot lately."

Adeline met her eyes. "Um, yeah," she said. "His workload has been heavy."

"Hmm," Jane said.

Adeline bit her lip. "And I kind of messed things up." Jude, bored, got up and walked to the window, looking out at the busy street below. They let him stay over there since the dining room was more or less empty.

"How?" Jane asked gently.

Adeline fingered her napkin. "I've been pushing him away."

"Why would you do that, hon?"

She lifted a shoulder. "I'm so afraid things won't work out. And then I'm left with all of this baggage, and..." She swallowed, slowly looking up to meet Jane's eyes.

"Well, the best way to be assured it won't work out is to never give it a chance," Jane said. "You can never be sure *anything* will work out, even in the best circumstances. But one has to try. I think fear has you in a vice-grip, hon."

Accurate. "What if he resents me?" she whispered.

"For having his child? Not likely."

"No, for being stuck with me. He..." She shook her head.

"Adeline." Jane reached across the table, covering her hand. "You *have* to give it a try. You'll never know otherwise. And you don't want to be my age someday, looking back and regretting."

The Williamsburg crew was almost finished with the fireplace in the library by the end of the month. Sometimes Adeline would just stand in the door and stare at its magnificent woodwork and lofty crest. She could imagine past Ravenel men hosting their neighbors in this room, smoking a cigar as they discussed the crumbling Union.

She seldom saw Adrian, who often worked late, but she started a routine with Jude on Thursday nights of streaming old PBS dramas. Jane had been staying late on Thursdays since Adrian was back to teaching his class. However, Adeline, with Adrian's agreement, started sending her home and bonding with Jude then. She enjoyed looking after him, which boded well for her happiness as a mother.

Then again, Jude was exceptional. One night while he sat enthralled with *Cranford*, she sat beside him, going over some numbers for the project. She whispered to herself in stream of consciousness, "What's fifty-three thousand times forty-eight?"

Without looking up from the TV, Jude said, "Two-million five-hundred-forty-four thousand."

Adeline blinked. She pulled out her phone and did the calculations and then looked up at him. "Jude, how did you do that?" she breathed.

"You just add zeros. I mean, to fifty-three times forty-eight."

He wasn't even seven yet. She touched her middle and looked down, getting a sinking feeling. What if she had another child prodigy on her hands? She wouldn't even know how to help it meet its full potential—if it was gifted in science or math, that was. She blamed Adrian. He hadn't warned her about this.

To her surprise, Jude snuggled up beside her on the leather sofa and returned to the show. He dropped off to sleep in about fifteen minutes, his head against her shoulder. She looked down, stroking his hair back, and felt her chest squeeze. She needed to stop pretending like she was just becoming a mom to her baby. She was more than half lost over Jude. And Jude's father? That was an altogether more dangerous line of thought.

# Chapter Five

As sunlight streamed through the lone, small window, Shannon awakened. She had been aboard the ship six weeks, enough time for her to know that the window was too small for its meager light to agitate her so much. She soon realized a headache had come upon her, so severe that she could do no more than stay abed and hope it would dissipate. As the morning wore on, the pain intensified to the degree that she, holding the porcelain bowl in shaky hands, cast up her accounts.

Feeling her temples throbbing intensely, Shannon touched them and wondered if she had perhaps caught something aboard the ship. This was possible. She often took walks on the deck with Lieutenant Simmons, her guard, and she ate in the dining hall.

Late in the morning, she managed to request some headache powders from the cook, which helped a bit. Still, she did not feel she could go down to breakfast or dinner. John Thomas had gone into Charleston. Because he did not return to his quarters that night, she had no way of asking whether he thought she ought to see a doctor. She decided that she must find him tomorrow. If this were an illness which had plagued some of the men, perhaps he would know whether she needed medical care or if it would pass.

It did not pass. Shannon's headache lessened marginally, but the nausea persisted into the second day with such intensity that Shannon was able to keep down none of the meals which were brought to her quarters. Naturally, she began feeling weak, and, racking her brains, she could not think what it might be. She did not ache or feel feverish, as she had with the influenza, but she was generally unwell.

On the third day, after losing her breakfast, she managed the rest of the day without incident. Although she did, by that point, feel far from well. That night, she fell asleep before John Thomas returned. She didn't know he had come in until she heard him dressing in the anteroom before dawn.

Knowing he must be needed in the city again, she rose, slipping the blanket around her and walking toward the adjoining door. She knocked on it, and in moments, he opened it, fully dressed in his uniform. "Shannon!" he said, apparently surprised. He met her eyes, seeming to hesitate. "Forgive me, I didn't mean to wake you."

"You didn't." She held the blanket together at her chest.

His brows drew together slightly. "Are you well?" he asked, taking one unconscious step toward her and making a survey of her face. He met her eyes then, questioning. "You haven't been ill?"

Her chest tightened, and she couldn't think what held her back then. She bit her lip. She did feel a bit better today. And she didn't want an illness to be the cause of him putting less distance between them. "No, I... That is, I was a little unwell yesterday," she said, wondering why she could smell breakfast cooking. She had never been able to do so before.

His eyes flashed with concern, his brows pinching. He stepped into the room, closing the door behind him. "Were you? What was—"

She touched her throat. "A little. Perhaps something I ate."

His anxiety eased, although he still looked concerned. "Oh, I see. You wouldn't be the first victim of ship's fare. I'm sorry," he said, touching her arm. "The situation isn't—"

"The situation doesn't trouble me," she said, covering his hand briefly. She glanced up at him. "As I told you before." She bit her lip. "Be careful in the city."

His face softened. "You have everything you need here?" he asked.

"Yes," she said faintly.

Nodding, his eyes lingered another moment before he said, "All right, then."

She went and sat in the chair, wrapping the blanket around her so that she was cocooned. As the morning wore on, it became evident that she had been too optimistic. Only the fact that there was nothing on her stomach, she felt, kept her from being ill now, and, simultaneously, she felt that fact contributed to her nausea as nothing else did.

And yet, as she sat her mind turned to worrying over John Thomas instead of herself. His form had filled out over the course of the war, but he was thinner than she would like to see him. She sat for quite some time concocting ways to fatten him up. And he was troubled, too. It did not affect his duties. She was awe-struck at the capable and confident commander he had become and only grew more admiring as the days progressed. But that she had turned his world topsy-turvy she had no doubt.

Getting up, she ate breakfast in her quarters and promptly retched. So, she merely sat, too exhausted to hold her head up, breathing shakily and wondering whether she ought to send for a doctor. Only, she did not think there was one on board, and she might have to go into Charleston. She didn't wish *to* go into Charleston. There, she would have to see one of her family's doctors, which was disagreeable to her on two scores. First, anything she did or said would be reported to her father, and second, she was the wife of a Union admiral.

Later, she asked Lieutenant Simmons casually as they walked on the deck whether there was a doctor aboard, and he confirmed that there wasn't. He told her that there was one on a nearby ship, however, who tended them. She held his arm, feeling weak and sweltering as the sun beat down on her. "I believe I will go down and rest before dinner,

Lieutenant," she said. He was happy to escort her, telling her that they had received word that the Admiral would be dining aboard the ship that night.

"Thank you, Lieutenant," she said, smiling briefly up at him.

She closed the door behind her, turning the lock and beginning to remove her day gown, which took such effort that it exhausted her. She unlaced her corset, wondering whether John Thomas might be very much irritated if she requested without his authority to have the Union doctor brought to her. As she removed her corset and loosened the fabric on her breasts, she experienced such pain that her eyes watered, and she gave a little cry.

She sat in a bit of panic on the bed, holding her corset up, trying to apply pressure. As two tears escaped and rolled down her cheeks, her mother flitted through her mind. Her heart flew in her chest until she remembered Marie saying that Louisa Ravenel had felt no pain until the very end. Shannon breathed a little easier, considering other possibilities, biting her lip to keep from crying at the tenderness.

She sometimes experienced something resembling this just before her courses. But then, it was such a mild version of this... She turned her head, thinking.

She blinked. It was past time. She rapidly counted. Long past.

She stilled. She felt as though there were a gentle butterfly in her chest, waiting to take flight. Timid and uncertain, her mind waved a feather of possibility. There was a fluttering in her heart that dropped down to her abdomen.

She took a sharp breath and released it unsteadily. She was frightened to let her mind... No, it wasn't possible. And yet... Before, she had been unwell in various ways that she wasn't now. In fact, years had passed.

Her lips parted as she looked down at her waist. She covered her bodice timidly with a trembling hand, almost as though she needed permission to do so. She sat, scarcely able to breathe.

And then, slowly, tears began to stream down her cheeks.

As she lay down, all she could think of was the wonder of it. But could it indeed be? She had suspected once before only to be disappointed. But this time was very different from the last, her symptoms so many and so strong that she was either dying or with child. Her heart fluttered at the thought. She couldn't—but she *must* be.

Yes. She was with child. *Their* child, hers and John Thomas's. *Oh, good heavens.*

Once upon a time, he would've been immensely happy. There would be no fear except for her health, no anxiety for the future, no discomfort of feelings. Why could timing never be as one would wish? She felt fear now. For they were estranged as surely as they had been during the war. What his feelings would be, she couldn't say.

When she finally came to herself, it was nearly dark. Getting up weakly, she dressed in her evening gown, wondering what supper would hold and whether she would have an opportunity to speak with him. She turned her head to the side, brushing away a tear and reaching for her reticule, into which she stuffed her handkerchief.

She wondered what her family would think. But just as quickly, a pain rose in her chest. She felt her mother's death keenly. She felt the lack of female companionship as never before, and that of her menfolk, too. Her heart fluttered with anxiety. She needed—oh, she scarcely knew what.

She turned to go, closing the door behind her and walking up the dimly lit corridor. The ship shifted on the waves, and her nausea intensified. The smell of lobster cooking struck her, and she lay a hand against her bodice, her stomach reeling. As she gathered herself, one of the junior officers escorted her deprecatingly in the direction of the captain's table where John Thomas was sitting, though when he met her eyes, he stood.

She walked toward the table, and he held her chair for her, seeming to study her. But she quickly realized that they wouldn't be dining alone. There were several other officers aboard, some of whom she had met, others not, and one other lady. The latter fact encouraged her until she realized the other woman meant to snub her. She was Mrs. Rice, the wife of Commodore Rice. John Thomas introduced her to Shannon, and Shannon said what was proper.

Shannon sat between the large Commander Harrell and the loquacious Captain Jay, as had been laid out for her. John Thomas sat several seats away, and she wondered whether the distance between them was due to proper ship's etiquette or something else entirely. In any event, she sat in silence, hoping she wouldn't be publicly ill.

As the dinner progressed, it quickly became borne in upon her that these people had fought and won a war together and that there was an intimacy between them in which she had no part. There were barbs aimed at Commander Harrell to which she wasn't privy. Everyone knew the names of the Rice children and asked after their studies in Illinois. Conversation flew rapidly and swept up in a tide in which she was hopeless to participate.

She was too Southern not to be glad for the ease of the dialogue. However, she was irritated when, after Captain Jay said something which ought to have sparked conversation between the two ladies, Mrs. Rice seemed to have nothing to say to Shannon. Alluding both to Shannon's Southern affiliations during the war and to her desertion almost in one breath, she then abandoned Shannon altogether.

She didn't think John Thomas had heard it, and, when she looked up, he was studiously talking to the man on his left as though hoping their eyes wouldn't meet. She did look up later, however, to find him looking at her, but he cut his eyes away quickly.

"I said, 'Are you quite well, Mrs. Haley?'"

Shannon looked over at Captain Jay, blinked, and gave an attempt at a smile. "The heat," she said. In truth, the meal was taxing her almost beyond endurance. She was weak, a bit light-headed, and the smells... She flashed a brief smile at Jay before cutting her eyes away.

Since there was nothing resembling a parlor on the ship, the guests lingered to talk and drink their wine at the table. Shannon stayed as long as she felt she could and then she rose. All of the men did, too, and she said, flushing faintly, "If you will excuse me, I am a bit tired and believe I will retire to our quarters. I...enjoyed meeting all of you and dining with you." She felt John Thomas's eyes upon her. She turned to go as some of her fellow diners said polite goodnights.

She walked toward her chamber. She had not made it far down the corridor when she heard softly, "Shannon!" She halted, turning around.

It was the first time he had sought her out in weeks. She met John Thomas's eyes, lifting her brows courteously and wondering what the other diners had thought when he had left. "I hope they were polite to you?" he asked, eyes flickering anxiously over her face.

"Yes," she said, feeling nausea pass over her in a strong wave. She had only eaten four bites at dinner. Each had been a mistake. She clutched her reticule. "Yes, mostly."

He hesitated as though choosing his words carefully. "I hope you weren't offended. Mrs. Rice...is very loyal to me, and—"

Shannon's eyes pricked, and, seeing her mortification, he flushed deeply. He reached to touch her arm. "No, forgive me, I only meant..." He didn't finish. He had meant that those who were loyal to him did not associate with her. And the truth of the notion pierced her.

She swallowed. "I...am very glad you had devoted friends. I imagine they must have been invaluable."

She looked up into his face, and, all else fading, she felt wonder anew. She took in every feature, marveling that he had only grown more handsome during the war. Would their baby—*heavens!*—have his nose, his chin, or his blue eyes? He probably thought her mad, but her hurt changed to happiness in an instant. All vestiges of despair fled to be replaced by a gentle look in her eyes and a slight smile which just barely touched her lips.

And apparently feeling that she no longer needed his support, he was prepared to recede again. For when she said, "John Thomas, I...," he gave his tight, distant smile and said, "If you are sure you are well, I really ought to return then." He turned to go.

"John Thomas!" she called urgently.

He halted, his blue eyes registering surprise. "Yes?"

She took a deep, unsteady breath. "If I might have a moment?" she asked, willing her voice to sound stronger.

He frowned and returned quickly. "You are not unwell again?"

"That is what I need to speak with you about," she said in a small, quivering voice. Good heavens, she must gain control of herself.

"Shannon," he whispered in dismay. He touched her arms, searching her face intensely. "What is it? Tell me."

"Not here," she said, glancing around.

"Of—of course," he answered softly. He looked around

them, seeming to regain his senses, and led her back to his quarters. He closed the door behind them, turned up the lamp, and stood in front of her. He looked at her in deep anxiety, standing just a few inches away, her skirts brushing the trousers of his blue uniform. "Shannon, tell me," he implored.

She swallowed, standing still. She held his eyes for a long moment, her heart flying. "John Thomas, I think…" She swallowed again and gathered her breath. She met his eyes. She couldn't say it.

"Shannon," he whispered, pale. "What is it?"

"I am with child," she said. As the words echoed off the walls, she watched him. A silence descended and reigned. His lips parted at the first comprehension of her words. "And I need a doctor," she added into the silence, her voice breaking.

"What?" he breathed in the thinnest whisper, his eyes never leaving her face. His expression was a mixture of shock and something else that she couldn't discern.

He whispered in disbelief, "With child?" His eyes searched her face as though within her features he might find answers. She had never seen a man look so stunned. But at last, he blinked, shaking his head, seeming to realize that whatever his surprise, he had no right to it. "Yes. Of course," he whispered, regarding her in awe. Then her other words occurred to him, and he met her eyes with intensity, gripping her arms. "You need a doctor? What is wrong?"

She moistened her lips. She felt, suddenly, acutely embarrassed. "Nothing…of immediate concern. But I have been very unwell, unable to eat, and...very unwell." Her lip trembled, despite herself.

He looked her face over and seemed overcome. "Why haven't you—" He broke off and walked her to the bed, where he helped her gently to sit down before bringing her a glass of water. "You are unwell now?" he asked, taking her gloves, which she had been holding, and watching her progress with the water.

"John Thomas, your guests. If you might simply think on it and send whomever you think best—" she began. He left, closing the door behind him, heedless of her speaking. Shannon sat on the bed, her mind whirling. She cast aside her reticule as her illness grew stronger. She covered her bodice, closing her eyes. *Good heavens.*

He returned in five minutes. Taking one look at her face, he hurried with true presence of mind to fetch the basin. He kneeled beside her and held the porcelain as she retched and then as dry heaves shook her frame, over and over. When she was at last able to lean up, exhausted, there was deep concern in his eyes. "Shannon, how long have you been this ill?" he questioned raggedly.

"A few days," she answered.

He paled further. Standing, he removed the bowl and found her a cool rag. He asked whether she would like to lie down, but she shook her head, holding the rag tightly in her hand. "I don't think I ought."

It was perhaps thirty minutes later that there was a knock at the door. John Thomas had taken himself to a chair, elbows on his knees, and he was watching her intently and seemingly thinking rapidly. He startled to attention, going to open the door and inviting the person in. Shannon saw at once that the man was in Naval uniform. So, she surmised that he must have been brought from another of the ships which currently stared the Charleston harbor down. In his hand was a bag, and he appeared to be self-possessed. He was handsome, perhaps in his early forties, with dark, silvering hair and laughing eyes. He looked between them with a twinkling smile which revealed that the reason for which he had been sent had already been communicated to him. "Admiral Haley," he said, showing proper deference, but the devil never left his eyes.

"Doctor Schafer, you are not acquainted with Mrs. Haley." John Thomas walked back to her and lay a gentle, protective hand on her back, kneeling beside her and taking her hand comfortingly.

The man might have said that he had heard so much that he felt them to be acquainted. Instead, he greeted her with elegance and kindness, talking of simple nothings only a moment before shutting the Admiral out of the room and getting down to business.

John Thomas took himself to his office, where he could not sit still. He paced first one way and then the other. Dragging his hand through his hair, he tried and failed to gain his bearings. He had gotten himself into such a state that he nearly pounced the doctor when the man opened the door. John Thomas said hurriedly, "Is she all right?"

"Indeed," Schafer said, entering and putting his bag on an old, battered table. As John Thomas watched him intently, he added, "I wouldn't lie to you, Admiral Haley. If I believed her to be in danger, I would say so." The doctor opened the bag, from whence he pulled a few bottles. "These will help her. I've explained to her how to use them." John Thomas gripped them, holding his eyes.

After a moment, the doctor added, "She seems to be in a stable condition. The child, too, as far as I can tell."

He felt light-headed. "The child," he repeated.

"It is a great deal to take in," Dr. Schafer said soothingly. "Have some wine."

"What?" John Thomas looked up, awakening from his reverie. "No, of course I don't need wine."

"Ah, well, then," the doctor remarked breezily.

John Thomas met his eyes. "You say that…the child is safe?"

"I see no immediate troubles," he confirmed.

John Thomas released his breath, feeling relief there, at least. "But Shannon. Why is she so ill? My sisters were not." He felt as though he needed to pace, as though his blood would burn through his skin, but he stayed still.

"Weren't they? They were fortunate. I trust the illness will pass soon enough, Admiral, and that you have no cause to be more worried than any other man."

John Thomas swallowed. Looking up, meeting the doctor's eyes, he said, "My wife has had…troubles in the past, pain and...very difficult courses." He experienced disbelief that he was discussing such things with another man, but one would never have known his discomfort, for he didn't flinch. "We lived together nearly two years, and no child was conceived."

"Well, sometimes these things mend. It has been a few years, has it not?"

"Yes." He hesitated a long while. Finally, he added, "Her first cousin was lost in childbirth."

Looking at him with compassion, the doctor said, "Don't borrow trouble. She is unwell, but as I said, I find no cause for undue worry. However, you know where to find me should you need me."

John Thomas drew a hand through his hair, his mind whirling. "Thank you. I must get her off the ship."

"That would be wise. You might send her to Massachusetts to your family..." the doctor suggested.

John Thomas shook his head. "I couldn't do that," he answered softly, his mind on Shannon in the other room. Was she ill this very moment? He tangled his fingers in his hair. "You are likely aware... That is, you can scarcely be *un*aware of the troubles of my marriage," he said. "My family does not yet know that Shannon has...returned to me, much less that..." He flushed slightly and looked up to find the doctor with laughter in his eyes again.

"Well, if she needs me again, you'll send for me," Dr. Schafer said at length, closing his bag.

John Thomas looked up quickly. "You'll take her under your care?"

The doctor hesitated. "If you intend to set up a house in Charleston, Admiral, it would be wiser to find a doctor there. If one can be had," he added reflectively.

John Thomas studied him. "Doctor, we have served together these past two years, and I have the highest respect for your skill and confidence in your abilities. I am on foreign territory, and I won't be popular with the natives. If there is a man of medicine who can be induced to attend my wife, it will be out of respect for her, and not for me. And I don't desire her to suffer."

Dr. Schafer shook his head. "You are very kind. But I haven't seen a female patient in four years, and I imagine Mrs. Haley will feel more comfortable with her own doctor. I recommend that you try and see what may be accomplished in that direction. But of course, in the interim, you will notify me if I may be of service."

Shannon sat up as the door opened softly. John Thomas entered quietly as though he had feared she might be asleep. Seeing her awake, he straightened. She met and held his eyes for a long moment in the flickering candlelight. And then he came forward and knelt in front of her bed. Tentatively, he reached for her hands, looking from them up to her eyes. "I'm sorry," he rasped. "Please forgive me. I feel so ashamed…"

"Shh—no," she said earnestly, pressing his hands.

There was such remorse in his eyes that he looked ready to throw himself into the ocean. "I didn't know you were ill. I saw you looked fatigued but thought it must be...something else," he whispered.

"No," she answered, flushing. "I didn't know myself what it was at first." She looked up at him shyly. It was such an unfathomable moment. The eyes meeting hers told her John Thomas was aware of that fact, but that he intended to act rationally, however stunned he was.

"Do you need anything?" he asked, his voice searching. "Are you ill now?"

"No." She swallowed thickly. "I am sorry if—"

His head jerked up, anguish in his expression. "Sorry?" His grip tightened on hers. "I'm not sorry, except very much that you are ill," he whispered. "Are you?" His eyes searched her face rapidly.

She shook her head, tears rising to her eyes. "No," she breathed. "I couldn't be. Only, I know that we have only just reconciled, and I feared you would..." She broke off, unable to finish.

"Shannon," he whispered, aghast. "No, my darling," he said, cradling her face. The candlelight glinted off his golden hair, his blue eyes shining with unshed emotion. He stroked his thumbs over the twin tears that tracked down her cheeks as though her skin were the most delicate thing imaginable. He said passionately, "It means as much to me—every bit as much—as it would, had you told me in the first months of our marriage."

She bit her lip, and a teardrop trickled down her cheek. "Do you mean that?" she whispered.

He took a shaking breath. "Oh, Shannon. *Yes.*"

The next day, John Thomas escorted Shannon into the hot sun on deck, off the ship, and eventually out of the boat which had taken them to the edge of the city. He held her hand in his and glanced anxiously at her as they made their way down the wharf. They met with the curious stares of the people of Charleston all the while. Until a more permanent situation could be found, they would be staying at the mansion which had been made headquarters by the Union occupation.

As she set foot for the first time in nearly two months on dry land, Shannon knew there were treacherous shoals ahead.

# Chapter Six

Jude's room was finished in two weeks. After his furniture was moved back in and the curtains were hung, Adeline spent most of her time working in the living room. She couldn't seem to get the boys to call it "the parlor."

*"Like a funeral parlor?"*

*No, Adrian. Gah.* She had designed bookshelves that closed the TV in so the room would look historically accurate. The added benefit was that by keeping the TV, she wouldn't be thrown out of the house. Football season was underway, after all.

Joe and José spent the better part of a week installing shelves in the living room and painting them white to match those in the library. Adeline got rid of the furniture and installed more appropriate pieces. The new sofa wasn't really an antique, however, and she made sure it was just as comfy as its predecessor. Still, the room looked like it was right out of *Southern Living*, and even Jude approved.

Taking a stroll through the downstairs, she was almost emotional sometimes at how pretty it looked. She felt a rush of gratitude for Adrian. She would likely never have such freedom on a project again.

Maybe it was something about the cooling of temperature combined with her emotional neediness, but she felt less and less inclined to push him away. He was a little quiet around her, and she knew she needed to apologize for a month's chilliness.

When she awakened on Saturday morning, Adrian was already up, and the sun was slanting through the period-appropriate screens she had installed. The smell of something cooking reached her senses, and she was immediately filled with hunger.

She put on a gray dress and went downstairs, finding Jude perched on a barstool in his pajamas. Adrian was in jeans and a T-shirt putting fruit on plates next to bowls of oatmeal. If a girl wanted bacon around here, she'd have to go somewhere else, but that was okay.

Adrian looked up when he heard her enter. His expression was hesitant. He was probably thinking she'd grab her plate and go. She smiled, and he said, "Morning."

"Morning."

"Hungry?"

"Starved." She sat next to Jude. Since they were settled, Adrian stood across from them and ate, letting Jude chat them up, amusement in his eyes from time to time at something Jude said. They discussed the LSU game, which would start at noon, and then Jude asked if he could name the baby.

"No," Adrian said. "Now go up and dress. Not shorts, okay?"

"Okay!" Jude answered, jumping down from the barstool and scampering off.

Adeline's eyes danced. "He can name the baby."

He looked up from wiping Jude's part of the counter. "I don't think so. He had a goldfish once. Angus."

She laughed. "Should we do something matchy with his name? He's Jude Thomas, right?"

"He is. I can't really answer that without giving it away. Can't even suggest names because I'm bound to put more energy into the real sex than a decoy name."

"Hmm. True." Sometimes she regretted not knowing the sex, but she wasn't about to tell him that. It had been a sort of competition between them, to see if she could hold out in her resolve.

She bit her lip and looked up to find Adrian studying her. She wanted to bring up her apology, but it didn't seem like the right time somehow. He was too guarded. It might not even sound genuine. "So, I was thinking about going shopping for the baby. Is white furniture okay with you?"

"Sure, whatever you want." He laid the dishrag on the sink and looked up. "Do you need help?"

"No, I was thinking about having whatever I order delivered in November. Jane just mentioned that the baby might come early, and—"

He scowled. "That was an awful thing to say. Is she trying to scare you?"

"No, I don't think she meant it that way."

He didn't look appeased. He said, "Are you sure you don't need help?"

"Yeah, I don't think it would make me very popular, with the game and everything." He met her smile, which was a good start. "Anyway, I guess I'll see you this afternoon."

His eyes followed her to the door. "Okay."

She went out and got a huge reality check on the prices, but in the end, she slid her credit card anyway. She saw some little clothes in the store, which made her chest squeeze. She was excited to hold her baby in her arms; she couldn't even imagine what that would feel like. She tried to picture it, Little Adeline or Little Adrian, but couldn't quite.

She bought some groceries while she was out, determined to cook dinner for once. And since the boys were absorbed in a double overtime, she almost got away with it. Adrian came in halfway through, brow furrowed. "Adeline. Why didn't you say you needed help?"

"I don't," she said. "I'm not fragile, and you have a pot filler, so I don't even have to lift. See?" she said, running it for good measure.

He sighed. "LSU lost," he said, lifting the pots and draining them for her.

"Oh, boohoo. North Carolina always loses."

"True," he said.

She swatted him with a dishcloth, and he laughed. He rested his hand on her waist to reach around her for the silverware, maybe so she wouldn't hit her hip on the drawer.

Don't mind her. She was just over here pretending a normal touch didn't give her shivers. The good kind of shivers, not the creepy kind.

"I think maybe it's too cold to eat outside," she said, clearing her throat and striving for normalcy. Adrian had on a gray LSU sweatshirt. It wasn't summer anymore.

"Yeah, I'll set the table over here," he said.

"Thanks." She started to lift the dishes and take them to the table, but Jude came in, offering his services. She held her breath while he carried them, but he made it. "Me and Daddy can get the drinks, Adeline," he offered.

"Quite the gentleman," she said, handing him the glasses and going to sit down. Adrian smiled with her. He was thawing. Maybe she could apologize tonight.

"Have you ever been to Baton Rouge, Jude?" Adeline asked. She figured Adrian had taken him to a game.

He nodded. "Last year. With Daddy and Uncle Harris and Mr. John."

"How was living in New Orleans while you were in school?" Adeline asked, turning her attention to Adrian.

"It was great," he answered, handing Jude a napkin. "But I prefer Charleston."

"What did you do while you were there?" *Open up. Just a little.* She innocently took a bite.

"Studied mostly," he said grimly. "But the restaurants were great. Jackson Square, trips to the bayou... The history was interesting, admittedly," he said.

"And my mama would come visit him," Jude said.

Adrian looked at his son, and there was a slight silence. Adeline didn't think Jude was old enough to have any designs of making her uncomfortable. She thought, instead, that he was able, little by little, to talk about his mother and was testing the waters. "That's right, buddy, she did," Adrian said, wiping Jude's mouth for him.

Adeline looked at Adrian, letting him take the reins. She wasn't going to move on if he thought Jude needed to dwell. He seemed to be waiting for Jude to make that decision.

"And you went to this place in the French Quarter where the chef came out and screamed at everybody," Jude said quietly, now as if just talking to Adrian, his eyes lighting with amusement.

Adrian studied him. "Yeah, that's right," he said softly. "You have a good memory."

"That's what Ms. Richardson says," Jude agreed, ready to turn the subject.

"Don't be conceited, Jude."

"Okay," he said, taking a drink, unabashed.

Adeline smiled, meeting Adrian's eyes. There was a slight apology in his, but she continued to smile.

Later, when he came into their room, he glanced at her. She had attempted to read her book about Abraham Lincoln but had already lain it aside.

He noticed this and lifted his brows. "Feeling okay?" he asked gently.

She snapped out of it. "Oh. Yeah," she said, smiling.

He sat down next to her, neck attractively giving way to sweatshirt, making you want to see beneath. Or maybe that was just her. He was leaning on his hand, the one with her ring on it.

"Adrian, can we maybe talk?" she asked softly, feeling embarrassed for inexplicable reasons.

Concern flickered in his eyes. "Sure, what's up?"

She pressed her lips together. "I know I've been pushing you away, and I'm sorry." She shook her head, heart pounding because he was looking at her so closely. "I didn't mean to, and then once it got started..."

"Adeline, I said I would give you space to figure this out, and I meant it."

She hesitated. "Yeah, but... I don't think it's that simple anymore, is it, Adrian?" She bit her lip. "I basically cut you off from all contact, and that was...not cool."

He smiled a little, warmth in his expression. He touched one of her curls, fingering it. "Not cool at all," he answered softly.

"Sorry," she whispered. She didn't think she had to explain herself. She could see from the forgiveness in his eyes that he already knew she was a mess.

He initiated a soft kiss, sweet in its gentleness, devastating in its effect. He lingered but never deepened the kiss. Instead, he leaned back, surveying her. "You're sure you've been feeling okay?"

"Yeah, we're fine," she said, covering his hand, giving a smile. He looked down at their hands. She slowly retracted hers. His eyes flickered back up to hers in surprise. She shook her head, blinking. "Sorry. Doing it again."

He kissed her temple, drawing her against his chest. "It's okay," he whispered.

"No, it isn't," she whispered back, feeling odd sinking into him, liking it, but also intensely aware of every flaw in her body.

They settled against the headboard, and he drew her into his side with his arm around her. His hand rested lightly on her middle. The baby fluttered and she turned her head to look up at him. They smiled together.

"I keep wondering what it'll be like," she said, getting less uncomfortable by the minute.

"He'll probably be a little worrier, keeping us on our toes with tough questions."

She laughed softly, knowing the inspiration for that thought. "Definitely a prodigy." She smiled as she dreamed of it. If it were just like Jude, that would be fine with her.

Adeline paused. Worrier, prodigy. He.

She blinked, sitting up. She pinned him with a stare. His eyes were closed, his bottom lip between his teeth. "Adrian!"

"Sorry," he said, exhaling the breath he had been holding, squeezing his eyes together.

"How could you do that?" she demanded, whacking him with her pillow.

He caught the pillow, laughing. But he looked at her with true apology in his eyes. "I'm sorry. So sorry. I think I must be tired."

She looked at him, her expression changing. Suddenly she was sappy like she was looking at kittens or a favorite childhood toy, newly rediscovered. "Aww, we're having a boy!" she said, almost emotionally, blinking away tears.

He smiled, meeting her eyes. "We're having a boy."

"We're having a boy," she repeated, wiping her eyes. She could suddenly picture it all so much better. Her sweet little boy. She looked up so she could see Adrian's face. "Are you happy? Is that what you wanted?"

"It didn't matter, but after the nurse told me, it seemed perfect."

She smiled, tears filling her eyes, and she nodded. She looked at him, overcome by emotion, almost swept away. "Yes. Perfect."

The end of October closed in, and Adeline pushed her crew hard. She hoped to be finished by the November deadline she had set after they had penciled in more time for the library fireplace. She wanted to finish this for Adrian and look back on a job well done. She wanted to nest and for the men to be able to move on to the small job she had taken in Columbia. They would be restoring a ballroom in a hotel. She would go up occasionally and make sure everything was in order. The job would tide the crew over until the baby was born and would be easy for her to manage.

Everything was finished—not to say pristine yet—except the Silk Room. She was waiting to see how the final coat they had put on the fabric settled. It hadn't looked promising the day before when she and Joe had looked it over.

But in other news, she was having a boy. She and Adrian had agreed to keep that fact to themselves until the birth and still let Jude tell everyone then.

"What am I going to name you?" she asked as she walked toward the massive double doorway of the Silk Room where Joe and two of the crew members were.

She looked first at Joe, whose face didn't give her a good feeling, and then to the walls. They were still streaked, scarcely less than when they had first started, and she knew immediately that it wasn't going to work. She did a slow turn around the room, feeling a weight pressing her shoulders down and a sinking in her heart. She covered her mouth, shaking her head, trying not to embarrass herself in front of the crew. Then again, they looked scarcely less broken-hearted.

Joe cleared his throat after a long silence. "I've been thinking, ma'am, that it's probably time to send that scrap to England for reproduction."

She nodded after a moment, her hand on her throat. "Yeah. That's..." She swallowed. "Thomas, will you find a good piece to pull?"

He nodded. "Yeah, I'll get right on it."

She inclined her head once. "Well. No use worrying over it, I guess. Thanks, guys. I'll get back to work." She made a regal exit, went into the kitchen, closed the door, and cried.

She was still crying thirty minutes later when, much to her surprise and chagrin, the back door to the kitchen opened and Adrian strode in. She looked up, clearly a mess, and tried to wipe her face hurriedly. He scowled. "Adeline? If my mom called, I swear I'll—"

"No, it's not that." She tried to laugh. He was coming toward her, kneeling beside her and taking her hands. She had paired Adrian's kitchen speaker to her phone and had been listening to fun music in an attempt to lift her spirits while she wept. The plan had not worked. "I can't save the silk, Adrian," she whispered.

He sighed. "Adeline. Do you think I care about that?"

"*I* care about it, Adrian."

"I know," he said softly.

She met his eyes, biting her trembling lip. What was wrong with her? "I promise you, I don't usually throw a tantrum when something doesn't go my way on a project." More tears spilled out, and his thumbs stroked the soft skin of her wrists. She cried embarrassingly for about a minute before saying, "And I'm going to be a terrible mother."

"You're not going to be a terrible mother," he said calmingly, apparently not questioning where that thought came from.

"Yes, I am." She sniffed. "I...should probably tell you that I don't want to breastfeed." She hiccupped on a sob.

He looked like he was suppressing a laugh. "Adeline, I don't care," he said.

She swallowed, blinking rapidly. She needed to pull it

together pronto. "We're going to send a sample to England for reproduction, so it'll probably take another couple of months. The crew can come back one weekend and—"

"Adeline," he said. He had stood, and a smile was hovering—unusual for him. "Can we not talk about that?" She bit her lip. She was doing it again. Getting hyper-focused on work. She wasn't sure why he stuck with her.

Sam Cooke's *Wonderful World* had just started playing. Adrian reached for her hands, and she looked up at him. She put her hands in his, standing, and he brought her against him. She didn't know why he was surprised that he was a natural dancer. The way he had moved had always mesmerized her, and he was surprisingly athletic. She laughed at a move, smiling up into his face, and he was smiling, like he had on Sullivan's Island. Like in the pictures of his first wedding. Like he did when he was happy.

Adeline studied him. She needed to be very careful. Nothing about this was simple anymore. She hadn't anticipated this. And she would bet he hadn't either. Now the question remained: was he just as scared of her as she was of him?

# Chapter Seven

The house which had been invaded by the Occupation was a large mansion that had once been inhabited by some of the Pinckneys. Likely, it had been abandoned and confiscated. It was brick and sprawled with rotundas and halls and chambers, providing plenty of room for more than thirty Army staff who either lived or worked there. Shannon and John Thomas brought with them two of his aides: Lieutenant Georgeson, who was his secretary, and Captain Jay.

Admiral and Mrs. Haley had been greeted by the Army with great hospitality. They were given a suite of two rooms, both of which were bedchambers. One of them was styled more like a sitting room with a small bed and a handsome desk, which John Thomas took, leaving her the more lavish. He settled her into bed himself as soon as they arrived, running his hand over her hair. The feather bed was her undoing, and she slept almost two days, scarcely waking.

When Shannon fretted that John Thomas ought to leave her established and go back to his ships, he told her that it was becoming impractical anyway and asked whether she truly believed he would entertain the thought of leaving her. The ships, he assured her, would be left in the charge of capable captains and would await further instruction from Charleston.

Charleston was experiencing occupation not of any concerted government effort, but of the military fashion, like any of the Southern cities which had fallen throughout the war. The current mission of the officers of the Army and Navy was to stabilize the city and, more broadly, the eastern seaboard and Atlantic, a task which kept them all busy from dawn until dusk.

John Thomas, hanging close, asked whether Shannon wished to send a message to her family.

She shook her head. "I know it might be difficult to understand or sound silly, but I... My father hurt me greatly. He never would've closed his doors to a son, and I thought he loved me enough..." Her voice broke. She looked away.

His face tensed in sympathy.

He had asked her immediately after their arrival which doctor she preferred. Too ill to give it much consideration, she had mentioned Dr. Travers, since he had always been her family's doctor. It would prove to be a mistake that she would regret, and she wasn't even aware of the cool greeting afforded to John Thomas below stairs.

The doctor had stridden past the occupier, asking to

be told where John Ravenel's daughter was, and, upon being directed, had gone up to her without further ado. John Thomas, scarcely caring as long as Shannon was well-treated, paced in the green library below.

The house was rather thin of its occupants. Most of the Army men went out to the encampments at least once a day, for which John Thomas was grateful this day.

He paced continuously, wondering how the meeting was progressing with the doctor, and whether Shannon felt alone in this perilous situation. His chest tightened at the thought. Ought he to go up? Would she consider it an intrusion? The examination seemed to go on forever as possibilities played themselves out in his fevered mind.

At length, the doctor emerged, and John Thomas met him immediately at the bottom of the steps. He took Dr. Travers into the library, paying him and asking what his thoughts were on the matter. The white-haired man was silent for a moment, his mouth pursed in distaste at the Yankee household. "I take a very unfavorable view of the case," he said finally.

The blood drained from John Thomas's face. His lips parted as he fixed his eyes on the doctor's.

"I should, in any event, do so. But you may not be aware that your wife took a very bad cold following her forced march, half-naked, into Charleston. She has struggled with her health ever since."

His heart stuttered. "No," he whispered, barely audibly. "I didn't know." He thought of Shannon without him and ill, and after such a painful experience. He would've given anything not to have had such an image in his mind. "You believe she may be in danger, then?" He drew a thin breath.

"If she produces a healthy child next winter, I should be very much surprised," the doctor said, and John Thomas could feel bile rising in his throat. His hopes sank to the floor. "If the process does not kill her, I should be even more surprised. In short, *Admiral* Haley, the chances of both your wife and child surviving are narrow." John Thomas gripped the edge of the desk, his knuckles going white as the doctor continued speaking. "It gives me no pleasure to tell you this. But the blockade so cut us off from proper nourishment that many women are finding it difficult to bear their children, and Mrs. Haley is no different. My felicitations, Admiral. All over the South are women who will be killed and children who will never be born because of the shameful acts your government enacted upon an innocent populace."

Ravenel House was shrouded in peacefulness until the boots of the gentleman began pounding against the wooden floors. Frederick Ravenel threw back the doors of the library, and they slammed against their respective walls. "Father!" he called, seeing that gentleman standing near a window with his hands clasped behind his back.

Mr. Ravenel turned, lifting his brows in surprise and displeasure. His son was standing several paces away in a green coat and riding breeches, a folded scrap of paper in his right hand, his jaw thunderous. "Shannon is with child," he announced, eyes sparking in anger.

Mr. Ravenel blinked. He could not at first speak. "What?" he breathed.

"Travers's servant told July, who told me, and I have had it confirmed from Travers himself," he said, waving the letter. "You have sent her back, and this is the result! How can you justify it, Father?" he demanded. "You closed your doors to her, and she went back. She is now living in the house of the Army Occupation. She is alone and with child, and a more precarious situation can scarcely be imagined. Can you live with yourself?"

Color heightening, his father exploded, "Do you mean to suggest to me that *that young man* would *dare* to take my daughter without her consent? If you *do*, then you may collect your shotgun as well as mine, and I will see him into his grave before the sun sets."

Frederick paused, blinking. "No," he said, unnerved. He shook his head. "No. But it is not that simple, as you know full well. If she returned to him, she must eventually end in his bed."

His father stared at him, looking forbidding and shaken all at once.

"You were thinking like a man," Frederick said, jaw clenching. "You were thinking there would be no repercussions, but for a woman there are *always* consequences. Now her whole life is determined. If she wanted to leave him, she couldn't," he said, eyes flaming. "And what choice she had in the matter, I cannot see."

"I cannot live under his roof any longer, Elizabeth," Frederick said. She lay against him, his arm around her. One candle flickered, but otherwise their chamber was in darkness.

"Oh, Frederick." Elizabeth sighed as she stroked his chest. They lay in silence a long while. Finally, she said, "Did you ever think perhaps Shannon was glad?"

"She despised him so much that she fled from him right into a war. I was the first to condemn her for it, but we came to terms, and if I don't support her now, who will? What if she felt trapped? She is *irrevocably* tied to him now. All rights to the child will belong to him, and Shannon's no fool. She knows that."

Elizabeth pressed her lips together, taking a long breath. "Frederick, there is something I must tell you," she said, lifting her head. His brows drawing together, he looked into her eyes. She hovered above him with her hand on his chest. He covered her hand. "I understand why Shannon felt it necessary to break ties with us. She is spirited, and...I might have done the same myself." She paused. "I have kept this from you because Shannon told it to me in confidence. But she intended to return to him before ever your father forced her to it. Not perhaps that moment, but she did intend to return." His brow was still furrowed as he searched her face. "I believe she realized that she had made a mistake. She wanted to tell her husband that she still loved him—to reconcile, I mean, if he would have her. Obviously, his answer was yes. So don't repine about the baby, my dear man. When you told me, I wanted to shout for joy."

Frederick was much relieved, and his mood lifted—until he received a letter three days later which read, "*Come to me at the Old Pinckney Mansion. I have need of you. Shannon.*"

He knew two things at once. First, that Shannon was going to ask him to take her away, and second, that he would have to do it. Removing a man's wife from under his very roof (and that roof a house of occupation of a victorious army with which he had, quite recently, been at war) was something he had no notion of how to achieve. It would be a shocking thing, one of the most regrettably shocking requests Shannon had ever asked of him. But he would do it for her sake, he thought, grimly and bitterly resolved.

It occurred to him (not for the first time) as he tied his horse outside the mansion that he might be arrested for stepping foot on the property of occupying headquarters, something that added to his grim look. He merely hoped he wouldn't be taken as hostile. Considering how to do it, he decided to carry it off with a high hand. He strolled up to the door and, when a Negro woman opened it, told her that he was Mrs. Haley's brother, and he would be obliged to her if she would take him to her.

"Why, yes, sir," she said, seemingly surprised. She glanced up at him quickly and then away before setting off toward the stairs.

He followed her through the hall, past rooms where he saw many blue coats, none of which saw him. He glanced around, seeing that they had set up house, but not fully. There was furniture missing, large maps and scrolls lay here and there, and other pieces of furniture were seemingly stowed where they ought not to be. The Negro woman knocked on a door and announced him.

Frederick walked in to see Shannon lying like a queen in the bed. A tray of food the likes of which he hadn't seen in ages lay to her left, a newspaper was spread open to her right, and a stack of books was before her. Any visions of her in a neglected state fled. "Frederick!" she exclaimed, extending her hands as tears started to her eyes.

He walked forward, taking her hands. "Now, what's all this, Shannon? I ought not to be here."

"You won't be arrested: I'll see to that."

"Handsome of you," he said. He spoke irascibly before remembering her condition and saying, "Never mind that. Lying in bed at noon?"

She smiled but said, "I have been ordered to stay here. I am ill, and if Charleston is even a ghost of its former self, I imagine you know the cause."

"Ill?" he asked, pressing her hand.

"Yes, but that is being seen to and is not the reason I sent for you."

He braced himself. She studied him, her fair brows and lashes seemingly even lighter. She looked weak.

Moistening her lips, she pronounced, "I need you to speak with John Thomas."

"What?" His eyes snapped to hers. "Shannon, I cannot! You know perfectly well he oughtn't to speak with me, to fraternize with the enemy."

"We are not at war anymore," she said firmly. "And whatever has happened, that isn't his way, as you know perfectly well. The very first thing he asked me was whether you survived the war."

His throat tightened, and he looked away. At length, however, his brows drew together. "Well, in any event, we shouldn't see one another until the fate of the Confederate officers is decided. And I should not be seen here at all. I imagine you are already under suspicion. What are you about, Shannon? What do you want me to say to him that you cannot say yourself?"

She bit her lip. "I have been most displeased with Dr. Travers. Frederick, I think he must have said something awful to John Thomas, for he looked so shaken when next I saw him, though he tried to hide it and still does. He will not leave this house, despite that there are many occasions when he ought to do so. I think he has taken a leave from his duties, for he is very rarely out of calling distance. He says he doesn't want to leave me alone, which is absurd when others are here, and I am not so very ill. Jeptha—one of the maids—says he looks like he's seen a ghost. Well, I *know* it was Dr. Travers, for he did not want to come to this house. He let me know what he thought of *my* fraternizing—he was quite vulgar—and said he only came because he felt a sense of duty to my father. I was within an *inch* of mentioning Marie's death to him and reminding him that we never blamed him, though we could have, and if he crosses this threshold again, I will *bite* him!"

Frederick looked startled and, seeing her flaming eyes, said, "There, don't upset yourself. I will talk to him and tell him you don't want Travers back."

"*Thank* you," she said, eyes shining. "And you must undo whatever Travers has done, for John Thomas is barely even eating, and I worry this has entirely overset him. I have never seen him like this, Frederick. You will know what to do."

Frederick nodded, pressing her hand. "Things...must be resolved between you." When she flushed, he did so as well, hastening to add, "I mean if you are so worried for him!"

There was a long silence. "No," she said softly, looking down and picking at her blanket. "No, but he doesn't deserve to feel as Travers has made him feel. He has been through such a great many trials, much of it my doing, and I shan't let him suffer anymore."

Though Frederick started to speak, he seemed to decide against it. He then took his leave of her, asking where he might find John Thomas. She lifted a bell, sighing, and said, "Jeptha will take you. She seems to have been assigned to me solely, as everyone here seems to believe I am dying." When Jeptha came within moments, Shannon said, "Please escort my brother to Admiral Haley. And if anyone has any questions, please direct them to me. Please do not mention his name, or our relationship. Thank you, Jeptha."

"Yes, ma'am," she said, glancing at Frederick before escorting him downstairs. She took him to a quiet part of the house to what appeared to be a small study. There he saw, like a vision from the past, John Thomas sitting at the desk, his elbows resting on it, his head in his hands.

Frederick's coat brushed the door facing, and John Thomas looked up. His lips parted. He blinked. "Frederick?" he asked in disbelief. In just a moment, he came to his feet, looking toward the door, his face paling.

"No, she is well!" Frederick hastened to say. He added, "She asked me to come."

John Thomas's look turned wary. Frederick knew he was thinking the same thing he himself had, and that was the first proof Frederick had that things were indeed not rose-hued between them. "She merely wished to see me."

It struck him that John Thomas was still watching him, that he hadn't spoken more than his name, and Frederick wondered if he was on solid ground.

Finally, though, John Thomas came to himself. "Great heavens," he said, shaking his head to clear it. He walked toward the door, and, after glancing out, closed it. "Still bold as brass, I see!" he said, turning the lock and looking at Frederick in shock at his behavior.

Frederick couldn't help grinning. "Shannon assures me that I won't be arrested—just as though she has authority!"

Walking back into the room, John Thomas asked as he

observed Frederick, "What did she need? I don't understand."

Frederick cleared his throat. "She wants me to ask you to dismiss Dr. Travers."

A mildly confused look entered his distracted eyes. "Travers? Does she? I wonder that she didn't tell me herself," he mused softly.

"She thought you might be offended, having brought him in to her," he hedged.

John Thomas's brows drew together. "He is the man *she* chose," he said. After a moment, he added, "But in any event, I am reluctant to dismiss him. He knows her health; he was present at her birth." He dragged a hand through his hair. Then he, sinking to his chair, said in agony, "He thinks Shannon and the baby won't live, Frederick, and what is to be done, I don't..." His voice trailed off. Saying the words aloud seemed to throw him into a near-manic state, for Frederick had never seen him look just so. But John Thomas looked up after a moment, stricken. He swallowed, collecting himself, and said, "Dear God, to say such things to you—forgive me!"

Frederick shook his head. "No, no. There is nothing to forgive," he said softly, looking at him with compassion.

John Thomas studied him. Frederick felt the silence grow and knew he was thinking of Marie. Frederick knew also that he wouldn't say anything, though, because John Thomas always grasped when he would prefer not to speak of something. A war and years of separation wouldn't have changed that.

Frederick cleared his throat. "Now, listen, Haley, he can't know that. No one can know at the outset a woman's fate, let alone the child's."

His former friend sat silently, lips compressed, his mind receding, it seemed.

"I mean that," Frederick pressed.

John Thomas lifted his face, a haunted look casting shadows in his eyes.

Frederick moved closer to the desk. "Where is the fellow who used to tell me that with God all things are possible? That nothing is a foregone conclusion?" he demanded fiercely.

John Thomas held his eyes, and, slowly, a sheen of moisture filled his. He looked away, seemingly trying to collect himself. At length, he said quietly, visibly shaken, "Yes. Yes, you are quite right."

Frederick let him sit in silence for a moment. "Now, don't go thinking it was a crisis of faith, Haley, for I know you. You are worried for your wife, and there is no shame in that."

A flicker of a smile appeared, to Frederick's surprise. He said, voice cracking, "I've missed you, Frederick."

Frederick's throat tightened. He cleared it. He held the other man's eyes for a moment, the years of war, the unspoken enmity, and the state of John Thomas's and Shannon's marriage hovering between them. Frederick could see that something still weighed on him, and he said, hesitant because he feared he didn't have the right, "Come, what is it?"

John Thomas seemed surprised at his question but only for a moment. After a long silence, he shook his head.

"I've put Shannon in a terrible position, Frederick," he said. "Estranged from her family, only just reconciled to me... I don't want her to feel isolated for a single moment, but I would imagine she feels nothing *but* alone. I am all she has, and she can't want that."

"Has she said so?"

"No," he said, voice quivering. He cleared his throat, and his eyes tightened. "She has been sweetness itself, whereas I..."

Silence reigned, and birds sang outside. Frederick was inclined to grip his shoulder, for the man's pain was palpable. John Thomas never would've imagined himself in such a position. His love for Shannon had been as real as anything. To think of an estrangement between them would once have been absurd, especially at such a moment.

As seconds passed, Frederick instead said calmly in a voice of reason, "Shannon is not estranged from her family. My father wants reconciliation. It worries him day and night, their falling-out."

John Thomas seemed to come to himself, but he hesitated. "I fear, given her feelings on the matter, that reconciliation will be a long time in coming, Frederick. I know she misses you and your family, however."

"We miss her, too, especially my daughter."

John Thomas said after clearing his throat, "Shannon tells me that Rose is a fine little girl, and very beautiful."

"She would say that. She's her very image," Frederick answered, but pride gleamed in his eyes.

"Is she?" John Thomas asked, wonder in his expression.

"Nearly identical. In face *and* personality. Elizabeth says—" He halted, meeting his eyes.

"I knew," John Thomas said, nodding. "I always liked Miss Middleton very much. I pray you have found happiness with her."

"Yes." He flushed. "Perhaps in a better day you can meet her as my wife. I ought to take my leave of you. Only be sure not to let Travers see Shannon again. She thinks his—err—politics are clouding his judgment." As a clincher, he added, "And she won't have it. Says she'll bite him if he crosses the threshold again."

"Bite him?" John Thomas asked faintly.

"Yes. And I believe she meant it."

"Well," John Thomas responded, perhaps the barest twinkle touching his worried eyes. "I suppose that won't do then."

*Charleston*

*July 1865*

*My Dear Mother,*

*I pray all of you are doing well. I will write to the others when time permits, but for now, I wished to give you news of me. I am in Charleston still.*

Naturally, this placed me in proximity to the Ravenels. Wishing to reconcile, Shannon sought me out in April, and she is with me now. As you are aware, she has suffered a great deal during the war, as have I, and we are eager to put the past behind us.

To this, we have an added joy: Shannon has told me that she is expecting our first child in January. My happiness is only tempered by concern for Shannon. She has been very ill. It is upon this subject that I write to you, despite what I know will be a shocking letter for you. I beg for your advice. I know you, if you were with her, could make her better. But as that is not a possibility at present, I hope you will tell me how I may do so. She is not able to eat, or, if she does eat, she is afterwards very sick. This state of affairs has led her to become so weak that she has been confined to her bed.

She has been seen by one of our physicians, Dr. Schafer, who believes the sickness will pass, despite the belief of a local doctor that she and the child stand in grave danger. The former has taken her under his care and has provided some relief to her, but I would prefer still more. I should be very grateful for any advice you may have to give.

Convey the news to my brothers and sisters and give them my love. Tell me everything concerning Charles.

I remain your loving son,
JTH

# Chapter Eight

A month passed, and Shannon began to grow stronger. She was able to rise from her bed on most days. While she did not go out often, it was a welcome relief merely to take advantage of the mansion's well-stocked library, which its previous inhabitants had left more or less intact. They had likely been unable to expend the time or effort to try to sell the collection.

She had exchanged two letters with Elizabeth: one in which Elizabeth had asked if she might send Shannon's clothes and shoes to her (to which she had replied *no*) and another in which Elizabeth had said she was sending them anyway. Shannon could not be altogether sorry, even if it meant accepting trunks from her father's household.

On a Sunday afternoon, she sat in the window seat of the parlor, the library's solitary volume of Shakespeare open in her lap. She had watched out the window the throng of worshippers walking, riding, or taking carriages to their churches. And all she could think of now was how weary the people looked, how bedraggled and low.

And yet, the Negros were, in some respects, jubilant. Their children were allowed to attend classes for the first time in schools opened by Northerners, and they could assemble any time they chose. The former slaves' festivals of freedom were still taking place in the streets.

They had raised funds to make a proper cemetery for the Union soldiers who had died at the Washington Race Course, which had been a prisoner of war camp. Shannon had seen a fundraising pamphlet on John Thomas's desk, detailing the endeavor. Thousands of Negros had come out to support the effort, and they had done all of the work. They raised more than two-hundred-fifty graves, made markers, and built a tall fence to protect the cemetery from grazing animals.

Shannon finally heard a door opening and a stirring and looked up to see several men file out into the foyer in their various shades of blue dress uniforms. John Thomas had been in a meeting with several officers, of both Naval and Army variety. She leaned to look through the crack of her door and heard murmurs and whispers.

"The lynching across the state simply must stop."

"But with matters so tenuous, the populace so unsettled—"

"I don't care if we have to use the full might of our military power. It must stop, and this people must be brought to understand that they are no longer the law. They are in *violation* of the law!"

"Indeed," came another, more languid voice, "but until Congress devises a resolution, it is all very well for the President to say *keep the general order*. But how we are to do so among a people still unwilling to submit—"

Someone broke in, saying something too low for her to hear. She then heard John Thomas's voice for the first time, saying something to settle tempers. In moments, the Army men dispersed, on their way to a review of the regiments.

After a few more seconds, she heard a woman's voice. Catching the accent, Shannon quickly discarded the idea of it being any of the servants or the General's wife, so she knew it must be Mrs. Rice. She was likely bringing her husband's noonday meal to share with him. This Shannon confirmed when she recognized Commodore Rice's voice.

"I did go up to call upon her, but she wasn't there," Mrs. Rice said in a hushed tone, almost a whisper. "I imagine that the creature has slipped the leash and gone to church among her own people."

"I have not known her to do so. Perhaps tomorrow you might see her. I believe it would mean a great deal to him if you could make an effort in that direction, my love. You must see that he is in a difficult situation: cut off from our homes as we are and yet unable to send her to her own kinswomen for care as one usually would."

"I see he is in a difficult situation, yes," she answered in a clipped whisper. Her tone was heavy with innuendo.

A brief silence. Shannon cocked her head, leaning toward the door.

"What do you mean?"

"Didn't the Admiral tell you that they anticipate the child's birth in January?"

Another pause. "Yes. I believe so." She heard confusion in his lowly spoken reply.

"Well, might she just as easily have been with child when she boarded the ship as not, in that case?"

Shannon tried not to sharpen her breath. She heard movement, like a man taking his wife's arm and pulling her away from danger, which she gathered to be the other door. What they didn't know was that they had drawn closer to her own door.

"Amabel, your dislike carries you too far!" he hissed. "Haley is no fool. If he claims the child, there can be no doubt of its sire."

Apparently duly chastened, no more except an unintelligible low mumble was heard from the lady. After a few moments, Shannon heard the footfalls of their retreat.

Shannon, leaning back, knew that it was in large part jealousy. She imagined that when Amabel Rice had joined her husband during the war, she had been the highest-ranking officer's wife present. She also imagined that, since Mrs. Rice was safe in a pious, middle-class marriage, John Thomas had felt comfortable lowering his guard with her as he had with few other women during the war. He had offered his friendship to the wife of a friend he held dear. Mrs. Rice had made certain that Shannon knew that John Thomas had become attached to the Rice children during the war.

And the woman had heard, of course, every rumor regarding Shannon—her beauty, her familial status, her betrayal. The latter with which, of course, Shannon had given her perfect ammunition for hatred. She imagined that Amabel Rice was a little in love with John Thomas, not in a dangerous sort of way, or even in one that truly betrayed her husband, but rather in the manner of a young girl idealizing a storybook hero.

Now she had been thoroughly deposed, for an admiral's wife sat higher on the table than a commodore's. And if there was an honor to be bestowed (such as the General taking a Naval lady into supper) it was likely to be upon Shannon. Captain Jay liked Shannon, too, sending her bouquets every day she was unwell and talking all the time of their evenings spent together before the war. And now, the whole headquarters was bending to accommodate her illness. This was an occurrence which Shannon knew to be more in deference to John Thomas than to herself, but it must have been difficult for Mrs. Rice to watch, nonetheless.

Still, it was a good story the lady had speculated into belief, one with a startlingly authentic ring to it, especially if one already despised Shannon. There was no doubt the woman could do a great deal of damage if she chose. And yet, Shannon didn't think she would be so bold.

She sat, her book laying forgotten on her lap, her lip between her teeth. She must suppose that John Thomas did not share the woman's suspicions. And heaven forbid he ever did.

Ten thousand people went to watch the dedication of the Martyrs of the Race Course Cemetery, most of them Negros. Two military regiments and a military band had been there, too. Shannon, occupied with the hospital during the war, hadn't had time to give much thought to the prisoner camp, which was located on the site of Charleston's once-grand racecourse.

But she thought of it now. On the day of the dedication, schoolchildren had led a procession and adorned the Union graves with flowers. Despite the large crowd, only a few had been allowed inside to dedicate the cemetery, all of them former slaves. The gates were closed, and white Charlestonians were expelled.

Shannon looked around now as she was handed down from the carriage, fearing she would not be welcome still. But no one was about. The place was peaceful and quiet. John Thomas did not know she had made this outing, but she intended to go home straight away.

She clasped the bouquet, glancing up at the soldier who had brought her. Quietly walking to the gates, she waited while he opened them. Then she glanced across the rows of markers, struggling to stem her tears.

She went to the nearest grave and knelt, placing her flowers and touching the ground with her gloved fingers. *Timothy Payne, Kentucky*, the marker read. Lowering her head, she closed her eyes and offered up thanks to God. For it might just as easily have been her husband.

It was nighttime, and Shannon felt well enough to attend supper below stairs with the officers. She was not the only woman in the house: old General Robertson's lady had come to be with him, and, while the Rices had lodgings elsewhere, they often came to dine.

While Mrs. Robertson's manner wasn't precisely warm, she did accept Shannon as an officer's wife. Mrs. Rice, however, would hardly speak to her. The room was not a scene of elegance, since men were running the household. Any proper etiquette at all was due to Mrs. Robertson's efforts.

Shannon listened as the officers argued civilly over how severe the punishment must be for those who violated the lives or liberty of the freedmen. It was startling, if true, how deep the brutalities had run across the state. There were none in Charleston just now (at least that she had heard) with the freedmen having the majority and the military presence being strong. But she wondered how long that would last.

"You're telling me that you think we ought to turn a blind eye," Captain Jay said, eyes kindling. "When a colored man was dragged from his bed, his wife and children watching, and strung up from the nearest tree?" Shannon was beginning to think that, over the course of the war, the word *Negro* had gone out of fashion in Northern circles. She took mental note of it. It would not do for Admiral Haley's wife, of all people, to seem backwards.

"No," Colonel Rittenburg replied, arms stretched out languidly with palms on the table. "I merely suggest that to hang the perpetrators likewise would be to incite a rebellion amongst the whole populace of South Carolina."

"Then let rebellion come!" Commodore Rice exclaimed, apparently aghast. "What in the name of *heaven* have we been fighting for if we are only to give them reign of the whole the territory once more? Do you think there will be a freedman alive, much less able to flourish and prosper, in six months' time?"

"I believe you exaggerate," a languid major intoned. "And it is their territory. What right have we to reign in it more than they?"

This caused an uproarious reaction of loud opinions such that the General, sitting at the head of the table, raised his hand in benevolent grace and asked for order to be restored. All the while, John Thomas sat unflustered by the commotion, occasionally talking quietly either to the person on his right or his left.

"What do you think, Mrs. Halcy?"

Shannon almost jumped. She looked around and realized it was General Robertson himself who had asked. The table had gone silent. They could hear the distant clang of the silver in the kitchen. She glanced across the table at John Thomas. He had stiffened and was not taking his eyes off of her. She felt mostly certain that it was a protective stance, but she could not be sure, of course.

After a pause, she turned her head toward the General. "I believe Commodore Rice is right," she said quietly in her lilting accent. But somehow her voice seemed to resonate through the entire room. "You must act swiftly and harshly in such instances. Nothing else will be effective to protect the freedmen." It was God's truth, however much a traitor she felt.

Silence reigned for almost a full minute. But Shannon experienced the feeling for the first time in her life of knowing her words would be heeded.

Shannon felt rather exhausted by the time she made it to her bedchamber. Trying to light a lamp, she couldn't get the wick to burn immediately, but eventually she managed it, turning down the knob and resetting the glass. She realized then that she was very warm. Walking toward the windows, she unlatched the lock on one of them as she looked down into the estate's park of live oaks below. But she couldn't force the window to budge so she turned away.

Sighing, she began struggling in the lamplight to unbutton her dress. Most of her day gowns fastened in the front and presented no obstacle, but her evening gown required a smooth bodice and possessed tiny buttons down her back. This was more difficult to manage alone.

There was a knock from the hall. She straightened, walked to the door, and opened it. John Thomas stood outside.

He was looking at her intensely, searching her too closely. It went on so long that she lowered her eyes. "John Thomas," she said belatedly, rather short of breath, though she didn't know why. She stepped back to allow him to enter. His presence made her lofty chamber feel small. He continued to regard her as though she were a foreign and an unusual creature. "Do you... Would you mind opening my windows?" she asked.

He almost jumped. "Oh—! Yes, of course!" Pulling at his collar, he seemed to suffer in the heat, too, probably more so than she. He slid the window up all the way to the top in one fluid, maddening motion. She heard the ropes pulling smoothly as he repeated the action with the other. At length, he turned back around to look at her. "You...are feeling well?" he asked haltingly after a pause.

"Yes."

He nodded, drawing his hand through his blonde hair, looking away for a moment. Looking up, he said, "Would you like to go outside? Perhaps a breeze—"

"No," she said. After a moment, she added with a touch of humor, "I am half-undressed already."

His eyes dropped finally to her hand where it held her dress closed. And lingered. At length, he looked back up, swallowing, meeting her eyes, and not moving. "Do you... Do you need help?"

"Yes," she said softly, barely above a whisper.

Holding her eyes, he moved forward, going around behind her. He touched the first button. A long silence followed—the clock ticking, the lamp whistling, his fingers against the fabric. "I hope you didn't feel attacked at supper," he said, his voice cutting through the silence. He cleared his throat.

"No," she answered, her cheeks heated.

"I didn't think you did," he returned gently. She didn't know what to make of that statement. He reached the button nearest to her skirt, the last one. Then he slid the sleeves over her shoulders, and she waited while he, after a slight pause, began on her laces. His fingers seared her wherever they brushed. She moistened her lips and clasped her hands at her middle.

He finished, and there was nothing left for him to do. He paused a moment overlong and then stepped away and around to face her. "Well, then," he said softly, regarding her, taking in her eyes. He had always been fascinated with them.

Her heart quickened. "Well, then."

He looked as though he wished to say something, but he didn't. "I... Goodnight, Shannon."

She studied him. "Goodnight, John Thomas." Her eyes followed him as he left.

John Thomas knew he was caught between waking and sleeping in his bed, but he was just enough asleep that he was powerless to wake. The sun was not quite up; he noticed that fact before he knew he was slipping into unconsciousness again.

In his dream, Shannon was sitting at the table across from him. He was so struck by her beauty, he could scarcely breathe.

"What a picture you paint of me, Papa. I am neither so quiet nor so effective." She smiled at him. "I am merely Elizabeth Bennett—are you acquainted with her, Mr. Haley?"

"Quite personally," he said, holding her eyes with a sparkle in his own.

"Then you will understand that I am of 'an unsocial, taciturn disposition, unwilling to speak unless I expect to say something that will amaze the room, and be handed down to posterity with the éclat of a proverb.'"

John Thomas awakened suddenly. He listened to the sound of his own breathing for a long time, feeling his heart beating. Finally, he got up. It was still very early. Only the guards posted outside were awake, and there was a stillness to the house. He walked to the desk, picking up the letter that remained open on it from the night before.

*Harmony Grove*
*July 1865*

*My Dear Son,*

*I hardly know what to write and find my thoughts*

in turmoil. I was naturally very much shocked by your letter. When last we were together, you bore my misuses as few children would have, and I can only offer as my excuse that I was grief-stricken and thank God for your forgiving nature.

The other news which you conveyed must have been a delightful and pleasing surprise. The child which is to come will be a very welcome addition to our family. It sounds as though Shannon is having a difficult time. I wish I might come to you, but Charles's condition is such at the moment that I am unable to do so. I will write you more on that subject later. But I have enclosed several recipes from which I hope Shannon may derive relief.

And now I must entreat you, my dear son, to hasten in sending her to us. She will benefit from the cool climate and the company of other ladies, and I solemnly vow to you that we will, all of us, put past differences behind us for your sake and the sake of the child she carries and treat her as one of our own.

You will, of course, visit her when you are able, and you may safely commend her to our care. I do not like to think of a woman in her condition in a war-torn land living amongst none but military men with little access to proper medical care or supplies. I know *a little of these things from my time abroad, and I can promise you that these circumstances are difficult for gently bred ladies.*

*But, of course, the decision is yours, and you have always exercised sound judgment. You must tell me if there is any way in which I can be of use to you.*

*Until next time,*
*Your Loving Mother*

John Thomas looked up, holding the letter, and leaned against the window casing. He watched as a guard relieved another from duty, the gold buttons of their uniforms flashing as the first vestiges of sunlight glimmered. And at length, he turned to take his mother's recipes down to the kitchen.

Shannon lay in bed, vaguely ill. She had heard John Thomas leave his chamber before the sun was quite up. He had left a note for her saying that he hoped that by joining them early at the ships, he would find himself able to return midday to handle his correspondence and to see that she was well. In the meantime, she must send word to him if she needed anything at all. He remained hers, etc.

Shannon sighed, absently running her handkerchief through her hand when she heard someone walking in the hall. Her door cracked open. Jeptha said in hushed tones, her head toward the hallway, "She's in there, ma'am."

Sitting up, Shannon heard Elizabeth's voice say, "Thank you," and her sister-in-law appeared, hesitating in the doorway with clear and concerned eyes.

"Elizabeth!" Shannon cried, tears flooding to her eyes. "My dear friend!"

"Oh, Shannon," Elizabeth said emotionally, going forward and leaning down to embrace her. "Dearest, have you been unwell today?"

"Yes," Shannon sighed. "Though all of last week I was much better."

Elizabeth stroked her cheek, looking her face over worriedly. "I know I ought not to be here, but I thought you might need me."

"I shall *always* need you," Shannon said earnestly, catching her hand. "Though you *shouldn't* be here, of course."

Unheeding, Elizabeth sat on the bed, retaining her hand, her lips trembling into a smile. "Oh, *Shannon!*" she whispered as tears filled her eyes.

With fresh, answering tears, Shannon smiled, tightening her hand.

"I cannot imagine either your surprise or your joy," Elizabeth said earnestly. "I know the timing... But your husband must be happy?"

Shannon shook her head. "He feels it as he ought, but he has been too worried for me to be happy," she said. "I have been ill, you see, and that fool Travers... I suppose Frederick told you. He informed John Thomas that he has killed me and half the women in the South. I finally dragged that out of an orderly who was listening in the hallway."

Elizabeth's eyes sparked. "Infamous!"

"Yes, I should like to give him a piece of my mind," Shannon said, looking militant. "But what of all of you? How is my dear Rose?"

"Mischievous," Elizabeth said succinctly without hesitation. "And so precocious we haven't any notion what to do with her."

Shannon wiped stray tears, beaming, and Elizabeth laughed at her. "Oh, my dear." She slipped her handkerchief from her sleeve for Shannon, blotting her eyes gently as she smiled.

"Oh, Elizabeth, I *miss* her!" she mourned.

"My dear! It is too terrible, but I don't suppose we *can* see one another just yet."

"No. I don't believe Frederick ought to be seen here, nor should the wife of Admiral Haley be seen in Captain Ravenel's house. Is there still no word on whether the officers will be arrested?"

A shadow crossed Elizabeth's face. "No," she said softly. She turned her head away.

Shannon gripped her hand, laying her other against her middle as nausea stirred. "Well," she said softly, "it can do you no good to be seen with me, in any event. I daresay I am loathed in Charleston?"

Elizabeth hesitated. Shannon asked, "Because I returned to my husband? That is how I thought it might be."

Her friend shook her head. "No. My mother tells me it is generally believed that your father forced you to do it." She bit her lip, meeting Shannon's eyes and saying gently, "It is because of the baby."

"What?" Shannon breathed.

"I believe Dr. Travers must have conveyed his distaste for your fraternizing (as Frederick said he put it) to a select few people, and now it is all over Charleston."

Shannon lay silently for a time before saying quietly, "Perhaps they believe me to have secured a life of luxury for myself amidst the hardships."

Elizabeth shook her head. "I don't know, my dear friend. It makes me writhe with anger. How they can adore you—nearly worship you—and then turn on you—"

"They venerated my virtue. And now they believe I have none, I suppose."

"Yes, and it is a great deal too much from people constantly droning about a woman's wifely duties to her husband!" Elizabeth exclaimed.

Eyes kindling, Shannon agreed. "Yes, by heaven, and if one performs one's duties, how is the other to be prevented, I should like to know?"

Elizabeth flushed instantly, and, to Shannon's lifted brows, she said, "One hears of certain things to prevent—but that is neither here nor there." Quite red while Shannon regarded her, Elizabeth squeezed Shannon's hand, clearing her throat and saying seriously after a pause, "My dear, I fear your privacy has left you and may never return. Your husband is a person of fascination here. They discuss him all day long in their parlors. And you, too. You…have been thrust into a life of fame and consequence."

Shannon hesitated. "I believe that may be the case, but it is hard to tell just at this moment, stranded as I am."

"Well, in any event, I assure you that my mother and I do all we can to quell the vicious tongues."

She met Elizabeth's eyes. "Thank you. But I have learned that there is only One opinion which matters, and if the people of Charleston think that honor belongs to them, they are deeply mistaken."

Elizabeth smiled, and just then they heard a horse riding up the lane. The morning had slipped away, and Shannon said, "That will be John Thomas, I imagine. He has been in meetings. All of the others were reviewing the troops, I believe."

"I know. I saw them ride through town." Elizabeth got up, going to pull back the curtains and watch as he handed his reins off to the aide who had accompanied him home. She stood in silence for a few moments before looking over her shoulder. "Is it my imagination, or has he grown more handsome over the years?"

Shannon burst into silent tears, nodding and groping for her handkerchief. "And he will scarcely come near me!"

"What?" Elizabeth looked at her quickly.

Shannon nodded. "It is the severest trial, Elizabeth!"

"Because of your illness, surely."

Shannon shook her head. "I think he is afraid of me, of

my power over him, so he is determined to allow me none."

Elizabeth studied her. "He is kind to you?"

"Oh, endlessly. But he doesn't trust me, Elizabeth. To pretend otherwise would be folly."

John Thomas crossed his room in the flickering candlelight the next night, going to a window and thrusting it up. He had forgotten how unbearably hot summer nights in South Carolina could be. He paced until he realized he was growing warmer and stopped, sighing and drawing his hand through his hair.

He looked at the adjoining door before going to it and knocking softly. He heard Shannon's voice call softly, "Come in."

He opened the door and saw her sitting at her vanity, her red hair wisping about her face, the cream she had asked him to order from the North in front of her. Apparently, she could no longer obtain it here. She had been in the act of rubbing it on her hands. He wondered if that was what made them so impossibly soft.

She was looking at him with a slight flush rising, and he realized he must have been staring. She closed her dressing gown more securely and said, "Good...evening."

She seemed a bit on her guard. Good heavens, did she think he had come to... How to set her at her ease? Her hand was on the back of her vanity chair, her spine rather straight. But she couldn't be afraid of him, could she? There had been an instance or two, early in their marriage, when he had thought she might be, although he couldn't explain them. He looked into her eyes. No, she wasn't. She was merely embarrassed.

"Good evening," he said earnestly, belatedly. "I...had hoped we might discuss something." He took a step forward.

She had risen. Her dressing gown was very thin, from age more than deliberate choice, and it left little to the imagination. Sweet heaven, her form was beautiful. His mouth went dry, and he lost all conscious thought.

"Do you mind if we sit?" she asked sweetly, innocent of his thoughts. "By the lamps? I cannot see your face."

He snapped to attention. "Yes. Yes, of course." He moved with her to the collection of furniture before the fireplace which, thankfully, was not burning. He moved a pillow from the sofa and guided her to it before taking the wing chair, sitting on its edge. "I know you need your rest, so I won't keep you long," he said. "How are you feeling tonight?"

"Very well, thank you." She should not have to thank him. His jaw tightened for a moment. She looked confused at his expression and a bit worried. "Did I...?"

"No, no!" He shook his head. "I was thinking of something else." Now she would think he found something more important than her health. He was handling her like a callow youth. He drew a breath and sighed its release, his hands clasped tightly. "I think you should let me take you to Massachusetts." He looked up, weighing her reaction.

But she sat calmly, apparently studying his features. "Do you?"

He sighed. "Everyone believes I should."

She continued to survey him. "On account of the baby?"

"Yes. I had dismissed it as prejudice, but many of my friends and fellow officers, those with our interests at heart, have encouraged me to take you away from Charleston. And my mother..." He swallowed nervously, looking at her, choosing his words carefully. "I told her of our reconciliation, and your condition. In her reply she says the same. I cannot deny that I am wholly inexperienced in these matters, Shannon, or that there seems to be some merit to their arguments."

"Better access to the country's finest doctors?" she asked, studying him.

"Yes, that is one of them."

She lifted a shoulder. "We have Dr. Schafer."

"More supplies, things we cannot obtain..."

Her brows drew together, and she lifted a finger to interrupt. "Forgive me, but what supplies are needed in childbirth that we could not obtain?"

"I confess I couldn't imagine, but I also admit my knowledge is limited."

Her lips twitched. "Go on: what else?"

"The climate..."

She waved a hand. "Born and raised..."

He studied her beautiful face, her firm jawline and sloping nose. How he had missed her features. And how well they matched her disposition—did God design humans so? And had He designed it that he should be drawn to her, body and soul, with such overwhelming force?

"Yes, I had thought of that," he said softly. He hesitated. "Will Elizabeth be here for you?"

She looked confused for a moment, but, realization dawning, she said, "We have not discussed it, but yes, I'm certain of it. Why, don't you intend to be by my bedside?"

"Of *course*, if you wish it," he said, reaching to take her hand seriously.

Her eyes twinkled, knocking the breath from him. *Magnificent..* "I'm joking you. What else? Were there other objections to the place I choose to give birth?"

His hand was still holding hers, and it tightened. "Our unpopularity here. If I thought anyone meant you true harm, I would remove you tomorrow, but I don't. And yet, it isn't going to be easy for you here anymore, Shannon. We both know that is true."

She met his eyes. They hadn't spoken of it, and it was easy to pretend public opinion didn't exist while they remained separate from the population of Charleston. "Do you think it will be easy for me in the North, John Thomas?" she asked, not meeting his eyes.

"Well. One can never say."

"No." There was a pause. "Do I have a voice in the matter?"

"Yes, forgive me. I didn't mean to imply otherwise."

"Well, then. I wish to stay here with you and return to Massachusetts when you return."

"You're *certain*? Shannon, this isn't a whim? You have truly thought of it, of what it will be like?"

"Yes." She moistened her lips. "I have no wish to undertake

such an arduous journey, John Thomas. I fear that to do so might endanger...my health."

"Shannon!" he whispered, reaching to clench her hand again. "Do you?"

"Yes."

"Then there is no question of it," he said firmly. "You ought to have stopped me immediately!"

"Is it what you wish, for me to stay here?"

"Of course!" he asserted.

She smiled gently. "I mean, setting aside what I just said. Will you mind it, that your child is not born in your home?"

His eyes softened. "That is unimportant. Since my posting here seems to be indefinite, perhaps I might lease a house, as the Rices have done. They'll send guards for us, so you would be safe."

She seemed to cheer just at the thought, and he knew that he must make an offer to lease the house he had seen on Tradd Street. It was located amidst many which had burned, but it was intact.

"Would you..." She bit her lip as though she were uncertain.

"Yes?" he urged sincerely, watching her.

"Could you perhaps convince Jeptha to come with us as our housekeeper? I don't know whether you can afford it, but I was considering that I won't be able to keep things for you as I should once the baby comes, and—"

"Shannon," he said tenderly. She stopped, looking up at him. "I can afford it. And I will ask her."

"Well, then," she said.

"Perhaps by the end of September."

She nodded.

He released her hand gently. "I ought to let you get your rest." He stood. "Goodnight. Sleep well, Shannon."

There was a long pause. "Goodnight," she answered softly.

# Chapter Nine

Adeline got up quickly to take the bowl of chili from Jude as he tottered toward the table with it, cute in his posh school uniform. "Thanks, Jude!"

"You're welcome," he said. "Are you going trick-or-treating with us?"

She glanced at Adrian, who was spooning salad onto plates. "Um...sure!" She was grasping in the dark here. Wasn't sure she was invited, but... Yeah, Adrian wasn't responding. He seemed deep in thought.

"Pa and Nana usually come on Halloween to see me, but Pa has a cold this year, and they don't want to give it to you. He feels bad. He didn't go to work today."

She smiled at his chattiness. "Aw, I'm sorry to hear that, Jude. We'll send lots of pictures."

"Gigi and Pop want them, too," he added conscientiously.

Adeline glanced up at Adrian. His back was still to them.

"We'll be sure they get some, too! I'm sure they have no idea you've become Dr. Jude Ravenel at so young an age."

Jude giggled and said, "Daddy, I'm hungry!"

"I'm coming, buddy," Adrian said softly, carrying the other bowls.

They settled at the table, and Adeline closed her eyes as Jude said the prayer.

They were more or less finished with the house. The crew was only fine-tuning everything, and she was doing nit-picky design stuff to make it perfect. She could easily finish the Silk Room when the wallpaper arrived at the beginning of December. Her British friends had seemed hopeful about reproducing the pattern. It was a huge relief. Now she could get started on the nursery.

"Good job," Adrian said as they crossed themselves. She bit her lip. Was little Henry going to be raised Catholic, too? They still hadn't talked about that. They hadn't talked about a lot. And Henry clearly wasn't going to work. Zane? No, too modern. She was failing at this.

She was going to need Adrian's help. He'd talk to her about *that*. As long as the discussion wasn't about himself or the future, he was good. Okay, maybe she was panicking because he was quiet tonight. She really needed to get a grip.

Looking over, she saw Adrian reaching to wipe Jude's mouth, as he did at almost every meal. Her sweet, dysfunctional boys. Adeline smiled, wanting them, wanting this so badly her chest hurt. Why did that scare her so much? Why was she so afraid she would lose them? If she was determined to give it a go, as she was, why the insecurity?

Doubt knocked again. What if he wasn't all in? *What are you talking about, Adeline? You just said he looked happy.*

True. But... *Her?* She wasn't really his type. At all. She was pretty insecure about that when it came down to it. But that wasn't all of it. Why didn't he ever talk about forever? She admitted she had been about as easy to pin down as a feral cat; so maybe he was afraid to get too close. But what if he was just doing the right thing here? What if—?

"You okay?"

Adeline blinked, looking up, realizing they were almost finished with the meal and she hadn't said anything. Adrian was studying her. His phone beeped with a text, but he didn't look at it.

"Yeah. I'm good!" she answered. Actually, beyond freaking out about her relationship, she was worn out. Her back ached, and she was still hungry after eating more than was really acceptable when your husband was that sexy.

"Jude, run up and put on your costume," Adrian said. "It's almost dark."

"Yes!" Jude said, squeezing his fist victoriously.

Adeline smiled at him. "Your lab coat should be crisp, and your daddy can help with your stethoscope."

"Okay!" he said, skittering off. She heard his little feet pounding the stairs and smiled.

Adrian looked down at his phone. After a minute, he looked at her, eyebrows lifted with a surprised and slightly intrigued look in his eyes. "Harris has a girlfriend."

"What?" she asked, surprised. "Did he tell you?"

"No. My mom has spies on the ground everywhere."

"Very interesting," she said. "I take it we don't usually make it to girlfriend status?"

"No, not usually. Not recently."

Adeline popped a cucumber slice in her mouth. "Who is this paragon, then?"

He looked at his phone. "Mom thinks she's from Savannah. Not sure about her job. First name's Jacqueline. Maybe Jackie."

"Very intriguing," she agreed, laughing at his mom's skills while stifling a yawn.

"Adeline, why don't you stay home?" Adrian suggested gently.

She looked at him. She hadn't realized he was looking at her, all thin and handsome in his white shirt and loosened tie. "Do you want me to?" she asked softly.

His brows lifted. "No, of course not." He smiled a little. "There's nothing like trick-or-treating on The Battery. But you feel tired, don't you?"

"A little," she admitted. She sat back, studying him. "Are *you* okay?"

He looked surprised. Then again, he was good at feigning things. He had to know he'd been quiet. "Yeah. I'm fine."

She bit her lip. "If, um…it's okay with you, I'd like to go. I'm…kind of getting attached to Jude, Adrian." Her heart was pounding. "I don't want to miss this."

He studied her. Yeah, this was awkward. He kind of

looked deer-in-the-headlights. She sensed they both knew they weren't just talking about Halloween. His arms were still crossed, and he sniffed in that way he did when he was buying time. "Yeah, that's great, if you're sure you feel like it," he said, getting up. "I'm going to go...help Jude with his stethoscope."

And then he was gone. Running.

# Chapter Ten

Adeline and her sister sat on the couch in the living room with the fireplace going the night before the baby shower. Annie had driven in that afternoon after working a half day and would be spending one night. Adeline was excited to have her and had treated her to one of her husband's delicious meals.

Now the air was thick with things unsaid, and Annie looked like she had finally worked up to saying what she'd been holding back all day. Maybe it helped that Adrian had taken Jude out for ice cream and a walk on The Battery.

"Adrian's...wow, Addy. And Jude, and the baby..." She looked around her. She was a little smaller than Adeline, her hair blonde, too, but longer and flat-ironed straight and then curled into big coils. Her bone structure was more delicate than Adeline's; maybe that was why men had always rushed to protect her. "This amazing house... Seems kind of perfect."

Yeah, it kind of did, but Adeline said what she should. "You know nothing's perfect, Anns. Even if we do have a pretty social media feed."

Annie smiled, but it quickly fell away. "I... I didn't want to tell you over the phone, but I...called off the wedding three days ago. So, you have nothing to be grateful for. This trip saved me."

Adeline was shocked. She glanced down, only now noticing her sister wasn't wearing her engagement ring. "What? Did you have an argument?"

"No." She swiped at her eye. "I...got to thinking after you said something about how long we'd dated—"

"Annie..."

"No, I needed it. I thought I was just being sensible and cautious. Not bad things, but...I knew it wasn't right. I'd just convinced myself right could feel like that. But, I mean, there was no excitement left, and we didn't really talk about *things* anymore. We were always together, always talking, but..."

"But you weren't in love with him," Adeline said.

Annie bit her lip. "I mean, I loved him. Still do. It'll take a while to get past that. But..."

"Did Brad realize things had been dissipating once you told him?" Adeline asked.

"No, of course not," Annie said with a bitter little laugh. "People only do that in movies. He was entirely blindsided and *very* angry."

"He'll understand someday if he meets the person he's

supposed to be with," Adeline said, squeezing Annie's hand. "He might even thank you."

Annie gave a short, unhumorous laugh through her tears, vulnerable and a little lost. "And so here I am, thirty years old and starting all over again. Mom thinks I've lost my mind. And I'm scared." She bit her lip, looking up at Adeline with blue eyes swimming with moisture. "You've always been braver than I have, Adeline," she whispered. "You never minded it. But I don't want to be alone."

"What you did was very brave," Adeline said. She paused. "You'll find him, the right guy. And he'll take your breath away." She bit her lip. "And scare you half to death. But he won't bore you."

Annie held her eyes. "Addy..." She looked like she would say more but decided against it. Adeline was grateful.

Adeline reached for her sister's hand, pressing it and smiling. "Thanks for coming." She didn't mention other names. But maybe her mom and grandma really had the flu.

"I wouldn't have missed it," Annie said, smiling genuinely.

Adrian stood in the kitchen at his parents' house in States-boro, leaning against the counter. He looked through the double doors into the living room, where there were a bunch of women. Adeline sat near the fireplace opening gifts. Apparently not all that uncomfortable with the situation, she was friendly but dignified, warm but with a becoming touch of reserve. Her sister sat to her left, listing the gifts and who gave them, surprisingly supportive. Her mom hadn't been able to make it. Adrian clenched his jaw.

Adeline bent to lift something that was way too heavy, and he started for the door. Why weren't they helping her? Harris caught his arm. "Adrian. It's fine. Mom won't let her hurt herself. And those women have known you since you were a baby. They'll be nice."

He sighed, leaning back against the counter. "They can be kind of...uppity."

"They're eating out of her hand," Harris said, looking back that way. "They've never met someone that cool."

Adrian laughed, shaking his head. He looked out the window where his dad was playing in the yard with Jude. Jude was diving into the leaves, coming up with them sticking to his dark hair, and encouraging the neighbor's dog to do likewise.

"He's doing really well, Adrian," Harris said. "You've done a great job."

Adrian grunted. "Adeline has been good for him, too. And the idea of a baby."

"Why do you say it like that?" Harris asked with knitted brows.

He had said it kind of darkly. He met Harris's eyes. But he didn't say anything.

"You're afraid she's going to leave," Harris said. "After the baby."

Adrian just stared at him before looking away.

A second or two ticked by. "Do you have feelings for her?"

Adrian snapped back to attention. His eyes flicked

over his brother's face, but he didn't respond. He merely said haughtily, "I don't know why you think I would answer that."

Harris rolled his eyes, sighing before leaning against the opposite counter. "You're welcome, by the way," he said moodily, "for the sacrifice of my Saturday to help with this shindig."

"Thank you," Adrian said softly.

"Never mind," he said, apparently embarrassed. He smoothed his dark brown hair. "Listen, Adrian. You know back in the spring when we all thought you were dying or something? When mom sent me to flush out what was going on?"

Adrian nodded once.

"Well, when I talked to you, you already knew about the baby," Harris pressed. "So it would be natural that you'd be distracted. But when mom saw you at Jude's graduation... If my timing is right, there's no way she could've told you about the baby yet. And yet, she still said you looked just like you did after Lauren died: distracted."

"And I've told you that if I was distracted back then, it was because Jude was injured," he said firmly, an edge of warning in his voice.

"That's not my point," Harris said, unabashed when most would've curled in the corner in shame. "I'm talking about Adeline." He held Adrian's eyes forcefully. "You had already slept with her then, and—again, if I'm not mistaken—agreed to go your separate ways. And it was tearing you up."

"Don't be ridiculous. We hardly knew one another then," Adrian said, beginning to get angry at the intrusiveness.

"Because you have to know every detail of a person's life and character to fall in love with them," Harris said ironically.

"I didn't say that. I'm saying I didn't know her then. And that we're still getting to know each other now. She asked me not to put labels on what we have, and I'm not."

"Really? Is that what it is?" Harris demanded ironically. "When you dated Lauren for six years and were married to her five, and you *still—to this day*—can't admit that her death affected you? Seems to be a pattern here, Adrian." He slapped the counter.

Adrian scowled. "You were there. Front and center, remember? She almost *killed* our son. Do you think I could possibly have any feelings left for her after that?"

"You were in love with her, Adrian. You always had been."

"Yeah, well...things change. You don't know what it was like...those last few years."

Harris studied him. "No. I don't. But I think you're still holding a grudge, Adrian. You need to forgive her," he said, meeting his eyes. "For Jude. For the baby. For Adeline."

Adrian held his eyes for a long time before sighing. "I don't know what forgiving Lauren and loving Adeline have to do with each other," he said softly.

"I think you do," Harris said, brown eyes not leaving his.

Adrian looked away. A full minute, maybe two, passed. The air was thick. His eyes and throat hurt. He crossed his arms, looking out the window for a while. "What am I going to do, Harris?" he asked softly.

"*Tell* her," Harris answered.

"It's not that simple."

"Then show her."

Adrian met his eyes and held them for a long moment before looking back out the window, sniffing.

"Listen, I have to head back to Savannah," Harris said, squeezing his arm. "I think y'all can handle it from here."

Adrian looked at him quickly, standing upright. "Do you honestly think we're not going to talk about your—uh—new girlfriend?"

Harris sighed. "I don't have to run who I date by you, Adrian."

"Of course you do. I'm your elder brother."

Adrian was nailing him with a look. But Harris gave in eventually. "All right, fine. Her name is Jacqueline Johnson—Jackie for short."

"And?"

"And... She's a paralegal at a firm we have a lot of interaction with. She's...divorced. Don't tell Mom yet."

Adrian lifted his brows but decided it would probably be best not to say anything.

"She's thinking about going to law school." He hesitated. "She makes me want to do crazy things like offering to send her," he said, looking up at Adrian. It was said in a joking manner, but with an under layer of vulnerability.

"Offering more than that, if I'm not mistaken," Adrian said, brows lifted.

"Yeah, well..." Harris cleared his throat. Trying to change the subject from that serious line of thought, he said, "Any advice? Besides using protection, I mean."

Gritting his teeth, Adrian shoved him as Harris laughed. "Hush, she'll hear you," Adrian seethed, looking at the double doors.

Still laughing, Harris said, "All right, all right. Cool your engines. I'm going to say goodbye to Jude and Dad."

Adeline sat among a pile of boxes and gifts in the Ravenels' living room while Adrian's mom and Annie saw the guests off. One of the kitchen doors opened, and Adrian appeared. He looked different somehow.

"Hey," she said, smiling, trying to read him.

"Hey," he responded, walking toward her. "Tired?"

"A little," she said, heart thumping. He pulled her up, resting his hands on her sides and kissing her forehead. Okay, she was going to pass out. He lay his forehead against hers. "Were they nice?"

"Oh, Adrian. Yes. And so generous." She got a lump in her throat just thinking about it, and about how much they loved this family. His hand stroked her back. Someone was feeling affectionate.

"I can see that," he said, a smile in his voice.

The door opened, and before they could pull apart, Virginia was standing there. Adrian didn't shove Adeline away or anything, which wouldn't have been the greatest. But she had a feeling he wasn't comfortable getting cozy around his mom. Or maybe that was just her. She squeezed his hands and took a step back. To her surprise, she saw that Virginia's look was more interested/benign than disgusted. "Oh, I'm sorry," she said, turning toward the door.

"No, that's fine," Adeline said, releasing Adrian's hands and going forward. "Virginia, thank you. It was really wonderful, and everyone was so kind." She hugged her, and the woman looked touched.

She made an elegant deprecating noise. "It was nothing, my dear." As she pulled away, she patted Adeline's tummy. "Only the best for our grandson."

"Mom," Adrian protested. "Honestly."

"It was as plain as the nose on your face from last week's sonogram." Was it? Adeline still wasn't very sure what the head looked like. "I won't tell anyone," Virginia said patronizingly. Adrian looked appeased until she added, "Except your father, who originally pointed it out to me." Adrian sighed.

Adeline laughed. "That's all right. Jude can still announce the name."

"Speaking of... He is staying here tonight," Virginia said, transferring her attention to Adrian.

"Mom. I can't—"

She held up a hand. "We'll bring him back to Charleston tomorrow. He has clothes here. I've just been to the Beaufort Bonnet Company. Their winter line was excellent."

Adrian looked like he was wavering, but his dad came in. "Hey kids," he said, looking slightly dazed at the mess of his living room.

"Hi, James," Adeline said.

"Convince your son to leave his child here," Virginia said.

Dr. Ravenel lifted his brows. "Yes, of course. Why shouldn't he stay, Adrian?"

"He still has dreams sometimes—"

"He did very well during your honeymoon, and if he has a dream, we'll bring him home tonight."

Adeline smiled, looking up at Adrian. "I'm going to go see Annie off."

An hour later, Adrian and his dad had loaded everything up, Jude had been kissed goodbye, and she and Adrian were heading back toward Charleston. Her lips were twitching, and she had to look out the window.

"What?" Adrian said. She looked at him, and there was a slight smile in his eyes.

"I was just thinking... The last time we left your parents' house alone, we...um...made a baby."

He gave a single laugh, seemingly struck. "So we did." He touched her middle gently, meeting her eyes before looking back at the road. "I don't regret it for a single second."

She swallowed and whispered, "Me neither."

A tear tracked down her face, and she looked out the window, hoping he wouldn't see.

He saw. "Adeline," he said softly. She thought his voice cracked. "What is it?" He sounded miserable.

She shook her head. "Nothing—nothing! Sorry."

"Is it... Are you unhappy, honey?"

She shot to attention at his endearment. Her eyes flickered over his face. "No—no, no! Hormones." His eyes roved her features. He didn't believe her. But she couldn't tell him the thing that upset her: that she didn't know where this was going, that if it didn't work out these moments would haunt her the rest of her life. So, she said something else that was true. She looked at him. "I...didn't picture it this way with my parents, you know. The first grandchild. I thought they would be a part of it."

He scanned her face thoroughly, slowly, between glances at the road. His neck was really attractive from this angle, but that was beside the point. His hand found hers. "The situation may not be ideal to them. But I promise you," he said, looking at her, "the moment they meet him for the first time... All of that will fade. They'll be completely in love."

She blinked, fighting tears. She squeezed his hand, pressing her lips together and looking down. He didn't say anything else, just held her hand, absently stroking it with his thumb. Literally, he was trying to kill her. Such a casual touch shouldn't make her head swim like she was going to faint.

After another mile, he said, "And just so you know, you successfully rerouted that conversation. But someday I want you to tell me what really made you cry."

She looked at him, lifting her eyebrows. "I don't know what you're talking about," she said. She might as well be consistent.

He gave her a derisive look. She bit her lip, deciding it was best not to respond. But it hovered in the air between them, his belief that she was unhappy. And in one sense, she was. She had a decision to make.

Sometimes, like now, she felt like he would have chosen her if he had the choice. Sometimes she felt like she needed to leave the Asheville job she had been offered on the back-burner. She just didn't know how to talk to him about those things openly. He was wonderful in almost every possible way. But sometimes he still felt like a stranger.

# Chapter Eleven

Summer had finally faded into autumn, and Admiral Haley and his lady had been set up on Tradd Street for close to a month. The house John Thomas had leased was several streets back from The Battery, and Shannon supposed she must have passed it many times in her former life. Everything looked so different now with all of the rubble from the great fire of 1861. Churches, factories, houses—so many were hollow shells. The bombardments had added the finishing touch. They were fortunate to have found a home in good condition.

Their house was modest: gray with three stories, three windows across each of them, all sitting in elegant casings. There was some lovely molding at the roof line and a balcony off the side in Charlestonian custom. The home was fronted by a brick fence, painted the same color, which led onto steps up to the house. She had thought, as John

Thomas led her up them away from the carriage, that it was in keeping with his quiet taste. But he wouldn't have been able to have afforded it before the war. That he had offered a fair price, she did not doubt, however crippled the economy. She must assume, therefore, that his finances stood in a better state than did her father's. This was a surprising turn of events.

A cool breeze from her cracked windows fanned her cheeks now as she studied the hopeless disarray around her. Upon learning that Shannon had been letting her dresses out as the need arose, John Thomas had showered her with bolts of cloth ordered from Massachusetts. Her time was quite taken up in making new gowns since she thought it would be unwise to engage a Charleston dressmaker. Or so she had supposed until one day Jeptha told her that it might be a great help to a woman in need. And hadn't Admiral Haley given her permission to expend as much as necessary to have them made up?

"Yes, but I am the wife of a Union admiral, Jeptha," Shannon said, reclining on the chaise in her bedchamber. "And wouldn't it be only to fan the flames of wrath to bring these beautiful fabrics into such an establishment?"

But Jeptha had been born free and raised among a free community, and she knew a different Charleston. "There'd be women willing enough to do it, ma'am." She held her eyes with a boldness that never failed to surprise Shannon. "Women like me."

"Oh," Shannon said, reaching for her necklace. "I see."

"They wouldn't be opposed to making dresses for the wife of Admiral Haley, ma'am."

Shannon sat up, and her awe had to have been evident in the expression of her face. "Good heavens, when you think of it that way, half of Charleston is on our side, isn't it?"

Jeptha smiled mischievously. "A good bit more than half, ma'am."

Shannon sat up more fully. "You know of a woman? A fine seamstress, Jeptha, for Admiral Haley has gotten into some very lofty circles. I was beginning to fear it would never be finished and that I should be left without anything to wear," she said, looking around the room at the daunting piles of fabric.

"Well, that wouldn't be proper, ma'am, would it?" Jeptha said, making Shannon look at her and give a gasp of laughter. "I know of someone, ma'am," the housekeeper said.

Shannon stood, relieved, and decided to leave off drudgery for Shakespeare. She stopped at the door, touching her bodice and looking at Jeptha. "And something for my poor baby. I can't allow her to be naked either."

"No, ma'am," Jeptha answered, laughing and folding up the fabric.

John Thomas came to Shannon in the sitting room one sunny autumn Saturday with hesitance in his expression. He told her that there was to be a grand festival of freedom for which several prominent abolitionists were to come from

New England to attend. She knew that he was thinking that these events were a great affront to people like her family, and he was unsure of her reaction.

He had asked her whether she would feel well enough to host a dinner at their home. When she hesitated, he had looked chagrined, telling her that he was a fool and that of course she must not tax herself. "No, no," she had said, reaching to cover his hand. "I am well enough. I merely question whether I am the right woman to host." His eyes strayed to her hand on his, and she received the impression that he was not quite comfortable. Flushing, she removed her hand quickly and turned her face away.

She felt his eyes upon her, felt his regret, and his acceptance that to say anything would be to agitate the moment. "It was thought... My family is very well-known to most of the people who are coming," he said softly, still regarding her closely.

"Oh, well, in that case— Yes, I see." She swiped her eye quickly.

"Shannon—"

"There will be no trouble in it, John Thomas," she said hastily. "None at all. If you will merely let me know how many are to attend and what day and time will be most suitable, I shall manage the rest."

There was a long silence. "If you're certain." He hesitated further still. "William Lloyd Garrison will be in attendance, Shannon."

She looked at him, eyes widening.

"If it is too upsetting, you must tell me. You have a perfect right to say who may come into your home."

She shook her head. "No, he is welcome," she said softly.

His head went back a bit as he looked at her, completely stunned. It seemed he had not forgotten her horror that night when they had attended a lecture by Garrison and Frederick Douglass. Shannon held his eyes. "He is most welcome," she said firmly.

Shannon stood in a simple dove gray gown looking out onto the extraordinary scene below her window. Since the day the 54th Massachusetts had marched into Charleston and an elderly Negro woman had declared in the streets that it was the Year of Jubilee, freedom had been foremost in the minds of Charleston's colored majority. The freedmen, military, and abolitionists joined together in a march that was part of the months-long wake to slavery.

A hearse was pulled by a horse in funereal style, bearing a coffin labeled "slavery." The Negros marched in the most elite and aristocratic places, such as The Battery and the Citadel Green. There were so many thousands of people that the pageant took hours. There were dignitaries riding horses, fire companies following, and school children keeping step. Many former slaves would be recognizable to their one-time owners, who watched from balconies and windows. The tides were changing in Charleston; there could be no doubt of that.

Two young men held a banner that read, "We know no masters but ourselves." After that, there was a float of young women representing the fifteen slave states. They wore white to stress the purity of Negro womanhood. The Colored Regiment marched in line, and various songs were sung, including "John Brown's Body."

There was a mock slave auction on a cart and a reenactment of a slave gang with about sixty men tied to a rope. This led to merriment among some, but Shannon watched in horror as several freedwomen lining the streets burst into tears of agony, falling to their knees and screaming, "*Give me back my children! Give me back my children!*" Shannon covered her mouth as bile rose in her throat. Her hand went instinctively to her middle, and she was forced to turn away from the sight.

Shannon wore an exquisite gown made by one Miss Millington. It was worthy, Shannon thought, to be worn at a European court. The sleeves were very narrow and just off her shoulders, encased in the same gold lace which trimmed the entire top of the dress. The bodice was of cream satin, as was the skirt except the last twelve inches or so, which was a delicate gold, barely discernable from the cream. Over the skirt was net with exquisite and thick gold embroidery, which grew thicker as it drew closer to the ground. Her condition could not be hidden, and she didn't seek to. There was something about that which added to the beauty, too. She wore her mother's pearl earrings and a simple necklace. Her hair had grown just long enough that she could roll and pin it to give it the appearance of being long.

There was a knock at her door as she put the last earring into place, and she called, "Come in."

John Thomas entered, looking very smart himself in his dress uniform. She heard his intake of breath and smiled shyly.

He crossed the room and stared, awestruck. Softly, he said, "I hope I am not engaging in maladroitness when I say that I have never seen you look so beautiful."

"That is not maladroit," she answered quietly, a soft smile hovering about her lips.

He met her eyes. "But are you certain you feel able, Shannon?" he asked with concern in his expression.

"Yes, I am," she said, holding his eyes. She touched her middle quickly as the baby moved, surprising her. John Thomas's eyes dipped down to her hand in confusion and then up to her eyes intensely.

"Moving," she whispered. "Nothing is wrong."

She heard the softest quickening of his breath as he met her eyes with such wonder and love that she stood frozen. "Shannon," he whispered. She reveled in the sound of her name on his lips, in his nearness.

The door was heard opening below stairs. Jarred to alertness she said, "That will be our guests."

He did not move. He merely stared at her in earnest wonder. She felt herself flush as she looked down shyly, covering her middle. Then she looked up, her eyes smiling a bit. "We really ought to go down," she whispered.

He finally drew a breath. "If you feel the *least* bit poorly, Shannon—"

"I will tell you," she answered. "Will you fetch my gloves for me there across the room?"

It was fortunate that she gave him a task, for he was wavering. He collected them and even held them for her, watching her progress while she put them on. And then they descended the stairs.

As, one by one, the guests entered, it was plain that those of a military variety had forgiven her for her mistreatment of John Thomas. Perhaps no gentleman could treat with unkindness a lady in her condition. Perhaps they genuinely liked her.

"Commodore Rice," Shannon said. "A few months in your wife's company have done you good, sir. You look very well."

He flushed. "Yes, ma'am, indeed. And it is good to see you looking so well, too."

Mrs. Rice was on her husband's arm, her crimped fair hair parted and gleaming under the chandelier, her posture stiff. "Mrs. Rice," Shannon said, giving her hand. "I am so glad you came." She felt John Thomas lay his hand on the small of her back. Perhaps he was not unaware of the feline undertones to their exchanges. "When last we spoke, there was some talk of your governess bringing the children to you for Christmas."

"Yes, she will be doing so," she answered. And that was that.

The others were polite, particularly Lieutenant Georgeson. His secretarial duties brought him so often into their household that he was beginning to feel like part of the family.

Shannon was nervous as the Northern abolitionists, most of whom were from Boston, entered. Some of them, like Henry Ward Beecher, were famously vocal about anyone who had been connected to slavery. But they greeted her with civility.

She held her breath as she met William Lloyd Garrison. He had been sent the steps from Charleston's slave market, and he had climbed atop them at the Boston Music Hall to deliver a speech. She wondered what her father would think as she gave her hand to the gentleman.

There had been quite a crowd of Northerners who had come to Charleston in Mr. Garrison's entourage, and many were here tonight. There were others who had come to witness and report on the festivals. Some wanted mementos of slavery, which was a part of history now. John C. Calhoun's tomb had been desecrated for pieces of stone. Others had picked clover from the grounds of the now-burned Institute Hall where the Ordinance of Secession had been enacted. The slave-trading district had been combed for items like manacles, market bells, and Mr. Garrison's steps.

"Mrs. Haley," he said. "Have we met?"

Relying on her manners, for she could scarcely think, she smiled softly and said, "No, sir, but I attended one of your lectures at a church in Massachusetts. It was several years ago."

"Ah, yes," he said, pretending to remember. He gave his hand to John Thomas, and they talked so forthrightly and calmly that she realized Mr. Garrison was quite a close friend of the family. John Thomas was not at all in awe of having the famous abolitionist in his home, so she must suppose it had happened often.

Shannon presided over the table, catching the servants' eyes when it was time to change courses or when a glass needed to be filled. Those near here were quite polite and circumspect, careful not to mention her flight to the South during the war or anything to do with the war at all.

Shannon took a deep breath as dessert was brought, smiling fleetingly to reassure John Thomas when she noticed he was looking at her.

She glanced across her table at all of the prominent people there. She knew some Charleston ladies had attended a ball for the abolitionists, but she also gathered that they had been ridiculed by most of the white citizens. She knew she would likewise be scorned after word of this dinner spread.

No one had told her how the old aristocracy of Charleston was feeling, but she knew instinctively because she had been among their number for much of her life. They would be feeling as though the world had tilted upside down, as though their faces were being slapped at every turn when they were already flat on their backs. And she was sorry for their suffering. But some things simply must be, and she would no longer pretend otherwise.

She felt a hand on her shoulder and looked up. John Thomas knelt beside her chair as conversation continued around the table.

"Are you feeling well?" he asked softly.

He must have seen the turmoil on her face, she thought. She smiled to reassure him. "I am quite well."

"You will signal to me if you feel fatigued?"

"Yes, but I am well." She smiled again. "I promise you."

He studied her for a long moment before lifting her hand to his lips and whispering, "Thank you."

# Chapter Twelve

Shannon stood marveling over the Union Army's efficiency in her kitchen, where the week's supply of food
had been delivered by some Army ensigns. Jeptha, the housekeeper and cook, gently nudged Shannon away to the sitting
room. She said she would join her there in a few minutes
to plan the week's meals, and she thought Shannon ought
to be sitting rather than rummaging through dirty crates.

Shannon sighed and took herself there to read the
Charleston newspaper, as well as the Boston one to which
John Thomas had subscribed. It was as though the two cities
existed on different planets, so different were the daily lives
of their citizens and their take on events.

She got up and walked to the window, wishing she were
not so confined indoors. It made her restless, and her mind
was all too prone to wander to John Thomas, to worry about
their future. She had just begun to look out at the desolate

streets when suddenly the outer door was flung open, shattering the silence. Her head turned quickly toward her own door. In moments, a Negro man threw it back and strode in, breathing heavily as though he had been running. Startled, Shannon felt for a moment too shocked to think. Jeptha ran down the foyer, calling, "I tried to stop him, ma'am! I don't know him from Adam, and—"

Just then, the two sentries who had been posted outside rushed into the room as though to arrest the man. "Wait!" Shannon cried, trying to catch a glimpse of him, although it was difficult with them wrestling him. "He is July—one of the family!" The young men loosened their hold, looking at her for elucidation. "Captain Ravenel—my brother's—valet," she explained, going forward, and taking in the servant's sweating, breathless state. Anxiety grew in her eyes. "Is something amiss with Captain Ravenel?" she asked.

July shook his head, still trying to catch his breath. "It's Miss Rose," he said. "She's fallen off the balcony, Miss Shannon!"

A scream left Shannon's lips as she covered her mouth.

Jeptha, hurrying forward, asked quickly, "What are her injuries?"

"I don't know, ma'am," he answered, looking at Shannon instead as Jeptha helped her to sit. "I'm sorry, Miss Shannon. Captain Ravenel sent me for you right away. He wasn't himself."

Someone's throat gave a guttural sound that Shannon later realized was her own. She said, voice shaking, "Take me to them. Will you, please? We will use our carriage." When July hesitated, she said, "I'll see that there is no trouble for you."

One of the guards protested that he would drive her, and Shannon said, "Very well, but let us make haste!"

In moments, they set out, the houses growing grander by the moment as they drove toward The Battery, but Shannon saw none of it. When they arrived, she was lifted carefully down by the guard who had been most sternly charged with her care by Jeptha. He led her to the door, where she applied the knocker herself as she trembled from the outside in. When no one came, she reached for the knob, turned it, and stepped inside.

The servants were lined up in the foyer, some of whom had made their way back after emancipation. Among them, she saw John Tilman, Abigail, Rebecca, who had once waited on Marie, and Emma, the nursemaid. All were in various states of shock and anxiety. They did not at first notice Shannon and her Federal escort, who followed her in. But when they did, they straightened.

"Miss Shannon!" John Tilman said, coming forward hurriedly.

"Where is she, John?" she asked, voice trembling.

"They are upstairs with her, ma'am: Mr. Frederick, Mrs. Ravenel, the doctor, Mammy, and Matilde."

"How is she?"

"I don't know, ma'am. She wasn't dead when they took her up."

She drew an unsteady breath. "Mr. Ravenel?"

"He's not home, Miss Shannon. We've sent out looking for him."

She turned to her guard and said, "Thank you, I am safe here. Will you return to Tradd Street and tell Admiral Haley what has happened when he arrives home?"

He nodded. "I will, Mrs. Haley. You have only to send word if I am needed."

"Thank you," she said. Shannon began to feel the servants looking at her curiously, for they had heard it, all of it, of course. "I...I will go into the library to wait." She did so, where Abigail, her mother's maid, brought her a drink and gently invited her to sit as she paced. Shannon finally did so, the strength going out of her. "John Tilman spoke the truth, ma'am," Abigail said softly. "They wouldn't be up there now if he was wrong." Shannon nodded, unable to do or say more. Abigail, hiding nervous energy with her calm demeanor, waited with her.

At length, the door opened, and the butler came in, saying, "Miss Shannon? They wanted me to send for you, ma'am."

Shannon seemed paralyzed where she was, looking up to meet his eyes.

"Miss *Rose* wanted me to send for you ma'am," he said, smiling.

"Oh, thank God," Shannon breathed and quickly arose.

She climbed the stairs, passing a doctor she had never met on them. Seeing the most commotion near Frederick and Elizabeth's room, she went there. Through the open door, she could see Rose on the bed like a tiny queen. She stepped closer, and Rose caught sight of her. "Aunt Shannon, I *require* you," she said, extending her hand languishingly.

A smile of relief blooming, Shannon went forward, glancing at Frederick and Elizabeth, but her concentration was on her niece. Rose had her leg wrapped, along with her wrist. Various scrapes and bruises graced her porcelain skin. "My *darling*," Shannon said, voice quivering. "How did you fall?"

"Minnie Perkins said at Mass that I could not walk along the railing like a cat, and I told her I *could*." Frederick shaded his eyes, and Elizabeth placed her hands on his shoulders. "And I *did*, only there was a bird, and it *startled* me. I thought I could catch at the tree and not fall to the ground, only I *did* fall, and now I am in the utmost *misery*."

Elizabeth said gently, "And you know that you must never attempt something so dangerous again, Rose, darling?"

"Yes, I would *never*," Rose said, reaching for her handkerchief weepily. "And Papa will *not* spank me, like Mammy said, for I have learned my lesson, and I *hurt!*"

"My precious!" Frederick exclaimed. "No, of course I will not. Where do you hurt?"

"All over!" she cried, growing fussy, but her father looked horrified.

Elizabeth met Shannon's eyes and came around Frederick to kiss Rose's face, hushing her and telling her that the medicine would very soon make her feel better. And indeed, the doctor must have given her some laudanum, for her eyes began to grow heavy, and she drifted off to sleep.

Shannon leaned forward, closing her eyes and dropping a kiss on Rose's brow.

Elizabeth turned, smiling gently at Frederick, going close to him and touching his face. "There, my dear man, she will be all right."

Frederick nodded miserably, turning his head to kiss her hand. "Elizabeth, when you screamed..." he whispered.

"We have all had a shock," she said, agreeing. She touched his chest while looking over her shoulder at Shannon.

Frederick looked up. "Shannon!" She smiled. "Yes, I sent for you, didn't I?"

"Yes," she answered. "Oh, my dears, such a jolt you have had." She stepped forward and took one of their hands each, feeling Elizabeth's returning pressure.

"Shannon, for heaven's sake, sit down," Frederick said.

She did so, sighing while Frederick looked between her and Rose anxiously.

In a few moments there was a knock at the door and, seeing that Frederick and Elizabeth were still addled, Shannon went forward to open it. John the butler was standing there and said to her, his voice cast in a whisper, "Miss Shannon, your husband's here." He paused, obviously sensing the import of that statement.

"Mr. Frederick is quite safe from him, John," she answered quietly, though it did seem almost unimaginable that John Thomas was once again in Ravenel House. Her pulse quickened.

"He's in a state, Miss Shannon, worried about you and the little one."

Shannon flushed fierily. She was indeed feeling rather exhausted, but there was no cause for John Thomas to worry. "You told him Miss Rose is well?"

"Yes, ma'am. It was the first thing he asked, and I told him, and he looked so happy you'd think she was his own, but he set to worrying again so quickly you'd have thought I told him just the opposite! Well, he's cold, ma'am, and doesn't show his emotions, but I know what he was thinking."

Shannon was still flushing, but thankfully, Frederick came forward. "What's this?" He looked at Shannon. "Is Haley here?"

"Yes, he is," she answered and saw that it gave him pleasure.

Elizabeth patted Frederick's arm. "Go down and make him welcome, my dear. We will sit with her and send for you if anything is needed."

"Yes, and tell him that I am quite well," Shannon said.

He nodded, slipping out quietly after one last glance at the sleeping angel and closing the door behind him. Elizabeth looked at her, too, and then at Shannon. Smiling, she went forward with arms extended, saying, "*Dearest*."

Shannon embraced her, eyes misting, and when Elizabeth pulled back, she was smiling. "Oh, Shannon!" she said tearfully, touching Shannon's middle in wonder.

Shannon laughed, and they cried together, embracing, emotions spent from the day's events and from their separation. "Dear Elizabeth! Such a fright she gave us!"

"Yes, it is not the first time she has done her best to kill herself, and I fear it will not be the last. And the thing that is perfectly lethal about her, Shannon," she said, wiping her tears, "is that she is *not* a tomboy. She is as delicate and exquisite as a fawn. Every little boy I can think of is perfectly enslaved by her. And what will be our state when she begins courting, I can't imagine. Your father believes that we must take her to Europe, but I am much more inclined to lock her up."

Shannon laughed, looking down at Rose's face and sinking onto the bed. Elizabeth adjusted Rose's blanket to cover more of her arm.

Shannon said, "I ought not to have stayed up here. He will be feeling uncomfortable, I imagine."

"With Frederick? Not likely." Elizabeth felt Rose's pulse and seemed to find it satisfactory. "We've missed you, Shannon," she said softly, meeting her eyes.

Shannon's eyes misted again, and she reached for her friend's hand, pressed it, and nodded. She looked at Elizabeth, elegant in a blue gown, her dark hair wisping about her face becomingly. When she was able to, she said, "I did not want to make trouble between Frederick and my father. I could not make him choose between us."

Elizabeth sighed. "There is no choosing between you, Shannon. Your father wishes to see you. I've never seen a man look so truly shaken as he was all the evening after Frederick told us of your condition. I can promise you that ho worrioo for you very much."

Shannon swallowed, looking once more at the sleeping Rose.

The initial moment of greeting had been a bit uncomfortable, but Frederick had suffered too much of a shock to worry greatly with more subtle emotions. Very soon grasping the situation, John Thomas made it his business to restore Frederick's frame of mind.

Frederick sat with the drink John Thomas had poured for him in hand, elbows on his knees, forehead in his other hand. "When I made it to her, the breath had been knocked out of her," he said numbly. "Elizabeth was feeling frantically for a pulse, and she wasn't breathing. And her leg..." He shuddered.

John Thomas listened to him with sympathy.

"She is better now. Says she requires Shannon, but she's asleep, so she won't know if you leave."

"I won't do that. It will be good for Shannon to visit with Elizabeth. She misses her dreadfully."

"Elizabeth, too... She speaks of it so often, and I feel most sincerely for her, but what can be done, I..." His forehead wrinkled. "She actually *walked* the railing, John Thomas! Like a *cat*."

He lowered a hand to Frederick's shoulder, gripping it. "She sounds very determined."

He shuddered. "And Elizabeth! Poor Elizabeth, to see it happen! What would we have done, how would we have gone on...?"

John Thomas allowed Frederick to talk on in this style several more minutes until his nerves were somewhat restored. Then he considered it wise to give his thoughts another direction. "Shannon looks better, I think," he said gently, sitting across from him. "Did you think so?"

Frederick looked up, lifting his forehead from his hand. "Yes, much better. I think perhaps she isn't as gaunt as she was."

"She is able to eat a little more," he agreed, not chronicling her progression, since he didn't believe Shannon would wish him to. "How is your father?"

"Well enough, though a bear to live with. Thinks *he's* killed Shannon." He sat back, sighing. "He'll be in a tremendous worry, and I hate it, but we didn't know when we sent for him whether..." He swallowed.

A silence descended. After a time, John Thomas said softly, looking around the room, finding it stripped of its valuables, "How do you get by, Frederick? I know the suffering of Southerners. Dr. Travers would have it that I did my part to cause it, and I can't fault him for that."

Frederick looked at him. "You did your duty, Haley, and let me hear no more about that. Travers is a fool." John Thomas smiled slightly. Frederick sighed, looking around absently. "How do we get by... Well, we've sold everything of any value. We saved some things, hid them in the fireplace. Now they've all been sent overseas. We cashed in every foreign investment we had. But the simple truth is, we're having to plan how we'll make a living. We were planters by trade, and that's all gone now, so we'll have to do something else. Only there *is* nothing else."

"But surely with your lands returned—"

Frederick's brows drew together. "Lands returned? Where did you hear that? It isn't true, unfortunately."

John Thomas's forehead wrinkled. His heart stuttered. "I...can't think," he said faintly.

Shannon hadn't given them the orders he'd drafted. His mind tried to wrap around that fact. He could think of no other reason one so fiercely devoted to her family would have failed to do so than to protect him. And that before he had even accepted her offer to return as his wife.

"Well, don't think of putting in a word. It would have the stench of nepotism and damage you. We've made our case, like everyone else."

He sighed, drawing a hand through his hair. "Very well. Will you let me loan you some money?"

Frederick looked at him. "I know you're better off than we are, but you can't be flush in the pockets yourself. You've been serving your country for four years—well, longer than that."

John Thomas lifted a shoulder. "I had a good salary during the war. *Have* a good salary. And my father left me a little."

"I am glad to hear that Shannon will be taken care of," Frederick answered stubbornly.

John Thomas sighed again. "Well. You know where to find me if you need it. Everything I have is at your disposal."

Frederick's prideful features softened. "There is one way you can help me."

John Thomas lifted his brows, looking at him.

"We have eleven servants—more than we need now,

but we feel responsibility to them, of course." His eyes cut away. "We can scarcely afford to feed them, let alone pay them. Rebecca was Marie's maid. When I married Elizabeth, my mother had already passed, and her maid, Abigail, outranked Rebecca. So, Abigail serves Elizabeth now. But Rebecca's skills are far above that of a housemaid, and it isn't right for her status to be so lowered. Well, I've been thinking about Shannon. She's refused to have a lady's maid since Phoebe was killed." He hesitated. "I know you're not much for servants, but—"

Quickly, John Thomas said, "On the contrary, I wish very much for Shannon to have everything she needs. I have encouraged her to hire a lady's maid, but she becomes terribly upset when I do so. But she would hardly deny Rebecca the opportunity to have a fair salary, and it would relieve my mind very much."

"Very well," Frederick said. "I'll send her to you tomorrow." Looking conscious, he added with a flush, "If she's willing, of course."

"Yes, we can discuss her wages then," John Thomas agreed, pretending ignorance.

Frederick started to speak, but just then, the door opened. Mr. Ravenel entered, his appearance neat as always but his expression disordered. "Frederick," he said, striding to him and gripping his arms. "My boy, is she all right?" he cried.

"Yes, Father," Frederick said, standing. He clasped his arms reassuringly. "Yes, I'm sorry to have given you a fright, but when we sent for you, we didn't know."

The man gave a great sigh of relief, bringing forth his handkerchief and wiping his brow. "Nothing broken then?"

"Oh, yes. Her leg. But not her spirit, I can assure you," he said wryly. He glanced nervously at John Thomas, who had also come to his feet.

Mr. Ravenel took in the room then and, seeing John Thomas, he straightened, lowering his arms from Frederick.

John Thomas had not seen the man in six years. He would, he imagined, have been in bad standing with Mr. Ravenel since Shannon's flight four years ago. John Thomas had stood among presidents, testified before Congress, and faced off against military giants, but they were nothing to Shannon's father, who was just now looking at him with a piercing blue gaze, alarmingly reminiscent of his daughter's.

"Haley," he said. He straightened further.

John Thomas inclined his head. "Mr. Ravenel. A pleasure to see you, sir."

"I imagine my daughter is here. I only hope such travel may not have harmed, from what I hear, her very fragile health."

"Father," Frederick said, acutely embarrassed. "What, to drive three streets over? Of course it has not! John Thomas and I were just discussing her health. It is much-improved!"

"Hold your tongue, Frederick."

Frederick looked outraged, and John Thomas jumped into the breach in his usual quiet voice. "Frederick is right, sir. She is feeling much better."

"What plans have been made for her lying in?" the man asked, eyeing him sharply.

There was a tick of silence. "My own doctor—a very trusted man—will attend her," John Thomas said calmly. "And I hope Mrs. Ravenel will be there with her," he added.

"Of course—" Frederick began.

"You ought to hire a midwife, too," Mr. Ravenel interrupted. "A woman would be a comfort to her and would be there in case something prevented this Schafer from coming to her," he said, revealing how little in the dark he had been about matters.

"Father, honestly, you cannot dictate to him in matters of his household!" Frederick exclaimed, skin mottled.

"Frederick, if you cannot curb your tongue, you will—"

"No, that is a good suggestion," John Thomas said calmly. "I will see what can be done."

Mr. Ravenel grunted. When he finally looked John Thomas over, he seemed to be surprised by what he found and not wholly ill-pleased. He told Frederick to pour him some wine. Taking a restorative breath, Frederick did so, flashing a brief, apologetic glance at John Thomas.

"You seem to have grown taller, Haley," Mr. Ravenel said gruffly as he sat. The young men sat tentatively as well. Shannon's father did not sip his wine but instead fixed his eagle stare upon her husband.

"I doubt it, sir," John Thomas said mildly.

The piercing gaze did not waver. "You intend to take her back to Massachusetts, then? Against her will, I imagine."

While Frederick choked on his wine, John Thomas said mildly, "I must follow my postings, as you know, sir."

"Very well for a bachelor, but not for a husband, and certainly not for a father."

John Thomas, instead of giving a cool reply, studied him, disquiet in his face. A silence developed in which Frederick flailed about in his mind for something to say. Mr. Ravenel, however, seemed to sense that he had gone too far, for he said, more quickly than was his custom, "How is your family? All are in good health, I hope?"

There was an overlong beat of silence until John Thomas said, "Most, sir. But my father passed last year. And one of my brothers was injured at the Wilderness. He suffers still."

Frederick sat up. "Charles?" he demanded.

John Thomas looked at him, nodding. "Yes. He was shot three times." He paused. "He lost the use of his arm. He still has great difficulty in walking, although we are told that may not always be so. As yet he is confined to his chair. He suffers relapses and is then confined to bed..."

"He is at home now?" Frederick asked.

"Yes, at Harmony Grove," he answered quietly.

They talked on for a time until something caught his eye, and John Thomas looked up to see Shannon standing in the doorway. He jumped to his feet. She stood with her hand on the wide, white doorframe, purposefully not looking at her father. Then she met John Thomas's eyes.

The other men had stood, too, and a thick silence hung in the air.

"I came to tell you that Rose is resting peacefully," she said with quiet stiffness.

They all watched her. Her father appeared at a loss, for once.

"That…is good," Frederick said, glancing at John Thomas.

She looked briefly at her father and then away. "John Thomas, will you take me home?"

"Yes," he said quietly, moving toward her. "Of course."

# Chapter Thirteen

Rebecca had been more than willing to become Shannon's lady's maid. To be elevated to her former role and to be paid for it was a joy to her. But more than that, she was happy because she had heard from Phoebe what it was like to live in Admiral Haley's household, where slavery was loathed. She knew there was a likelihood that she would be taken to Boston, and, having many friends but no family, she felt that the novelty of living in a place where slavery had been extinct for many years might outweigh the disadvantages of leaving her native land.

It was a good thing, for Rebecca quickly became a constant comfort to Shannon and, therefore, to John Thomas. Rebecca knew just what to do when Shannon was the least bit ill, and she treated Shannon with kindness and great care. At forty years of age, Rebecca was tall and slim and rather quiet, a talented maid and extremely capable in all matters concerning a lady's wardrobe and fashion.

She was in the room with Shannon when the midwife which John Thomas had procured was scheduled to meet her. It had been a month since Rose's fall, and the young lady was on the mend and driving her own household to distraction. She was chained to her bed in the nursery and most unhappy about it. Shannon visited her once while her father was away, and she had even taken Rose's handsome uncle with her, which cheered the waif immensely.

Shannon had not expected the sheen of moisture in John Thomas's eyes as he had met the child. His voice had been thick as he talked to her gently and encouraged her to speak of all the ships she had seen from the balcony now that the harbor had reopened. He saw Shannon in her, as well as Frederick's child, and Shannon had been emotional herself. She had forgotten how much children liked him. But then she remembered how his young siblings, Vincent and Sarah, had shadowed his every step at Harmony Grove.

Shannon bit her lip, lying in her bed now. If only she could get John Thomas to rail at her for leaving him, to force him to speak of it and demand answers of her. But he wouldn't. And so there must perpetually be a distance. She sighed. "I can't think what good this will do," she said.

Rebecca was folding linens at the dresser. "He's just worried for you, ma'am."

"I know," she replied softly. They heard the door open downstairs and voices murmuring. "That will be her now, I suppose."

"Yes, ma'am. Admiral Haley told me he'd bring her up."

They heard footsteps on the stairs, and in moments, Shannon's door opened softly and a woman walked in. She was Negro, which Shannon hadn't expected, but that was the least of her surprise. Shannon sat up, meeting the eyes of her father's mistress.

The woman looked at her boldly. She was a mulatto, with light brown eyes and a shapely figure. Her cheekbones were high, her jawline firm. She was looking at Shannon, not unkindly, but unflinchingly. Neither the apron she wore nor the imposed status of her people hindered her dignity.

Shannon was still leaning up anxiously, her hand cradling her middle, her face giving away her distress. She drew in a breath. "Rebecca… Will you go and assure my husband that I am well? He will be worried—he always is when the doctor calls." She swallowed. "And stay with him. I will come down to you once we are finished."

Rebecca looked doubtful, but after a glance at the midwife, she said, "Yes, ma'am," and left.

Shannon sat up. She was in her dressing gown since she had expected an examination, but she covered herself as though to put an end to thoughts that there would be any such thing.

"I'm sorry," the woman said. "I had hoped you didn't know."

Shannon met her eyes, aghast at her boldness. "How… How did he—my husband—find you?"

She looked at Shannon with compassion. "Your papa gave him my name."

Shannon stiffened. "My father sent his mistress to wait upon his daughter?" she demanded, aghast. "I won't believe you!"

The woman waited quietly for a moment. "He always felt," she said gently, "that if I had been with Miss Marie, things might have gone differently. I told him it wasn't true, but…"

Shannon's jaw tightened, and she looked away. "What is your name?"

"Justinia. Justinia Reed. Now, I can leave, and we can say we didn't suit, or I can have a look at you and your baby and be there for you when your time comes. I think I could be a comfort to you, but it's your decision. I'll leave if you want me to."

Shannon moistened her lips. She sat in silence a long time.

"You and Mr. Frederick are all he has left now—"

"You mean after my mother's passing?" Shannon demanded, looking at her coldly.

"Yes," the woman said calmly. "He loves you, and I love him, and I'd just as soon you'd agree for me to attend you. It would ease his mind."

"For you to be a spy in my household for him?"

"For me to help you when your time comes," she said, shifting her bag to her left hand.

Shannon turned her face away. She swiped at a tear. "Very well," she whispered.

The woman—Justinia—drew a breath and came forward.

When she was standing by the bed, she looked at Shannon. Shannon nodded once, and she began. "The baby's in position," she said after a minute or two.

"Dr. Schafer said so. What does that mean?"

"It means you won't have a cross-birth," she answered.

"That is a relief," she said, drawing a thready breath.

When she was finished, Justinia sat down, to Shannon's surprise, on the bed. She didn't cover Shannon's hand, but she looked like she wished to. "You have a big baby, honey," she said.

Shannon met her eyes. "I thought so," she whispered, emotion tightening her throat.

"Your figure will come back to you. You're one of the thin ones."

"Oh, I don't care for that," Shannon said, though she once would have very much. "And it means the baby is healthy, doesn't it? I worried so very much, for I was extremely ill in the beginning."

"Yes," she agreed. "It's healthy, from what I can tell."

"Will it hurt very much?" she whispered.

Justinia nodded. "I wish you'd go before your time, but you won't, I think."

Shannon laughed through her emotion. "I am glad to hear it. I don't mind a little pain."

"I didn't think you would," the other woman said, smiling kindly.

Still uncomfortable, Shannon shifted. "How...long have you been a midwife?"

"Twenty years," she answered, and Shannon wondered what mysteries this woman's life held, not the least of which was how she had become John Ravenel's mistress.

"Do you…" Shannon hesitated, her heart pounding. "Do you have any children?"

There was a second of silence. "No," Miss Reed said, not looking at her.

And somehow, despite everything, Shannon felt a chord of sympathy with her. Miss Reed cleared her throat. "Now," she said, getting down to business, "you're too thin, honey. The baby's taking everything you have. You might want to go right back into your dresses, but—"

"No, *truly*, I don't care for that," Shannon said. "If I could gain weight, I would, but if I eat a great deal, it won't stay down."

The woman nodded, asking what Dr. Schafer had prescribed for her nausea, before saying she couldn't do any better than that. "I'll leave you now, but your husband will know where to find me."

It was a cold, gray day, and Shannon sat in her parlor looking out the window. Christmas was close. She missed her family, and her mind grew more and more anxious by day. Her baby seemed to be healthy, but she fretted that she would never be able to bring it into the world with her paltry strength. She worried over everything, including very miniscule things like whether she ought to serve the partridges for supper with carrots or peas, and larger things such as when John Thomas would be called away from Charleston. She suspected that he had been reassigned already but had requested an extension for her sake. One of his aides had alluded to such, and she had overhead.

John Thomas had invited her to share his bed, telling her that his mind was fevered with the thought of her needing him in the night and his not hearing. She had agreed to it. But while he was solicitous, he never drew close or laughed with her. She wished heartily that things were as they once had been before she had left him and ruined both of their lives.

She sat looking out the window, thinking about her baby, wanting to protect it always as she could now. Slowly growing more and more upset, she was lifting her handkerchief to her eyes when she heard John Thomas's firm step going toward the outer door and then heard him talking lowly and even whispering with a woman. She grew wrathful almost immediately. *Who* was this female?

Footsteps sounded and were growing nearer. Looking toward her door, she waited until it opened. John Thomas looked in, his gentle eyes falling upon her, and he said, "My darling, I have brought someone to see you."

He stepped back, opening the door wider for someone. It was a young woman with pale hair and blue eyes. She wore a dove gray travelling dress and a darker cape, the hood hanging down her back. She had quiet dignity and a plain sort of beauty that sparkled as she shyly began to smile.

Shannon gasped, slowly getting up and crying, "*Lizzie!*" Tears flooded to her eyes and flowed down her face. She rushed forward, embracing John Thomas's sister, who whispered emotionally, "Shannon—oh, Shannon!" Lizzie returned her embrace, touching her face tenderly and looking into her features.

"But how..." Shannon looked up at John Thomas questioningly.

"Are you happy?" he asked tenderly.

"Happy... Oh, that doesn't begin to... But how long can you stay?" Shannon asked, looking at Lizzie, to whom she was still clinging.

"Until your precious baby is brought into this world," Lizzie said, as if there could be no trouble about that. Shannon had forgotten how bracing Yankee confidence could be, and she was immensely comforted. "My mother wished to come, and I am only her emissary, but I am *very* glad to be here."

Shannon embraced her again, looking over Lizzie's shoulder as she met John Thomas's eyes and smiled.

"Tell me everything," Shannon said, sitting on the settee in her bedchamber. She had slipped out of bed in John Thomas's room without awakening him and found Lizzie awake and already dressed.

Shannon had no pretensions to be so disciplined and instead still lounged in her rich dressing gown (which she had asked Miss Millington to make with her spare material).

Lizzie sat across from her in a dark gray wool gown which she had proclaimed much too warm for Charleston.

"You are fortunate to have come in winter. There are times one wishes one could go about naked, it is so warm." She touched her lips, thinking that she would do well to remember that Lizzie was not Elizabeth. "Forgive me!"

Lizzie laughed. "I am not shocked."

Shannon's eyes widened, for the Lizzie she had known would have stiffened at any hint of indelicacy. But she had passed most of the war in Northern Virginia as a nurse, and Shannon rather imagined that such work, as grueling as it came, had flattened any prudishness out of her. Seeing tens of thousands of men naked and bleeding and dying would have taken its toll. Shannon saw that truth in the way Lizzie's eyes stared into the distance when she didn't think anyone was looking. She was reliving a thousand horrors, Shannon knew. But the war had done something else, too. It had given her a new confidence, a decisiveness and firm set to her thin shoulders, and Lizzie was shrouded in an air of peaceful competency like the Haley she was.

"John Thomas has told me about Charles," Shannon said. "What news of him?"

"He is much the same, but he was a bit better, perhaps, when I departed. I left the hospital where I had been working at the end of the war to go and care for him at Harmony Grove."

"That must have been a great comfort to your mother," Shannon said.

"Yes, I think it was. But she knows how to care for him now, and she wouldn't have it any other way than that I should come here." She reached for Shannon's hand, stroking it. "He feels miserably ill-equipped, poor dear, to give you the care you need, and he is so worried for you, Shannon. I cannot tell you how glad I am that you have reconciled and that the proof of it will soon come to fruition."

It wasn't quite like that, but Shannon could not bear to say otherwise. She pressed Lizzie's hand. "You do not hate me? I so feared that you might."

Lizzie looked at her, hesitating. "I could never hate you, Shannon," she answered softly. "I was angry once—yes. But what is that when we have been through a war? I am heartily sick of any emotion remotely low or base. We do not have the energy to expend upon them in such times as these. And so, when you cut to the heart of the matter, which I think is the only thing you can do after we have seen six-hundred-thousand men die, my brother loves you. I love you. We have a history, and *that* cannot be cast aside."

Shannon gripped her hand, tears clouding her vision. She asked Lizzie to tell her about her family. Her ignorance likely conveyed to Lizzie everything about the state of things between Shannon and John Thomas that outright words had not, for she looked a little surprised.

"You know that Adams is married?"

"What?" Shannon gasped.

She nodded. "To Anna Renley. Her father is one of the senators from Massachusetts. They met during the war in

Washington, where he did very invaluable work at the War Department."

"Good heavens…" Still in shock, Shannon asked of John Thomas's eldest sister, "And Patience? Did Jonathan…?"

"He survived, although two of his brothers didn't. The Whitcombs are all in great sorrow still."

"And their little James?"

"Yes, he is a healthy child. I fear that I do not know him, but I hope to now."

"Go on: Miriam?" Shannon asked with interest. The sister a few years junior to Lizzie had been a sharp little minx who had shadowed Shannon's every step in Massachusetts.

"Miriam is married, too."

Her eyes widened. "No!"

"She is twenty-two."

Shannon blinked. "To whom? Have I met him?"

"No, but you have heard of him." Her eyes twinkled slightly. "Mr. Winthrop, the railroad man."

Shannon thought for a moment and then gasped, "*Your* railroad man?"

"Yes. Well, he wished to be my railroad man but later determined that he might just as well be Miriam's railroad man," she said, her smile growing. "No, don't look so shocked! His affection for her is sincere, and I promise you that she suits him far better than I would have."

"Yes," Shannon said slowly. "Miriam *would* like to be very rich. I am happy for her then if he loves her. Do they have any children?"

"A daughter, born last October."

"Oh! What did they name her?" she asked, eyes shining.

"Amelia Anne."

"Has John Thomas met her?"

"No, but Miriam and Mr. Winthrop visited him when last he was in Washington."

"Oh, I'm glad. Vincent? Sarah?"

"Vincent caught the end of the war. He is nearly nineteen now, you know."

Shannon blinked. "That cannot—yes, it *must* be true."

"But John Thomas and Adams don't wish him to make a military career, nor does he. He is to enroll in Harvard as soon as his regiment disbands."

Shannon breathed deeply. How must it have felt for them to send him off to war?

"Sarah is to make her debut into society this winter. She is in high spirits, and I hope she may not bleed Adams dry with all of her ballgowns and trimmings."

Shannon laughed. "I am glad to hear it. It must have been hardest for her to lose your father, still at home as she was."

"Yes, indeed," she said gently, her eyes faraway. "As for my mother, she and the other ladies in Boston spear-headed much of the relief efforts for war widows and orphans in Massachusetts. And now she cares for Charles and prepares Sarah for her coming out."

Shannon nodded, feeling a prick of tears. She had not been there. For their triumphs or sorrows. She knew she would have felt the same about her own family had she made the opposite decision, but she supposed she had never considered that she had left behind more than just John Thomas. She could have been a support to them, and she hadn't been. More than that, she had been an added worry. For she didn't think for a moment that her name had been kindly spoken in the past years, however kind Lizzie was now. Shannon swallowed. "I cannot tell you how I have missed them, untrue though that may sound."

Lizzie shook her head. "No, it doesn't sound false," she said, close to emotion herself. She reached forward, pressing Shannon's hand tightly. "Not to me."

The morning was gray and cold, but Shannon and Lizzie kept warm by the fire in Shannon's chamber, Lizzie knitting industriously and Shannon reading from her Bible. She looked up after a time, her eyes narrowed shrewdly, and said, "Did it *truly* not trouble you, Miriam's marriage to Mr. Winthrop?"

Lizzie looked up. "No, it didn't." She paused in her knitting only briefly.

Shannon studied her sister-in-law: her fair head lowered demurely over her work, her posture unassuming. One would never know that she had saved more men than any officer could dare to boast. Shannon turned the subject to compare notes on their nursing experiences. She asked whether Union policies had permitted treatment of Confederate men.

"Oh, yes. We treated all of the men the same." Lizzie went on to relate to Shannon some of the structures of the Army Nurses and Sanitary Commission. Shannon was impressed.

Her mind straying back eventually, though she had ordered it not to do so, Shannon said, "And it isn't the least bit awkward for you, seeing them together?"

Lizzie laughed. "No, truly, it isn't. Do not worry for me, Shannon."

Shannon said solemnly. "But I do." She looked away into the fire, imagining what it would've cost her to lose John Thomas, as Lizzie had lost her first love to cholera. Would she have died, too?

When she looked up at Lizzie, her sister-in-law reached forward and covered Shannon's hand. "I did not refuse Mr. Winthrop because I was wearing the willow for Albert, though I will always love him, I suppose. I refused him because..." She lifted her head up, as though thinking. "I did not love him, and I suppose that is reason enough. But I wanted to do something worthwhile, something of my own. I don't wish to be married."

Shannon clasped her hand. "I can understand such a feeling. I suppose I thought you might have met a man during the war who..." she intimated softly, half-jokingly.

Lizzie flushed, looking away as a high color stole into her cheeks.

Shannon's lips parted to speak when there was a light knock, and the door opened. John Thomas appeared, and looking from Lizzie to him, Shannon said, "Come in, my darling." Belatedly, she flushed at the endearment, but her mind was whirling with questions. And it seemed to bring John Thomas pleasure, in any event, as he smiled and bent down to kiss her cheek, whispering, "How are you feeling?"

His face stayed close as he waited for her answer.

"I am well," she said, getting momentarily lost in the blue of his eyes.

"Are you quite comfortable?"

"No, never," she responded truthfully.

His face looked pained, and he touched her arm. "Shannon," he said, looking her over as though there must be some solution. His fingers brushed her cheek, and he looked at her as he had all of those years ago. It became rather difficult to breathe. She lay her hand at her middle, continuing to look up at him, but she did touch his arm gently, for she didn't think he had seen Lizzie.

Seeming to read her eyes, he looked around, flushing slightly. "Lizzie. Good morning. I trust you slept well?" His thumb brushed Shannon's arm.

"Oh, yes, quite well," she answered, eyes twinkling.

He looked Shannon over again. "Did I interrupt? I will go if—"

"You haven't," Lizzie hastened to say. "*I* will go, if you wish to talk with Shannon."

"No, no. It pleases me to see the two of you talking as you once did." He studied Shannon. "I was on the point of leaving for headquarters, but..."

"I'm well," Shannon said sweetly. "I am told a little discomfort is not unusual. I didn't mean to frighten you."

He looked disgruntled. "I *want* you to tell me the state of your health. And you never do, Shannon."

Shannon's eyes welled, not of their own volition. "Forgive me, I didn't mean to keep anything."

His face looked horrified. "Shannon... Oh, my darling, how could I? Don't cry!" He leaned forward, covering her hand, his eyes flicking over her with anxiety.

Lizzie laughed, getting up. "You haven't made her cry, John Thomas." She patted his back, prodding him up. "The baby has, as you know perfectly well." He was looking at Shannon in perfect agony, but Lizzie shooed him toward the door.

Shannon said, "Yes, I am quite well! Don't worry." He stood at the door, continuing to look at her, and she realized that she must convince him. "I *promise*," she said softly.

He nodded slowly, and after a long, measuring glance at her, he took his leave.

Lizzie said, going to tie back the curtains to let in the light, "There was never any couple like the pair of you! I would knock your heads together if it weren't so amusing."

"Is it?" Shannon asked listlessly, fingering the fabric of her skirt.

Lizzie stopped, looking back at her. "Isn't it?"

Shannon hesitated. "It is painful sometimes, Lizzie. To know there is not an easiness between us." Because she could not look at her sister-in-law, she looked away.

"It will come, Shannon," Lizzie said simply. "There was

never anything like the way he looks at you either. Give it time."

Shannon lay back, her heart aching, and suddenly, she felt very tired. She thought of their intimacy before the war, how they had smiled together, lingered together, talked of everything, and bantered. It was wearying to know that something was possible and to feel that if one could just pull the right lever, or turn the correct knob, the thing would hum to life.

She supposed she would go and lie down on her bed. Perhaps she would have Rebecca douse her temples. But just as she was about to say so, Lizzie told her that she would help her to dress, and that they would take a walk with one of the guards accompanying them.

Shannon recoiled, touching her chest. "I was just thinking of taking a nap."

"None of your Southern die-away airs, Shannon. Your spine is made of iron, I know, so you won't fool me. I promised John Thomas I would have you in excellent condition to deliver the baby, and that means we must build your strength. You are as thin as a starved cat, and if your baby is a Haley, it will be big, unfortunately. At least, they usually are."

Shannon said stiffly, "I can assure you that the baby is a Haley."

"That wasn't what I was implying, Shannon," she said, dragging her up and bundling her into a walking gown before putting her through an exhausting course over the next few weeks designed to bring her into excellent health.

# Chapter Fourteen

It was three weeks later that John Thomas, working at headquarters, received a note from Lizzie. Rushing home, he threw back the front door and ran up to Shannon's room, where there seemed to be a dozen women milling about. He glimpsed Lizzie, Elizabeth, Miss Reed, and Rebecca before finally seeing Shannon in her dressing gown, sitting.

"Oh, John Thomas," she said, and the relief in her voice and eyes seared him. She was glad to see him, as if his presence were of the greatest comfort to her. "They think it is beginning," she said as he went down on his knee in front of her, gathering her hands.

"Darling," he said, stroking her knuckles, wishing there were any way he might take this on himself. "Has Dr. Schafer been sent for?" he asked, trying to keep the fear from his voice. He must have succeeded, for Shannon seemed to steady.

"Yes," she answered.

His eyes held hers. "Remember to trust God, Shannon. He is your strength."

She nodded. "Yes," she whispered. "Yes. It *is* a peace that passes all understanding, isn't it?"

His eyes welled with tears, for *that* was what he had always wanted for Shannon, nothing more. "It is, my darling. And He will sustain you, as He has sustained me."

Elizabeth, coming forward, said gently, "John Thomas, you must leave. It is very improper for you to be in here, you know. Your sister agrees, so you see that you are outnumbered."

"You are certain you don't wish me to stay?" John Thomas asked, unheeding, holding Shannon's eyes.

She hesitated, finally saying, with a press of his hands, "No, we will send for you when it is over."

He rose and kissed her cheek, lingering there a long moment. He told Elizabeth that they would know where to find him if anything were needed. "Yes, certainly we shall. Frederick is in the library, you know."

"Is he?" he said, insensibly relieved. He pressed Elizabeth's hand. "Take care of her," he whispered.

She nodded, holding his eyes, the gravity of the situation returning to him as discomfort settled into the pit of his stomach.

Screams rent the air from time to time as John Thomas sat with Frederick at the library table, his coat flung aside, his head in his hands. Frederick tried to comfort him, but John Thomas would break off talking every time a new scream arose and stay silent until it was finished, as though he must hear them all.

"How long did it take when...Rose was born?" he asked.

"Days," Frederick said, the whiskey making him a bit blunt.

There was another piercing scream. Frederick got up, poured out a glass and extended it to John Thomas, who shook his head. "If I have another, I shall be drunk," he said. Frederick raised a brow as if to indicate that was rather the appeal. But John Thomas shook his head. "If she should need me, it would be...infamous," he said softly, seriously.

Frederick nodded, seeming to mull this over before nodding again, tipping up the glass himself, and putting it down with a loud *thunk*, which made John Thomas sigh, disheartened. "Now *you* shall be drunk."

"I imagine my tolerance is rather stronger than yours."

"It would have to be," John Thomas said, looking up and meeting his eyes before Frederick laughed. But he sobered quickly enough as another scream followed by a long crying whimper shattered their peace of mind.

John Thomas got up and walked restlessly to the window, crossing his arms and looking out. He knew it couldn't be easy for Frederick, but it was going to kill him, his brittle, beloved Shannon, enduring labor. After all her trials of body and spirit. He closed his eyes.

Only, she wasn't brittle anymore. There was only

vulnerability, and carefully concealed vulnerability at that. He was only just beginning to see how changed Shannon was, as he could have seen earlier had he allowed her to come within touching distance—the miserable fool that he was. Not that he had needed her to change to adore her utterly. That was the very crux of the trouble.

Trying not to let his emotions overwhelm him, he said shakily, "I shall need a great deal of advice."

"On bringing up a child?" Frederick asked.

He nodded.

"Then you must ask Shannon. She raised my child. I know nothing of child-rearing beyond all-consuming fear for her safety, which no one has to teach you."

He studied him. "Shannon brought up Rose?"

"Yes, until my marriage to Elizabeth, for which I could never repay her. And she worked in the Roper Hospital, too, besides holding us all together when Marie died." The loudest scream yet rent the air, and Frederick, touching his temples, said, "Oh, God!"

Going to him and laying his hand on his shoulder, John Thomas wanted to tell him that it wouldn't be like it had been with Marie. That they were as different in form as could be imagined, so there was nothing about them being cousins that should make this situation similar.

But he couldn't say that, for the simple truth was that none of them knew. Why had he wasted a single, stupid day in fear? When she had been right by his side, as he had begged God to happen for years?

He had been afraid of going mad if he allowed Shannon any part of his soul, only to lose her again. He had never thought of losing her to death until Dr. Travers had given his verdict. Either way, he feared the result would be insanity. Dear God, if that were to be the case, why hadn't he enjoyed her, every wonderful, magnificent part of her, these past few months?

Hours passed, and he and Frederick alternated between them who was feeling the more hysterical. Finally, things grew quiet, and they heard a strong, lusty cry of what could only be a healthy baby rending the air. John Thomas gave an overwrought cry, leaping to his feet in joy and nearly running to the door.

Getting up and laughing, Frederick caught his arm and cried, "They won't be ready for you yet, John Thomas!"

John Thomas paused, looking at him in confusion, before flushing and saying. "Oh! Yes, of course!" He let out a shaky breath and looked constantly at the door over the next few minutes. "Do you think she is well? They would tell me if she were not, wouldn't they?"

"Yes, of course they would," Frederick said firmly, just before the door opened. Elizabeth stood on the threshold, smiling at Frederick and then looking at John Thomas, beaming. She said, "You are a father, John Thomas. And your wife wants very much to see you."

The relief coursing through him left him weak as he passed by Elizabeth, kissing her cheek in gratitude. He ran up the stairs with a knot of emotion in his throat.

"Oh, what is it?" Shannon asked after they told her that the baby was healthy. She struggled to sit up, still a bit short of breath, although her pulses seemed to be calming.

Miss Reed was finishing cleaning the baby, whose soft coos seized Shannon's heart as nothing else ever had. The midwife looked up at Dr. Schafer (with whom she seemed to have enjoyed discussing childbirth), and he said, "The honor is yours, Miss Reed."

She smiled at Shannon. "You have a son, ma'am."

Shannon blinked, her lips parting as she stared in confusion and uncertainty. Miss Reed was bringing the baby to her, and Shannon hesitantly held out her arms. "A boy," she said, visibly shaken for a moment before the child stirred and Shannon caught a glimpse of him beneath the tightly bound swaddling, just his face and a peek of his arm. She looked at him in fear. Then fear turned to wonder as she watched him yawn, despite the fact that he was already sleeping. She was terrified, but love poured out of her so fiercely that she feared the strength of it would overcome the fragile creature in her arms.

The door opened, and she looked up. Standing in the doorway was her husband. His eyes were fixed on her, his face haggard, his expression deep. It was everything she had imagined he would look before their rift. He took a step but halted, looking at her hesitantly as though not quite sure she wanted him to come forward.

But, slowly, she smiled her sweet smile. As his shoulders eased, he came to her and touched her hair with tender reverence. He swallowed his tears, looking her over. "You are well?" he asked, voice trembling.

"Oh, yes," she said weakly, smiling at him and holding his eyes. Something otherworldly happened when their gazes collided, and she seemed to be swept up, taken out of the present and into the divine. Only the door closing behind all of her attendants brought her down from such heights.

"Do you want to see?" she whispered.

He nodded, a tear trailing down his cheek, which he brushed away. She pulled back the blanket so he could see the baby's face. She heard his awed intake of breath as his gaze took in every feature. "'*He has turned my mourning into dancing. He has loosed my sackcloth and clothed me with joy,*'" he whispered shakily, laying his head against hers, kissing her hair.

Her lip trembled, and she brought her hand up to touch his face. "John Thomas," she whispered, closing her eyes in sweet bliss.

The baby fussed, which brought their attention back, and they smiled down on him tearfully. "Would you like to sit with us?" she asked. She winced as she shifted to make room.

"Shannon," he whispered in horror as he searched her features, looking over his shoulder as though wondering whether to call the doctor back.

"I am well," she said, laughing shakily. He concentrated

for the first few moments after he sat down on making sure she was not in pain.

But she lay the baby down between them, utterly capturing John Thomas's attention. She carefully loosened the blanket so that they could see him. And it was plain that every inch of him was a pattern of John Thomas: from the thick, fair hair to the eyes and stubborn little chin. John Thomas stared at his face, lost, before looking over the rest of their fine, tubby baby. He looked up suddenly at her.

She bit her lip. "Did you think it was a girl?" she asked.

"Yes, I don't know why I..." He smiled, as the baby stretched, yawning again, making a little mewling noise. Reaching to touch his face, he comforted him until he stilled. "Already I have misunderstood him."

"He appears to have forgiven you," she said, laying her head back, enjoying watching John Thomas's face.

"He is perfect, Shannon," he said. He swallowed with difficulty, looking at his son in wonder.

"I have a grievance with you, sir," she rasped when she was able. He looked up quickly. "He weighs every bit of eight pounds, and more according to Miss Reed's scale, and I never knew a Ravenel to weigh more than six or seven."

"Shannon," he whispered, dismayed. "Forgive me!"

She flushed, biting her lip. "Well, all's well that ends well." He met her smile lovingly before leaning to kiss her, lingering, and then kissing her again. "What shall we name him?" she whispered.

"Whatever you like, my darling wife," he answered, eyes still closed.

She hesitantly touched his face, but with the utmost tenderness. "Name him, please. I should like it so very much."

"Very well," he whispered, covering her hand against his face, savoring her. "I will." He gently helped her to lie back against her pillows. "You must rest, my sweet. Don't worry, I shan't let him out of my sight."

"I don't think he *has* Ravenel blood," Shannon said in bafflement two days later. The baby was in her arms, and John Thomas was sitting beside her. He had appeared in her doorway almost as soon as she had awakened, and Lizzie had left to go have her breakfast, sent on her way by a kiss on the cheek from her brother.

Shannon had looked up at him then, and she had seen his brimming excitement and joy as he took in her and the baby. But he was cautious, holding back as though fearing she preferred him at a distance. She had smiled and asked whether he would like to sit beside her, telling him that there was plenty of room. He had come, pressing a lingering kiss to her forehead. She could still feel his thankfulness for her life. And with it, his love.

"He would have to, wouldn't he?" John Thomas laughed gently, running a hand over the baby's extraordinarily soft hair.

"Yes, but it has been drowned out by quieter blood." She

studied him. He was a complex man, not always easy for her to understand. No one, seeing him two days ago, could think that his love for her had been extinguished. And yet, neither had their troubles resolved. If she could wave a scepter and make it so, she would. But no one knew better than she the ways of the heart and mind, and how long healing sometimes was in coming. She studied his profile as he regarded the child in her arms.

The baby wriggled, seeking a more comfortable position. Shannon anxiously rushed to accommodate him, too new in her role to feel unconcerned when he fussed. She lay back once the baby had settled, and they simply watched their son sleep, studying every curve and dip of his face.

She glanced up after a time, feeling John Thomas's attention. She met his eyes, and her breath caught. His gaze dropped to her lips, and she knew he intended to kiss her.

That was, until the door opened back, and Mr. Ravenel strode into the room. John Thomas leapt from the bed as quickly as possible without jostling Shannon and the baby, his face reddening. "Sir!"

"You will have to forgive me, but your men sought to deny me entrance, not accepting my statement of who I was. The fellows had the *gall* to turn their guns on me as I crossed the threshold—as if I should be afraid of mere guns!"

John Thomas stared mutely in shock until Shannon said softly, glancing at him, "John Thomas, if you might give us a moment alone?"

He looked at her and then nodded. "Yes, of course," he

answered before going to call off his guards, who were heard running through the hall.

Shannon bit her lip, holding the baby with both arms so tightly that he gave a mild protest until she loosened them. She looked down, soothing him, tears welling in her eyes. She looked up at length, and her father strode forward, saying, "Shannon, my darling daughter!"

"Oh, Papa!" she cried, quite choked by emotion.

"I was wrong. Forgive me. I acted out of love for you and what I thought best. But I ought to have listened and not decided for you."

"Oh, Papa!" she exclaimed, looking up into his eyes.

"My poor girl," he said. "Are you well, and happy?"

"Yes," she whispered, shifting his grandson so that he could see him.

He shook his head in admiration, studying him for a long moment. Then he looked at her again. "What are Haley's plans, Shannon? Will you take him up north, this grandson of mine, and I never see him again?"

Shannon held his eyes. "The President *has* transferred John Thomas to Boston, Papa. And I feel he has earned it, the pleasure to go home."

He nodded, although she could see emotion in his eyes. "Children ought to be raised in their father's home," he agreed grudgingly.

"But you will see us so much you shall wish to be rid of us. That is, if you will invite us for long visits and come to us, too."

"Of course, there is no question of that," he said, regaining his tone of mind. "What have you named him?"

She looked up, meeting his eyes. "Benjamin Ravenel Haley," she said.

He looked pleased.

*Ravenel* told her that her family would always be welcome in their lives. *Benjamin*, she knew, had been chosen for its Old Testament translations. And Benjamin himself was a living testament that rifts could be mended, that time would heal. Even if, in her heart, she knew it would be more delicate than she could wish.

And even if travelling to Massachusetts filled her with fear.

# Chapter Fifteen

Adeline was teased awake by the smell of breakfast cooking, and her eyes flickered open. The blinds were half-closed, but enough sunlight streamed through to attest to a sunny November morning, Charleston style. She sat up, looking around the room. Adrian's scent lingered, and he had left his phone on the nightstand. He must not have been up long. Good: he never slept in.

She got up and put on leggings and a loose shirt. Going to the dresser, she pulled her polka dot bandeau out, situating it on her curls so she could just deal with them later. For the first time, looking at herself, she wondered if Adrian liked girls with short hair. It didn't really seem to be his type. Add that to the list.

She grabbed his phone and headed for the stairs, still reveling in the feeling of the house around her, its pristine shine and deep historical feel. She walked down the hall and went through the kitchen door. He was standing behind the counter. He looked up and said, "Hey."

"Hey!" Not sure why she was feeling awkward, but she could deal. Maybe it was the really, really quiet house and the aloneness of it all. She just needed to move forward. "I brought your phone," she said, laying it on the counter.

"Oh, thanks." He studied her for a minute. "Sleep well?"

"Um, yeah." She hadn't realized what a buffer Jude had been until that moment. He was never spending the night away again. The stakes were higher when they were alone, the longing intensified, for her at least. There was no child-friendly home today. Just a super-hot husband standing right over there. If not for her boundaries, he could be putting his arms around her while she stirred the eggs, stealing a kiss. He could bring her down onto his knee and playfully kiss her. She could put her arms around his neck and lay her head on his chest.

Or in reality she could stir the eggs alone, and he could stand over there chopping the fruit, glancing at her once. The silence hung around, along with the tension and the conversation from last night. He might even be mad at her. She bit the side of her lip, absently flipping the eggs.

She suddenly felt a stabbing pain in her side and put the spatula down, pressing her hand to her middle and closing her eyes. She heard a dish go down hard on the marble countertop. "Adeline. What is it?" She opened her eyes, and Adrian had appeared at her side, his hand gripping her arm. His eyes washed over her face. The look in them was zero percent doctor, all husband.

"Um..." She looked up into his face, a little overwhelmed by his expression. She swallowed. "There was a sharp pain."

"Still?"

"No, I think it's... No, I'm fine now."

He watched her closely. Several seconds ticked by.

"I'm fine, Adrian," she said gently, smoothing her hand over his where he still held her arm. He looked down and, as if coming to himself, released her.

"Have you felt it before, Adeline?"

He was using intense, laser focus. It almost made her squirm. "No. It's okay, isn't it? Dr. Jay said something about it, I think."

His hand stroked down her arm, landing on her elbow. "If you weren't my wife, I wouldn't be concerned at all. I mean, unless it happened frequently."

Her heart turned over. She wasn't sure she'd ever heard him call her that before. The mother of his child, yes. But this... Her eyes roved his face. He was wearing well-fitting jeans and a blue sweater with the white collar of a button down peeking out beneath, looking as clean-cut as they came. And good. His legs never looked longer than in jeans. Well maybe that gray pair of dress pants when he was wearing the white shirt tucked in and no coat.

But the point was, none of that mattered right now. It was great, if daunting. But she had been, for some time, more interested in learning the planes of his face, the subtle expressions, the glimmers of his eyes. She thought that, through those, she knew him a little better.

He put his hand gently on her tummy. "Is he okay?"

"Yeah, he's great," she said, covering his hand, looking down. "Moving all morning—see?"

He nodded, hand slipping away and up to her neck, thumb stroking her cheek. His eyes had just dropped to her lips when the smell of burning permeated the air. He reached quickly to turn off the stove.

Adeline covered her forehead. "Gah, where is my brain?"

"It's okay," he said soothingly.

She winced. "They're ruined."

"Yeah..." He looked at her, having put out the almost-fire. "We can eat the fruit. Do you want to, you know, go out to lunch?"

"Oh, wow," she said. "Is this a date?"

He smirked. "We'll see."

She smiled.

They snacked on fruit, and then Adeline went up to get dressed, putting on a light gray dress, black booties, and a white cardigan. Adrian looked at her appreciatively as she came down the stairs, so her choice of clothing must have turned out okay.

They drove downtown, actually finding street parking for once, and he came around to open her door since it was on the street side. They held hands, fingers laced, as they walked in Jestine's Kitchen.

"Have you heard from Jude?" she asked once they had ordered their shrimp and grits.

"Mom sent a text this morning. She wants to take him to Mass with them, so it'll probably be early evening before they get home." He said it with long-suffering, but she smiled.

He sat back, surveying her. "What are we going to name this one?"

She sighed, fetching the long list of discarded names from her purse and handing it to him. He skimmed it quickly. "You don't like any of these?" he asked, looking up.

"I theoretically liked all of them before I decided to name my own baby. Our baby, I mean." Whoops. Luckily, he didn't bat an eye. "Any ideas?" she asked.

"Maybe. I'm not sure we would agree."

She gave him a look. "Hey. I can be just as classy as you. And at this rate, you're not getting a second date."

He smiled. "I didn't mean that."

She started to respond, but their food was brought then. She took a bite. *Delicious.* "This is wonderful."

"I know how to treat a date," he said, reminding her of Jude as he got a bite of shrimp.

She laughed. After a time, he reached for her hand, squeezing it and looking at her. "What if we think about it and confer when he's born. When we meet him."

"Sounds great," she answered, her throat tightening. He held her hand, and her eyes. He hesitated for a second, but he looked like he was going to say something. She didn't pull her hand away. "Adeline..."

"Yeah?" she said softly.

"Why don't you... Would you like to pick Jude up from

school and hang out with him until I get home? I mean, just a couple of days a week, or Jane'll freak out. And only if you feel like it."

She saw concession in his eyes and an unspoken apology.

After another slight hesitation, he said, "I want you to be a part of his life, Adeline. I just... It was just hard to let go, you know?" He swallowed.

"Oh, Adrian," she said, pressing his hand. "Of course I know."

"I...try not to be clingy with him, but I failed miserably with you. And I think I hurt you."

"No," she said softly, squeezing his hand. "I understood. I mean, you're his father. Of course you're protective. And a step-mother has to be handled delicately."

He shook his head. "No, not you, Adeline," he said softly, but earnestly. If the other patrons thought their intense conversation odd, that was okay. They were just going to keep on. "I told you a long time ago that no harm could possibly come to him from you. I hardly knew you then, but I knew that. I just..." He shook his head. She stroked his hand with her thumb. "I almost lost him," he said, eyes a little red. "And then he was so traumatized." He seemed to be struggling. "He couldn't sleep for months. The slightest noise made him nervous. And he...needed stability. I had to be that for him."

She blinked, trying not to cry. "Oh, Adrian. And then I came and—"

"No," he said, shaking his head. "He's fine. He's going to be fine. I know that now, but there was a time I didn't. And when we married, I was just close enough to that time that I...tried to shield him from changes."

She bit her lip. She couldn't think of anything to say and couldn't really speak without crying. She stroked her thumb over his hand again and again. "I'm so glad he's going to be okay," she whispered, holding his eyes.

There was a flicker of realization in his eyes when he saw how much she cared. His hand tightened a little on hers. "And we'll be okay, too, Adeline," he said softly.

She wanted to believe that. In that moment, she did.

She didn't know if it was the holidays approaching, or what, but people needed *a lot* of therapy, and Adeline didn't see much of Adrian for the next few weeks. So, she worked on the nursery, went out to buy items she still needed, and bonded with Jude during their Tuesdays and Thursdays together.

She and Adrian also hosted Harris and his girlfriend for an early Thanksgiving on a Saturday night. Jackie was a stunner with rich chocolate hair, perfect eyebrows, and a heart-shaped face. Excellent body, too, which Adeline tried not to dwell on at the moment. During supper, the girls got off on college while Adrian and Harris talked about football, chatting about the intricate details of their teams. Adeline didn't think she and Jackie would've been friends in college, or even after-work pals if they worked together now. But clearly the girl was head over heels for Harris, and it developed over the course of the night that she really wanted his family to like her, too.

She wasn't just casually nice to Adrian in a we'll-probably-never-see-one-another-again way. She had obviously taken the time to learn about his job and family. And to Adeline's surprise, she was included in that, too. Adeline didn't exactly feel like a Ravenel, but Jackie obviously thought of her as one. For that, she knew she had Harris to thank. To her, Adrian and Adeline were recently married and expecting a baby, and Adeline was part of the family. Nothing had been conveyed dramatically.

She was a little younger than Harris, only twenty-four, but that didn't seem to matter. He looked at her a certain way with a smile in his eyes, and she anticipated him and looked all sappy near him, especially when he was playing with Jude. It was a good thing they actually liked her; it seemed like an engagement was imminent.

Adrian was talking to Jackie about a certain restaurant in Savannah, tossing Jude's ball back to him occasionally as it strayed and glancing at him pointedly when he got a little rowdy.

"Harris," Adeline said, "there's no way the Ravenels still owned the island Santarella was on by the forties." They were sitting on one side of the room on the sofa, and Adeline's mind strayed to the mysterious matching necklaces they had found, one on the island, one here at Ravenel-Thompson. Harris had been helping her, but she felt no closer to understanding them.

Harris looked at her. "You're thinking the necklaces have to be a little older. I don't think the Star of David was widely used as a Jewish symbol until the twentieth century, though, or maybe in the decade right before? There has always been a Jewish population in Charleston, but I don't know how likely it would have been for a woman to wear that kind of necklace until—yeah, I would say after the forties. When I saw the first necklace, I guess I was thinking of the symbols Jews were forced to wear in Europe under Nazi regimes. But why did someone feel the need to hide them here, if that were the case? It doesn't make any sense."

"Yeah, it doesn't," she admitted, her shoulders slumping. This was extremely confusing.

"Can I see them again?"

"Yeah, they're in the safe in the library. Come on," she said, starting to stand.

He laid a hand on her arm, staying her. "I can go."

"No, it's fine! I'm fine," she said, looking over at Adrian. He had glanced at them as she stood, but only vaguely, so she didn't interrupt to tell him where they were going.

"She's great, Harris," Adeline said as they got out of earshot.

He glanced down at her, hands in his pockets. "Do you think mom will like her? I don't want her to terrify Jackie at Christmas."

"I think she's a match for your mom. I saw her back you down at dinner."

He smiled. "True."

They walked in the library, and she flipped on the carefully concealed light switch. The white bookshelves instantly came aglow. "How long have you been dating?"

"We were talking when you and Adrian married, but not really dating... Thanks for being nice. I need to thank Adrian, too. He's usually pretty skeptical of the women I date."

"It's just because you're his little brother," she said before telling him the code since someone had to get down on his knees to get to it, and he was better suited for the job. He scrolled the knob, saying, "Finally, access to Adrian's stock certificates."

She laughed. "I hereby make you my fiduciary for purposes of discretion."

"Killjoy." He found the necklace case and stood with it, opening it. He had good hands. Not as good as Adrian's, though. He took one of the necklaces out, handing the box to her. Then he turned the mysterious piece of jewelry in his fingers. He drew his thumb over the star, looking at it, seemingly deep in thought. "It's..." He started to speak and then thought some more. "It's not a Star of David." He looked up at her. "I think it's a North Star."

Adeline straightened, the wheels starting to spin. She opened the box and took out the other one. It *was* the slightest bit asymmetrical, the top and bottom points just a little longer. She'd never noticed it before. And it was an unusual thing for a necklace. "So...what does that mean?"

"That's all I had," he said, grinning. "Totally lost from here."

She smiled, her eyes focused in the distance in thought. "Maybe a romantic gesture?" she asked.

"How?"

She took the necklace from him, comparing it to the other. Identical. "Well, the North Star shines almost directly above the north celestial pole. If you get lost and can't find your way, you'll always know which direction is true north, even if there's nothing else to guide you, if you can just keep your eyes on the star. It's kind of a home base. If you can find north, you can find all the other directions, too."

"Oh my God, that's good." Another idea occurred to him. "Wasn't Shannon Ravenel's husband a sailor?"

"Yeah," she said.

"Well, that would've been pretty important, wouldn't it? There aren't a lot of landmarks on the high seas. No GPS... It would've been one of those navigational necessities."

She smiled, looking up at him with a lightbulb expression. "Why, yes it would, Mr. Ravenel."

"See, I know a thing or two."

She laughed. "I can see that." She bit her lip, looking away in thought. "But why were there two?" She looked back at him. "And did they ever reconcile truly?"

He lifted a shoulder. "I've read everything in the box. There's nothing about it."

She huffed. "That's a bummer. We gotta figure this out, Harris."

He laughed. "Yeah. We do. But I don't know how."

"Well... We will somehow."

# Chapter Sixteen

Crowds roared and cannons were fired off as the train steamed into the station. Shannon looked below and was, for a moment, taken aback. The platform looked like the sea, or perhaps stalks of rice blowing gently in the wind. Before she could assimilate the scene, John Thomas had stood to help her up. He glanced at the crowds of people below who waved their hats and handkerchiefs and screamed what she thought might be his name.

She looked up, meeting his eyes, and adjusted the baby, who slept against her shoulder. He touched her arm, looking at her regretfully. "Forgive me, I had hoped it would have died down."

"Apparently it has not," she answered.

He held her eyes for a long moment. "Are you warm enough?" he asked softly.

"Yes," she answered, tucking Benjamin's blankets more securely.

Then they turned and realized all the passengers of the train had stayed put, looking at them and smiling, waiting for them to be the first to exit. John Thomas inclined his head to them. He led the way, perhaps to shield Shannon, who was soon to be the object of such speculation as perhaps the Commonwealth of Massachusetts had never known.

The thunderous noise only grew louder when the beaming conductor opened the door and John Thomas stepped out. He reached his hand back to hold her out of sight for a few moments. The slaying of President Lincoln and attempted assassinations of Seward and Grant were still too fresh to make the situation entirely secure. The people were chanting, "Speech, speech, speech!" and quieted down long enough only for John Thomas to say, "Thank you, it is good to be home," before screeching applause sounded.

Taking advantage of this commotion, he loosened the pressure on Shannon's arm, and she came down the stairs to the intensely interested gazes of perhaps ten thousand people. A photographer's horrid camera made a flash, and it was this, of all things, to which Benjamin took great exception. He balled his little fists and waved them in the air with his face contorted. He gave wails which were swallowed up immediately by noise.

A thin man materialized through the crowd, unrecognized at first, but suddenly Shannon realized it was Adams Haley. It was useless to speak, but he motioned, and they began heading his way while people screamed and reached to touch John Thomas's coat. The police made their best attempts to keep the crowd off them, but Shannon thought they would have ripped him apart only to have a memento of him.

They were bundled into a black carriage. John Thomas reached immediately to touch Shannon's arm and Benjamin's face as he looked down at the baby in fear. The sound was still deafening for nearly a minute, but when at last her voice carried enough to be heard, she said, "It is all right. He is all right."

She settled the baby, and the little fellow stared up at her with liquid blue eyes. That accomplished, a thought struck her, and she gasped, "Rebecca! Jeptha—"

"They will be collected. We sent servants to find them... Shannon." It was Adams who had spoken.

Shannon took in her brother-in-law. Her breath expelled from her lungs. He met her eyes, and she saw all of it pass through—all that he had felt about her over the course of their acquaintance. But it was more than acquaintance, wasn't it? Once, they had been friends, and she had loved him with the tenderest sisterly feelings. But she knew perfectly well that she did not imagine his stiffness.

However, Benjamin began crying again, and Shannon lay him on her shoulder, patting his back, attempting to look at his face. She knew he was hungry but feared it would be vulgar to say so and merely hoped they reached the Haley mansion soon.

The horses trotted down the cobblestone streets until at last a house—large, brick, and flat with uniform windows—was reached. John Thomas got down from the carriage first. He was immediately overcome by servants and neighbors, although they seemed to be of a less vulturous variety than the guests at the station.

Adams then got down, reaching immediately to take Shannon's hand, holding her eyes for a moment with an apology in his. She smiled slightly, and he said softly but with New England efficiency, "Come, let us get the two of you in. The little fellow is hungry, I fear."

He helped her to navigate the steps, and she looked up, taking stock of the new scene. As Shannon watched John Thomas for a moment, she saw that the people truly *did* love him. This made her heart soar, even if only briefly, for Benjamin was now shrieking. She tried to comfort him. John Thomas attempted to break them away from the crowd of people. But since he could not, he ultimately sacrificed himself and motioned for Adams to take them on.

When Shannon and Adams crossed the threshold, she saw a woman in the foyer dressed plainly but expensively. The lady met Adams's eyes and then moved forward, looking at Benjamin in sympathy. "Mrs. Haley, you will want to go up to your chamber," the other Mrs. Haley said. "I will take you there immediately."

"Thank you, you are too kind," Shannon said distractedly, wondering if something were truly wrong with the baby.

Her hands trembled from cold and worry and fatigue. Adams's wife—she supposed she would have to be properly introduced to her later—led her to a room which was, blessedly, blazing with a fire. She had barely closed the door when Shannon, heedless of the lingering chill, almost ripped off her bodice and began feeding her hungry baby. She winced as he latched on with vigor but smiled as his tiny hands clasped her breast as though to prevent her from getting away. She cried as emotion and cold shook her, an inevitable reaction and a welcome release. She merely wiped her tears with her arm. Then she reached down to smooth the baby's kitten hair and let him drink his fill.

A few minutes later, the door opened, and John Thomas appeared. He hesitated at the door before entering with a stricken look in his eyes. He searched her face and then hurried to where she sat on the bench at the end of the bed. "You have been crying," he said in horror.

"I am well," she hastened to assure him. "Merely spent." He searched her face only for a moment before reaching for the blanket that lay across the bed and wrapping it around her shoulders. "You're shaking," he said fretfully, glancing at Benjamin, who was still bundled except for his little arms. He led her to a chair nearer to the fireplace, and the heat felt wonderful. John Thomas knelt beside her, stroking her arms for warmth.

He looked terrified. Was it because of the crowds, she wondered? She didn't think so. He had never had any fear of anything physical. And then she realized: he dreaded that at any moment she would feel that it was all too much for her. Her heart was pierced, and she wanted desperately to reassure him.

"I'll have them bring your supper on a tray," he said.

"That is unnecessary," she protested softly as Benjamin finished.

John Thomas hastened to effect the transfer of the baby, holding him while she covered herself and righted her bodice. Then she took the baby and lay him against her shoulder, patting his back softly. "John Thomas…"

"Yes?" He looked up.

She tentatively reached to cover his hand, which was absently on her thigh. "I knew. Even when you hoped it would not be so."

He shook his head. "I promised I would do my utmost to ensure you led a normal life."

"We will manage," she said in her sweet voice, diverting his misery by asking if he would hold the baby, telling him that her arms were tired.

"Of course," he said earnestly, taking the baby, blankets and all, and sitting as close to the fire as he thought safe. He watched Benjamin sleep for a moment, stroking a finger on his cheek before looking up. "Shannon, I will purchase a home in the country, and we will—"

Shannon had stood and was searching through her valise, but she stopped, turning to look over her shoulder. "Hope to fade into obscurity? For heaven's sake, you behave as though my family were humble middle-class gentry. My grandfather was the governor of South Carolina—during my lifetime. If we must lead a public life, we will simply lead a public life."

He was looking up at her from the hearth, and he swallowed. A long silence developed, and Shannon reached up nervously to touch her hair. She opened a second valise he had brought up and rummaged through it for her dinner gown and jewelry.

She lay her dress aside and turned around, studying John Thomas for a moment. Then she walked over and knelt beside him, taking his wrist in her hand. He looked up, surprised. "'*Some are born great, some achieve greatness, and some have greatness thrust upon them,*'" she said, quoting Shakespeare. "You have all three, my dear man," she added softly. "And I know it is difficult, and not what you imagined, but above all things, my dear, '*be not afraid of greatness.*'"

He reached to tuck an escaped tendril of hair behind her ear as he studied her face. He swallowed, seemingly painfully. "I'm not afraid of greatness, Shannon," he said softly. "I'm afraid that it isn't what *you* imagined," he whispered. "This," he said, bringing her hand to his heart, his other hand laying on Benjamin's chest and middle, "is too precious to endanger."

Her throat tightened. "It isn't endangered," she whispered.

He looked at her tenderly, his heart in his eyes. Cautiously, he leaned in, waiting as if giving her a chance to escape. Then he brushed his lips against hers once, and then again more deeply. He had no notion that she hadn't the slightest wish to escape. If only she could convince him.

The air was thick at the supper table, uneasy and quiet. The only sound to be heard was the occasional soup spoon tapping porcelain. Adams appeared to be deeply uncomfortable. He was too kind to be cold to Shannon, but he certainly didn't wish to be warm. And he was too shy to make eye contact since he was harboring such anger against her. Shannon glanced at him and then at Anna before taking another spoonful of soup.

Breaking the silence, John Thomas said, "Lizzie writes that she returned safely."

"Yes," Adams said, looking up at him earnestly, as if to let him know that his displeasure was not for him. "I...accompanied her to Harmony Grove."

"How was Charles?"

"Much the same. That is to say, not very well."

Shannon looked at John Thomas. There was a flash of pain in his eyes. She touched his leg, and he, looking at her, gave a brief smile.

After dessert, still a luxury to Shannon, they all retired to a formal parlor where the atmosphere was a little easier. "I'm glad to be introduced to you at last," Shannon said to her sister-in-law.

The former Miss Renley was petite, with fair hair and a pretty nose. She complimented Adams very well. "And I, you. I hope you found every accommodation you need for your son?"

"Yes, indeed. Everything was most thoughtfully prepared."

"Adams says that you sing well," Anna said, glancing

at the piano near the window while the men were talking.

"Then Adams has perjured himself profoundly," Shannon said. "But it is kind of him to say it. If there is anything that both of our husbands are, it is kind."

"Indeed, yes." Anna seemed to lower her guard for the first time, looking at Shannon afresh.

"Won't you play for us?" Shannon asked. "I know it is not proper for a guest to ask the hostess, but I will, for I see your music all about the instrument and know you must be much more practiced than I."

"Oh. Yes, if you wish it," she said and thereafter stood, her belled skirts moving with her. Shannon took note of the subtle flattening of the front of the skirt. She must study the newest fashion plates from the Continent at once.

The woman played beautifully. When she had closed her books and they had talked for a few minutes, John Thomas, looking at Shannon, suggested they go up to bed. She agreed. After John Thomas had collected her and the couples said their goodnights, Shannon paused in the doorway, looking back into the room.

Adams had stood and gone to Anna, and he was looking down at her, a shy smile in his eyes. She picked up his hand and kissed his knuckles before running her thumb over them gently. Shannon sighed, much relieved, for one couldn't really know how matters stood with them, such was their reserve.

Once in their chamber, Shannon and John Thomas found the maid watching over Benjamin, who was sleeping peacefully in his cradle. Shannon thanked her, and she left, asking

Shannon if she would like her to send up her lady's maid. Shannon opened her mouth to speak, but John Thomas said, "Thank you. But she will manage."

Shannon looked at him when the maid had closed the door, pursing her lips, a little smile in her eyes. "To what do I owe this honor?" she asked as he came around and began with her buttons.

"Rebecca is thorough, to her credit, but I knew she would be at least thirty minutes with your clothes."

"Well, now the maid, and I suppose Rebecca, too, think you mean to make love to me."

"Perhaps I do," he said.

She smiled, tilting her head away while he started on her corset ribbons. After a time, she said, "I do not like you serving me."

"You didn't mind it once upon a time."

She heard the smile in his voice and flushed, smiling herself.

"You endured labor less than two months ago. I merely wish to save you further fatigue," he said, dropping a kiss on her neck, an action which caused her pulses to speed and her stomach to warm. Pausing and turning her so that he could look at her, he said, "You are exhausted. Was it too soon to travel such a distance, Shannon?"

She looked up at him and then down at his chest, laying her hand there, "No, I am well."

He led her to sit down and, looking up to meet her eyes, helped her up with her chemise before he unhooked her garters and took off her shoes and stockings.

She said, tamping down her emotion, "John Thomas, is Charles going to recover?"

He looked up at her for a long moment, her bare foot still resting on his thigh. "We don't know," he admitted finally.

She bit her lip. "Then why don't we go to Harmony Grove? How long has it been since you have seen your mother, your sisters, and Vincent?"

"Too long," he answered, his voice constrained.

"And do you think there is any likelihood that we can escape your adoring crowds in Boston?"

"None at all."

"Well, then. You have a two-week furlough. Let us go away to the countryside."

He hesitated a moment. "Are you sure?" he whispered.

She let a beat of silence pass. "Does an ambush await me?"

"No," he answered gently. "But it won't be easy, my sweet."

"Very few things in my life have been, John Thomas."

He held her eyes, the emotion in his growing as he realized the truth of the statement. Putting her foot on the ground, he stood, drawing her to him. Touching her face with his other hand, he kissed her, once and again.

# Chapter Seventeen

John Thomas turned and helped Shannon down. She clung to the baby. She had grown more anxious the farther outside of Boston they travelled.

He wished he could spare her this. He lay his hand on the small of her back, meeting her eyes and holding them a long moment until she seemed reassured. She looked ahead to his family and the servants, and then back at him. Then he led her up the path.

His sister Miriam and her husband were in New York, but Lizzie and the youngest, Sarah, were present, along with Patience, her husband, and their little James. And Vincent, who had been released from his regiment as the military quickly demobilized, stood beside their mother. All of them were looking at Shannon and the baby.

John Thomas called down blessings on Patience's head as she came forward, embracing him first and telling him in her sunny way how glad they were that he was safely home. She truly did have tears in her eyes as she catalogued his features. "And your sweet boy—Shannon, he is beautiful!" she exclaimed, touching his blanket and peering down at him.

Shannon's lip trembled. "Thank you."

"Come, let's get him into the house," their mother said, fighting tears herself. "There is a warm fire in the nursery."

Shannon stood outside Charles's door, hesitating before knocking. She had settled the baby and now wished to see her injured brother-in-law. At his, "Come in," followed by a cough, Shannon turned the knob and entered. Charles was propped against pillows in his bed, for he had suffered another relapse just before they left Charleston.

Shannon was surprised by his appearance in many ways. He had transformed from a young man to a true man, his form filled out and broadened. But he was pale as could be, his eyes weak with ill health. His golden hair, shining with false innocence, nearly broke her. He was a year younger than John Thomas and bedridden.

"Shannon," he said with a slight smile.

"Charles." She sat down in the chair next to his bed. She covered his hand, surprised by the wiry blonde hairs there. It was difficult enough to see Sarah, grown and tall, and young Vincent (the very image of John Thomas) with weariness of battle. But Charles a man, without the glitter of youth in his eyes?

"Well, you certainly made the war interesting, didn't you?" Charles said.

Shannon bit her lip, but she quickly saw he was joking her. "Oh, Charles. What I put your family through," she said.

"They will have forgiven it all by tonight because you are a mother," he said with the sharp perceptiveness she remembered. "I always supposed the matter was between you and John Thomas, so you won't find judgment from me," he said. "I only ask one thing: that you make him happy."

"I will do my utmost," she promised softly. After a moment, she asked, "How are you, Charles?"

He coughed, wincing, and she pressed his hand. "Shot three times," he said, around coughs. "My right arm is useless. I may never walk again…" He cleared his throat. "The worst of it is I'm addicted to morphine." He flushed, looking up. "John Thomas wouldn't like me to say that to you. I forget to guard my tongue around the ladies. But the truth of it is, without Lizzie, I'd be dead." Something unpleasant crossed his features. "My mother, too. And the others bear with me during my additional illnesses when they can help."

"John Thomas has never sought to shield me from the realities of life. And I was a nurse during the war. You may say what you like to me."

He smiled fleetingly, choosing not to do so. "They say your son is a hale and handsome little fellow."

"Yes, indeed, he is. I see some of his Uncle Charles in him. I will…I will bring him to meet you once he has rested and you feel you are able to meet him."

He smiled. "You look well, Shannon. I'm sorry for what happened to you during the war. Ashamed, too."

"Never mind that." She gave his hand gentle pressure. "Charles...do you need a change of scenery?"

"Like I need my next breath," he said affirmatively.

"Would you like to come and live with John Thomas and me?" she asked, her eyes shining in the light in a way that made him smile.

But he shook his head. "Shannon. You have a child to care for and John Thomas's career and fame to contend with. They'll have him in politics before the end of it."

She looked truly shocked. "You are family. We will all do what we must to ensure your health and recovery."

He laughed softly, inducing a fit of coughing. "I love Southerners," he said, tears suddenly in his eyes, and she could not tell if it was from the strain or emotion. "Damned hard to kill them."

"Charles, your family feels the same way as I," she said firmly.

"Yes, I know. Though they'd willingly sacrifice their lives for mine rather than say it."

At length she prompted, "Well?"

He shook his head. "No. But I shan't forget you asked."

Shannon sat beside Vincent in the parlor after dinner, taking refuge in his conversation.

"Your brother tells me that you are to attend Harvard in

the autumn, following your father's tradition."

"Yes," he said, nodding once. She had thought, initially, that he was behaving coldly toward her for which she couldn't blame him. But she soon realized that she didn't enter the equation. And besides, he had been devoted to her since she had saved him from his father's wrath years ago.

"Don't you wish to? If you don't, I might speak with John Thomas."

He lifted a shoulder. "I am nineteen. I might as well go to Harvard as not. I have no objection to it."

Shannon studied him. "But...?"

He shook his head and said softly, "It all seems so useless. Every friend I ever had is dead. I've seen four major battles and countless skirmishes. Am I to sit tamely before an instructor, learning Milton, or accounting? Or to sit in my brother's office and read contracts—as if I weren't fighting just to stay alive eight months ago?" He looked away, his face wrinkling with emotion before he gained control of himself.

He was in trouble, Shannon thought, looking around the room. In fact, they all were, the Haleys, in their different and varying ways. Lizzie was quiet and pensive, what she had seen and the heavy burden of caring for Charles weighing on her. Patience was suffering from the strain of carrying the Whitcombs in their grief and looked tired about her eyes. Mrs. Haley obviously fretted day and night for all of them, Charles especially. Only Sarah seemed herself, but the fact that everyone else was so very much *not* themselves seemed to cast her into affliction.

Shannon supposed she had been naïve. After all, the North had won. The Haleys were victorious. Their house still stood. Their fields were not plundered. None of that was true for the Ravenels, and yet... Despite it all—the deaths, the loss of an entire way of life, and the heartbreak—time's incomprehensible hand seemed to have treated them better. They did not know from where their next meal would come, but they didn't really mind because they had each other. *Oh, God, you have blessed us,* she thought, her eyes misting. She knew but for the grace of God they would be in just such a state as all of their neighbors, and, apparently, all of the country.

Shannon looked up and saw her mother-in-law approaching. The formidable woman glanced at Vincent, and he obediently rose and went to sit with John Thomas and Sarah. Seeing Shannon wipe her eyes, the woman's face softened. "You look well, my dear."

Shannon was surprised at this opening line, but she tried to appear otherwise. "And you, ma'am."

"You always did have such lovely manners. Your mother's doing, I don't doubt, for she was the same." Her face bespoke her sympathy.

Shannon was touched. "I was most grieved, ma'am, to hear of your family's great loss."

She inclined her head, saying softly, "Thank you." She looked at Shannon, studying her. "We heard, as you are aware, some of how you passed the war. You shouldn't have been on the island, of course, but there was no cause for brutality, as I told the reporter who asked me on the street. They never printed it. I imagine it was thought to be damaging to the war effort."

Mrs. Haley paused, looking across the way at John Thomas. "I was with him, you know, when he heard. I thought he would faint, or perhaps attack the poor messenger. I've never seen him with such a look of murder in his eyes, or afterwards cast so low. And that was when I knew: he will never be free of his abiding passion for you. Don't stiffen up, child. I only state the plain truth, without judgment, I trust. And his love for you *is* abiding. I was not always certain; I feared he married you on too short an acquaintance, or that your beauty had its part. But I was wrong, as I should have known. He always knows his own mind. And...for all of it, Shannon—all that I have watched him suffer for your sake—I do not believe the sort of love he has for you can exist where there is uncertainty of its return." She met her eyes, and Shannon felt the weight of that statement.

"Or where there is uncertainty of the person herself," she continued. "'*There is something more to her than is immediately tangible*,' he told me, the only time I tasked him with whether he would divorce you. And he was right. I knew it then, though I didn't wish to." There was a pause, and when Mrs. Haley spoke again, her voice was softer. "I don't know why you did what you did, Shannon. I don't know what you suffered that could make you uncertain of such a man's love." Shannon's heart quickened unpleasantly, and she stiffened. "But I want you to know that you don't have to doubt *anything* my son ever says to you," she said, her eyes welling, and she looked away, wiping them with her handkerchief. "You have given him a child and made him very happy. You have made all of us very happy and given us joy in a time of great sorrow. Never, ever destroy it again, my dear."

Shannon sat nearly trembling. Her insides felt as though they were heaving, and she was overcome. She looked up and saw John Thomas looking at her with great anxiety. Struggling with her emotions, she said, "I don't doubt him. Not anymore. Not ever again," before standing and fleeing the room.

Rebecca helped Shannon change into her nightgown and dressing gown and departed. Shannon knelt by the cradle, watching Benjamin. His little chest rose and fell with sweet breaths, and she looked at him, feeling the awesome weight of responsibility for him. She felt emboldened and weak all at once.

She hadn't been kneeling long when the door opened and John Thomas entered. She looked over her shoulder at him. He came to her and helped her as she rose. "I came away as soon as I could. Did my mother upset you?" He looked her over as if afraid their truce had been damaged.

"No. Well... She does not hate me in any event. And she spoke the truth."

His jaw clenched. "Please know that anything she said was without my directive or consent."

"I can safely assume that from the way you are looking at me," she said gently, touching his arm, picturing how he must have appeared upon hearing what had happened to her. Her eyes welled, imagining him telling his mother that he wouldn't divorce her. She had assumed he wouldn't because of religious qualms. Not because, in the midst of it all, he still loved her.

Seeing her tears, he cradled her face with his hand. "Shannon... What did she say to you, my darling?"

She hesitated, loathe to bring it up. She answered haltingly, "She...told me not to destroy what we have again."

The air grew suddenly thicker, more tense. He studied her, not speaking. It was the one subject which had never been broached, except when he had refused to discuss it for fear of upsetting her. But he had said he wanted an answer. And she trembled to think that she must give it. Yet, conversely, she wished he would delve into those depths, blame her, accuse her, so that it might be behind them. For it hung as thickly between them as any brocade curtain just now.

He would never lecture her now, in the near wake of her lying in. Or when she was already upset. She knew him too well to think she could push him to that brink. And if she imagined that she could *ever* force him to it, she knew she deluded herself. He would demand an answer when he was good and ready.

"She said what she must, and I trust that with her, that will be the end of it. She is happy about the baby."

"We are all happy about the baby," he whispered, still studying her. He brushed back a stray tendril of her hair gently, gaze lingering on the short, rusty lock. Then he brought her against him and kissed her temple poignantly. Obviously seeking to lighten the subject, he said quietly, "I can't think that with my mother and your father for grandparents he can stand much of a chance, though, can you?"

She could scarcely breathe after his caresses. He touched her as though she were precious to him. "Much of a chance?" she said threadily. "My dear sir, if with such a heritage he has not conquered all of Christendom by the age of thirty, I should be very much surprised."

"Will you go for a drive with me?"

Shannon paused, having started to ascend the stairs with Sarah, and looked over her shoulder. John Thomas was standing in the neat, simple foyer, looking—nervous? The day was unseasonably warm, and perhaps he merely wanted to do what his military duties had prevented: spend time with her. That was a lovely thought. She smiled to set him at his ease. "Why, yes."

He smiled, and she felt deep affection stir at the shyness in his eyes. Sarah, thinking it very romantic, helped her with her coat and bonnet upstairs. Soon, Shannon was being handed delicately up into a phaeton.

While crowds had lined the streets from Boston to Weymouth on their initial journey out to Harmony Grove, their neighbors had more or less given John Thomas the gift of his peace. Therefore, they travelled undisturbed.

"It reminds me of when you used to drive me on Santarella," she said softly.

He smiled at her. "I never liked to drive on the island very much."

"No?"

"No. When I wasn't worried a rabbit or deer would run out and sacrifice itself, I was fretting that an alligator or snake would attack the horse—and then where would we be?"

Her shoulders shook. "How cautious of you."

He laughed, glancing over at her. "Are you cold?"

"Yes, of course, but I shall manage." John Thomas draped his coat over her shoulders, seemingly unperturbed by the chill himself. He also sacrificed his hot brick, placing it near her feet while he let her hold the reins for a moment.

They drove on, the countryside passing in a barrage of neat Colonial houses, well-groomed fences, and frothy sheep. There wasn't a battle-torn field or residue of a cannon's blast in sight. Shannon swallowed her bitterness. One had only to look at the Haleys to know that the worst of the war's ravages were not in material things.

John Thomas looked at her, and she gave a smile before looking away.

She supposed they must have gone miles. The land, acres of countryside that would soon be green as spring gently arrived, grew more and more uninhabited. They passed the occasional village of weathered wooden houses with brick chimneys puffing smoke. They saw along the way little boys running out to wave at them or sturdy folk chopping wood.

Then at last she realized they were in a driveway lined with some Massachusetts variety of tree, but not thickly. They passed a small, white Saltbox structure, obviously seventeenth century. They continued along the path that had a split rail fence trailing the entire way. Eventually, a house came into view.

The manor had a brick foundation but otherwise was of a white wood. Colonial in style, it was quite large with chimneys jutting uniformly into the air. Off the back was a large, rambling wing, and looking around, she saw that all of the requisite outbuildings were in pristine condition. When John Thomas pulled up some distance away from the structure, she said, "What a lovely site!"

"Would you like to get down?"

She lifted her brows but gamely put aside her rug and let him lift her to the ground. He still touched her carefully, as though fearing he would hurt her. This amused her, for she was quite recovered. He secured her cape, a garment which draped down to her wide skirts with slits on the sides. Then he took her hand, and they walked a little distance toward the house. He stopped, looking measuringly at her, and said, "It is for sale."

She gazed at it before his meaning dawned. Looking at him again quickly, she said, "Have you purchased it?"

"No, of course not. I must hear your thoughts."

That, she knew, was a luxury not many women ever enjoyed. She looked at the house again and then back at him. "Then you must be... I mean, *we* must be well-situated?"

"My father left me more than I ever anticipated. When Vincent mentioned the Moores were selling, I suggested he ride with me out to the house—Beacon Hill, that is what it is called. I thought of nothing more than to take his mind off the war, but when we first saw it... I could picture Benjamin here." Shannon's throat tightened, and her eyes misted as she looked across the lawn and house. "And I could see you here, Shannon. Three hundred acres surround it; plenty of ground for your horses. And there is a library, too."

"Yes. Oh, yes."

He stopped and looked at her, obviously surprised at her easy acquiescence. "Shannon, I don't want you to feel—"

"I adore it." She unthreaded her arm from his and walked on the ground, feeling as though she could breathe here. It did indeed suit her very much.

He studied her, and she could tell that he was pleased. "It isn't just that you know I like it? You are too kind and sweet to say differently, Shannon, but—"

She smiled. "You are perhaps the only person ever to say so. Your liking it would indeed be quite enough for me. But

I do adore it. And what are we, seven miles from Harmony Grove? Not so close that we will rub up against one another, but close enough that we can be of help with Charles. The only thing that troubles me is that your work is in Boston." She examined him, forehead wrinkled.

"It is only eight miles. You see, we have been driving toward Boston. And with the train—"

"I won't have you exhausting yourself or taking a chill by getting caught in a snowstorm," she said firmly.

"I trust Adams will shelter me should the need arise."

She walked back toward him. "Yes, I wasn't thinking of that."

He was hesitating, she was aware. "There is something else, Shannon."

She looked into his blue eyes, her stomach tingling. "Yes?"

"Senator Renley—Anna's father—has had poor health in recent days. Adams wrote to me of it this morning. He plans to step down before the completion of his term."

"Oh, no. I am sorry for her. Does she have her mother? Any siblings?"

He shook his head. "No," he said sadly. After another hesitation, almost as if weighing her feelings, he said, "Adams relays that there is a contingent in Boston which plans to nominate me to finish his term, if I will accept."

Her lips parted. She blinked in surprise. "How long is left?"

"The special election will be held in May of this year, and his term would have concluded with the inaugurations in March of next year."

She studied him. "And what would happen then? You would return to the Navy?"

He held her eyes for a long moment.

"Oh. You want to stand for election." The breath left her body as she tried to take this in. She paced several steps away, crossing her arms, chin on her hand. "What are our chances?"

"Good. Very good. I believe I will be unopposed, Shannon," he said softly, flushing.

Arrested, she said, "For the special election, or the general?"

"Both."

*Good heavens.* His election was no doubt what the people of Massachusetts desired. He was their hero, and war heroes stood for public office. It was only that she couldn't picture it, John Thomas without the constant toil of the Navy. It was all she had ever known of him. "You are leaving military life then," she breathed.

He took a step toward her. "No. Not if you have the slightest wish otherwise. I didn't want to trouble you, or to upset you. I might decline to serve altogether, for Washington, you know, is—"

"Oh, I'm not upset," she breathed, touching his chest. She fingered the wool of his coat. "Yes, that will suit you like nothing else." Still in utter surprise, she added, "I wonder that I never thought of it."

He shook his head, covering her fingers. "Will it? I suppose if I pictured myself in another situation, it would be as a professor," he said softly.

"Of the Classics, yes. That would be 'to be afraid of greatness' at this moment. And there is plenty of time for that." Trying to wrap her mind around it, she said, "I would be a senator's wife."

"A *Republican* senator's wife," he reminded her gently, resting his hand on her waist.

"Oh, good heavens, you don't think I still care for that?" she stunned him by saying, appearing to be calculating. "We will keep a house in Washington, too, then?"

"Yes. We would lease one while Congress is in session. Forgive me, Shannon, I don't mean to dictate our lives. And I won't. If you want to stay away from it all, the politics and intrigues—"

"No, to tell you the truth, there is nothing that would suit *me* so well," she admitted. "But do you *want* to be a senator? Obviously, it is what the people want, but *you* must choose your life."

He nodded. "The war isn't over, Shannon," he said softly. "The next phase will be fought on the floor of Congress as it always should have been. Johnson has strayed so far off course. And I...find that my political beliefs have strengthened over the course of the war. There is so much good to be done, suffering to alleviate... When Adams wrote to me, I knew it was right."

She smiled. "Yes. It is."

His eyes dropped to her lips. Then slowly, he lifted his hand to her face, and ultimately he kissed her. She moved closer, returning his kiss. And then she pulled back, looking up and meeting his eyes, burning with pleasure. "Now,

Senator Admiral Haley, if you will escort me back to Harmony Grove, I daresay your son will be growing hungry."

Forgetting Congress and admiralty and greatness, he looked appalled, saying, "Forgive me! Yes, how could I not think...? Come along," before hurrying her back to the carriage.

# Chapter Eighteen

Adeline and Adrian spent Thanksgiving Day with Adrian's parents. While they were there, Adeline got a call from her dad, who was very sweet, asking how she was doing, telling her to send pictures of their next sonogram and to let them know if she needed anything.

The next few weeks were busy. Jude was in a boys' choir and would be performing in a Christmas chorale that reminded her of the choir scene on *Home Alone* (a.k.a. awesome). So, it became her job on Tuesdays and Thursdays to take him to practice. She loved sitting and watching them in the candlelit sanctuary and helping him warm up on the way there by singing "Hey Jude," which always made him giggle.

And she continued to see little of Adrian, though he was attentive when she did. He had been a little baffled when she had sent the modern, adorable nursery furniture back and decided to go with a more manor house nursery feel. But he was supportive and happy with the overall effect, the mahogany crib with the matching swing cradle, the rocking pony, the antique toy chest, and the gray rug.

She folded all of the baby's little onesies and snuggly pants, putting them in drawers, and hung his outfits. If Jude's style was very Martha's Vineyard, Baby Boy's was a little more Royal Baby right now based on what she had gotten piles of at the shower. She thought she would gradually style him a little more boho, but it was okay if he started his life out extremely posh.

During her spare time, she researched a lot of North Star details but found nothing really helpful to explain their mystery. Going back to the room where she had found the necklace, Adeline looked at the red walls, thick molding, canopy bed, and brick fireplace. She searched without success for another loose brick and stared without inspiration at the lofty ceiling. She simply couldn't figure out why there were two necklaces, and until she did, she couldn't confirm whether their theory about the jewelry being Shannon Ravenel's was valid.

Adeline was still thinking about it Saturday morning when she and Adrian (asking Jane to keep Jude) went Christmas shopping at the big shops. Adrian's family still did it the old-fashioned way with a present for everybody. Hence, they had a lot on their list, not to mention everything for Jude and the gifts Adeline would be mailing to her family since it would be too late in her pregnancy to travel.

Sometimes when she thought about the fact that the baby would be here in a month, she nearly panicked. She tried not to dwell on her inadequacies and reminded herself that a lot of motherhood was instinctual. But she really didn't want to fail her little guy.

The new wallpaper arrived from England, and the crew had it up in no time at all. That finished, and her nesting more or less complete, Adeline spent the remainder of December actually doing stuff she enjoyed for the first time since— college? She read and binge-watched historical dramas. She made design boards online for future projects. She did make a trip to Columbia to supervise the progress on the ballroom, but the crew was right on track with it.

The next big thing that happened was that Adrian got a call one night during supper and got up to take it. Adeline tried to chat with Jude but was tuned in to the serious tone in the next room.

When Adrian came back, there was light in his eyes, and he said, "Guess who that was."

She lifted her brows. "Who?"

He leaned against the door facing, looking smug. "Ever heard of a magazine called *Southern Living*?"

She held his eyes, afraid to break contact. Did he mean...?

He smiled, pleased at her reaction. "They want to feature Ravenel-Thompson House in the April issue."

"What?" she breathed.

He laughed. "Yes."

"Oh, my gosh." She flashed hot and then cold.

Career-maker. Literally, how was she going to top this? All of the potential jobs her secretary, Janice, had sent her came flooding back, particularly the one near her parents in Asheville—Carrington Place, her dream job. And there would be so many more now. But very quickly, joy turned to consternation, like a train coming to a sudden halt. Her options were boundless, but... She started to get a sick feeling, and when she looked up at Adrian, she saw pride in his eyes, yes, but also something else that she couldn't quite define.

The next few days were spent preparing for the visit from the *Southern Living* interviewers and photographers. They ended up with great captions and excellent pictures for the five pages. The cover would be a picture of The Battery with Ravenel-Thompson House the center of attention, and several of the pictures would be devoted to Adeline's restorations. There was also a really cute picture of Adrian, her, and Jude in front of the house, looking pristine, if she did say so.

After the teasers were released, Janice was instantly flooded with requests in Charlotte and was constantly on the phone with Adeline to convey them. Sometimes Adeline didn't answer the calls. It was wonderful, but she was trying to do what Adrian had suggested and not worry about any of that, or the future, and just focus on herself and the baby. And of course, meanwhile, there was Christmas.

Jude's chorale was on the 21st, and Adeline sat with Adrian on the pew, her fingers laced through his. It was deeply moving, the little boys on one side of the massive loft, the girls' choir on the other, all sounding like angels. It wasn't your everyday children's choir production. Sometime after they sang the line "God and sinners reconciled," something clicked, and she looked over at Adrian. He was watching Jude, content to let his hand casually be held in her lap. But he seemed to sense her attention, and he looked over.

"We can raise him Catholic, Adrian," she whispered, feeling a burning in her eyes.

He lifted his brows, studying her face for a long time. "Are you sure?"

She nodded. "I want him to know God's love. That's all that matters, isn't it? We'll teach him the important things, and he can be like his brother."

His eyes misted, his thumb stroking the soft skin of her wrist. He leaned over and pressed a kiss to her cheek, and Adeline didn't care that his parents and five-hundred other people saw.

They went to Statesboro for Christmas Eve supper, where Jude was showered with gifts and general goodwill reigned. Adeline thought everybody was excited about how close the baby was and generally in awe of the miracle of life. Adeline was pleased to see that Virginia liked Jackie and also to learn that Jackie was holding some of the cards. She was decent and pretty, and Virginia had thought her son would never settle down, while simultaneously wanting more grandchildren. Therefore, as long as she made Harris happy, she wasn't going to intervene.

Virginia was also really lovely to Adeline, pampering her and acknowledging her, it seemed, as Adrian's wife. And, of course, James was his typical distracted but peaceful self, kissing Adeline's cheek as soon as they got there and telling her how proud they were of the impending magazine article.

They left a little later than they should, and Adeline and Jude slept on the way home. But that didn't stop the excited little fellow from being up at the crack of dawn on Christmas morning. Adrian groaned in bed beside her, covering his eyes with his arm, but he couldn't withstand the urgings of his elated son.

"I'm pretty sure he's been, Daddy."

"Are you?" he asked, yawning.

"Yeah, I thought I heard something downstairs last night."

Adrian glanced at Adeline, eyes twinkling, and they got up, Adeline reaching for her robe and Adrian smoothing Jude's hair down for the pictures. Jude ran down the stairs, exclaiming in joy at the sight of his baby kayak and the other wrapped presents. He proceeded to tear into all of them, polite with his exclamations even when the gifts were more functional than fun. Adeline sat curled up on the sofa, watching and laughing, delighting in him and imagining all that was to come.

When he had finished, he set about playing with every toy he had gotten amidst the pile of paper and boxes. He was sufficiently occupied when Adrian pulled a little box from the fireplace mantle and handed it to Adeline, giving her a little smile. He sat down next to her and took her glass of water so she could open it. "What's this?" She hoped it wasn't jewelry, because he didn't go cheap, and she had bought him a sweater. She smiled and slipped the bow off while he watched. When she opened it, she instantly recognized the box from a jeweler in Charleston, the one her engagement ring had come from.

She saw a pretty silver bracelet with a charm. On one side of the charm was engraved *Our first Christmas*. And on every link was a tiny pale blue stone. She looked up at him, smiling in a wobbly way. *First* indicated that there would be a second, yes? But maybe she was reading too much into it. She had a feeling everything would come to a head when the baby was born. Wasn't that what he'd said? *Let's just... get you through the pregnancy and go from there.*

But she didn't want to think about that right now. It was Christmas, and a new year hovered close. Anything was possible.

# Chapter Nineteen

*City of Washington*
*May, 1866*

*My Dear Friend,*

*My love to you and to all our dear ones in Charleston. In response to your question, we are indeed quite settled. The house is not as large as I had hoped, considering my hostess duties, but we are situated quite close to the Capitol, which very convenient for John Thomas. He is able to walk there and is spared the necessity of sending for his horse or the carriage.*

*The outpouring of goodwill of the Navy in sending him off was quite moving, and there was never*

anything like the fanfare of his swearing in. I
believe Pres. J fears him nearly as much as he fears
Gen. Grant, though his worries are amiss. JT is not
old enough to be president and is barely so to be a
senator. When I think with what patience he awaited
his thirtieth birthday, and how strong I now know his
political aspirations to be, I believe there is something
of his political forebearers in my husband after all.

You may tell Papa that his grandson grows healthy
and strong, and that I show him my miniature
portraits of all of you quite often. He is already
beginning to crawl, which I attribute to his sturdy
New England blood. I believe his constitution must
be of iron since I have not yet known him to have
so much as a bellyache. I began not to make enough
milk for him and so have passed that duty to a
wet nurse we have hired. It was of great sorrow to
me, but JT says he is glad, for he feared my health
was suffering. How is my dear Rose? Tell her Aunt
Shannon adores the drawing of the ostrich.

You expressed concern for me in my new role, but I
find that my training has prepared me well for it.
You would be amazed to see Washington City; it is so
much changed. There are very few Southerners here,
of course. And I must tell you, my dear, something
which will not break my husband's confidence, for

*it is generally and openly debated: I believe you
are all soon to be placed under military districts,
with tens of thousands of troops sent to the South,
and occupied for the foreseeable future. This is the
result, I believe, of violence against the freedmen.
But I do worry what it will mean for all of you. You
would tell us, wouldn't you, if you needed anything,
or if you found South Carolina too troubled and
dangerous to stay?*

*As for John Thomas and I, we get on splendidly. We
live in such a state of polite awkwardness that of
course we never argue. He is kind and considerate, as
always, and is naturally very much occupied with his
new position. I wish I might be of more help to him.*

*Tell me how you get on, and send my greetings to all
our neighbors who do not loathe me.*

*Yours, etc.,
Shannon*

Shannon had spent the spring ascertaining the political
situation. It seemed to her that the Democrats had a great
deal of sympathy for the South and the Radical Republicans none whatsoever. On the other hand, the situation
was reversed regarding the freedmen. It was unjust, in

her opinion, that the Southern states were not readmitted and had no representation, that everything was voted and forced upon them without their consent. On the other hand, the violence against the Negros must cease. She was obliged to admit that the situation was volatile, and that to the victor went the spoils of war, including power over conquered lands.

Tennessee's congressmen and senators were currently standing for their vacant offices after their state's readmittance to the Union. She was curious to see how they behaved and who they would be. They would be the only representatives from the entire South.

She was also watching John Thomas closely to see with whom his beliefs most closely aligned. She had always known him to be more radical than his quiet demeanor would, at first glance, suggest. He wanted full voting rights for colored men, along with full equality of citizenship.

What made a person radical seemed to be whether he was willing to take away Southern rights to ensure the rights of Negros. She knew her husband to be sympathetic to her family, but he wouldn't stand for slaughter, which was taking place throughout Dixie now, he told her. And so, she planned her defenses of him against charges of being a Radical Republican. She also considered how to help him in what she knew to be far more important than any Congressional debate: the machinations of the drawing room.

Many of their friends were now in Washington, and if Shannon's table was always heavily weighted with Navy bachelors, that suited her. John Thomas also thought it was of importance to seek counsel of Negro leaders, who helped him sharpen his objectives and arguments. These gentlemen Shannon welcomed to her table, relying on her manners to see her through, until she no longer needed to rely on them; their backgrounds might be as different as could be imagined, but it didn't take long to realize that much of what society had always taught her had been untrue.

The Rices, too, were in Washington for the Commodore's military duties and had taken a little house, finally reuniting with their children under one roof. Shannon was not altogether thrilled at the intimacy between the families that this induced. But she was glad for John Thomas that Commodore Rice was near to him, for they were close friends, and she never excluded the couple from her invitations.

All of this came to a halt, however, when Benjamin terrified them by developing a cough. For days Shannon thought it was only a little cold, but by the fourth day, when he began whooping, she found herself running to meet John Thomas as he crossed the threshold, yelling for him and telling him to come to the nursery. He had run to her, taking the steps two at a time.

The cough persisted badly for a week, and it severely rattled them both. But the sturdy boy began to recover, gently playing on his mama's lap or sleeping. And looking down at him, at his thick, blonde hair and long, fair lashes, Shannon resolved something. She might not know how to bring up a boy. The very thought might terrify her. But she loved him with all of her being, and she would simply do as she thought best, and trust God to provide the rest.

With the onset of the true heat of summer in the wake of Benjamin's illness, Shannon had gone to John Thomas's study to tell him what she felt to be a necessary change. She and Benjamin would go to Massachusetts for the summer, and John Thomas would join them there when the session was complete. It was difficult for him, she knew—difficult for both of them, for she couldn't pretend she liked to be far from his tenderness or away from his quiet presence.

But it was not difficult for Shannon to settle into country life at Beacon Hill. She rode the clipping little Thoroughbred John Thomas had purchased for her and stocked her library where there were deficiencies. She oversaw necessary repairs and renovations until her home was her own, a splendid combination of New England simplicity and Southern style. On Sundays, she attended the small Congregational church in the village.

Letters flew back and forth between Shannon and her family, and even Rose had begun to write to her on the complicated and often dramatic events of her life. These happened both at Mass and at the classes for the little school which Elizabeth and some of the other ladies with small children had begun to host in their homes. Elizabeth had written that the fees of governesses or private schools were quite out of the question for them.

Shannon visited the Haleys, and they visited her. She sat with Charles most Sunday afternoons and relieved her mother-in-law during any periods when she had to go to Boston. Letters came daily from Lizzie, updating Shannon on Charles's state, and she began to grow more candid about the horrors of trying to break his morphine addiction. Shannon spent more time than ever at Harmony Grove after that.

Adams, amusingly, seemed to feel it his duty to be paternal to Benjamin in John Thomas's absence, which generally included him patting the boy's head or asking after his health. His wife was shy but regal in her own way, and Shannon rather liked her tranquil company. However, Anna had to leave to look after her father's health not long after Shannon and Benjamin returned to the North.

Sarah stayed with Shannon sometimes, recounting her season in Boston and enumerating which of her suitors she liked, and which repulsed her.

Shannon's letters from John Thomas were golden to all of them, and she read such parts as she thought prudent after their dinners. Their abiding passion, all of them, had once been the abolition, and now it was the equal rights of the colored man, and John Thomas was the instrument for their ambitions.

And yet, they kept busy in the cause, too. Patience's husband travelled to Virginia to lend aid to the newly established Freedman's Bureau. Miriam convinced her husband to purchase an abolitionist newspaper, and their employees printed a great deal of equality propaganda in Boston.

The other ladies sewed for the Negro refugees pouring into Northern cities and organized charity events for clothing.

The elder Mrs. Haley seemed to have moved past her conversation with her daughter-in-law, briskly instructing Shannon while they baked and asking her to bring cuttings from the rose bush at Beacon Hill for Charles's room. There was still constraint and a general uneasiness, and Shannon knew she must again earn their full trust, but it was a beginning.

"Tell me, Shannon, is your family struggling?"

Shannon looked up from her soup toward her mother-in-law one night when she was dining in the Harmony Grove dining room. "Yes, ma'am," she said softly. It was impossibly hard to admit it, a great family brought low.

As her brothers and sisters-in-law looked on, Shannon wondered where the woman was leading. The subject of the Ravenels was not generally discussed, nor was Shannon's time in the South or the state of matters there now, except as it related to the freedmen. The woman's blue eyes pierced her. "What do they need? May we be of service?"

Shannon laid her spoon down. "John Thomas has already offered them money, ma'am."

"What are their chances for recovering their assets?"

"Not great, ma'am. The infrastructure of the entire South is in ruins. And with the confiscation of their lands, their greatest source of wealth and any chance of earnings in the future were taken at a single blow. The economy is utterly broken."

The woman looked at her while everyone else watched quietly. "I am sorry to hear it," she said finally. "But they oughtn't let their pride stand in the way of what might help them."

"They won't take anything, ma'am," Shannon said, wiping her mouth, feeling close to tears. "They simply won't."

Shannon spent many afternoons cultivating and preserving their vegetables with Jeptha like a proper Massachusetts woman, something which horrified John Thomas when she wrote to him of it. She merely smiled over that, sealing another jar.

She and Rebecca spent time preparing her wardrobe for the high degree of visibility she would experience in Washington. She was often invited to dinners, and everyone seemed to want to see Senator Haley's infamous wife. There was also a likelihood she would be entertaining foreign diplomats upon her return. The talents of the colored dressmaker in Charleston had seen her through her first stint, but she would require many more dresses now. With funds at her disposal, she (bred a daughter of wealth) knew precisely how to adorn herself.

She and Sarah let themselves be driven to the sea, and they stood on the green cliffs overlooking the breaking waters and derived great benefit from it. There, Sarah confided to Shannon that she wished to marry. To Shannon's astonished question of whether it was a man of fortune and consequence in Boston, she confessed that he was a child-hood playmate from Weymouth, a young Mr. Johansen. None of her suitors in Boston had turned her head, and she had finally, one summer day, realized why.

No, he was not extremely wealthy, she told Shannon, but he was from a good family. Did Shannon think her mother would ever allow it? Shannon did, indeed, for, while the Haleys would not want Sarah to marry very much below her station, they could not preach that the worldly things were all a matter of vanity and not practice their doctrine. And this Thomas Johansen sounded like just the sort of young man to whom a family would feel secure in entrust-ing their daughter: kind, loyal, with distinguished service in the Army, and, apparently, desperately in love with Sarah.

And so, before anyone else knew of the matter, Shannon set about planning for a wedding which would bring all of the Haleys out of the doldrums.

The summer, a warm one, passed pleasantly. Shannon played with her son in his long, sunny nursery, the windows open to allow in a fresh breeze. She noticed the first cool gust toward the end of August, much earlier than in the South. Although she had been contemplating a New England autumn and winter with some trepidation, the first sign of the cooling of the Earth was not unwelcome, for it meant her husband would return to her soon.

# Chapter Twenty

John Thomas rode onto the grounds of Beacon Hill, his pulses quickening, almost as though his heart could fathom her nearness. His horse, brought for him to the train station by one of the servants, clipped confidently up the drive. The temperature had reached eighty degrees, and the day was crisp and clear. He had missed summer in New England.

He dismounted and handed the reins off to the servant who had travelled back with him. He had started up the walkway to the house when he caught sight of the new gardens, which Shannon had designed, off either side of the house. He had followed their progress throughout the summer with great interest. Seeing them, and their thoughtful design and beauty, he questioned whether there was any talent God had withheld from his wife. He caught sight of movement in the east garden.

Turning his head that way, he saw Shannon, her belled skirt casting an elegant silhouette. She was carrying Benjamin through the garden, holding one hand under his little rump, her other hand curled around his. He would babble something and giggle, causing her to kiss him. And once, she let him down, kneeling and holding both of his hands while he stood. Only seven months old, this was the most he could manage.

His breath hitching, he started out to meet them.

Hearing a noise, she turned, her face lighting, which did his heart a service, and exclaimed, "John Thomas!"

Benjamin looked up from his dismantling of a hyacinth and smiled, squealing and bouncing, obviously recognizing him. Swallowing the knot in his throat, John Thomas went to them, kissing them both and smoothing a hand over Benjamin's silky hair.

"You are early!" she said.

"I excused myself from the dinner," he replied, studying her. She looked a bit tired. But the weight of the decisions for the property and Benjamin, not to mention caring for his family, had fallen upon her shoulders in his absence, so this was not surprising. He wiped a smudge of dirt from her cheek, resolving that she would rest for the remainder of the summer.

"You should not have."

"Shouldn't I? I thought perhaps my family might like to see me."

"Perhaps," she said, meeting the laughter in his eyes with a smile. "How are you?" she whispered, her eyes travelling his face.

"I am well. And you?" He brushed the backs of his fingers softly on her cheek.

"Quite well," she answered demurely.

She handed Benjamin to him, and he took the baby, kissing him once and again. Glancing down at Shannon, he thought she was a bit quiet and reticent. But as she reached to adjust Benjamin's dress and tucked her hand in his arm as they started for the house, he thought perhaps he had imagined it.

He had missed Shannon tremendously in his absence. He felt like the lovesick boy he had been upon their marriage, and he could not look upon her enough. He had insisted she nap when his impression of her fatigue had grown, and, laughing, she had obeyed.

He went upstairs to her bedroom that afternoon to check on her and saw her through the cracked door. She was standing, her blue skirts falling gracefully, her hand femininely against her tiny waist. Her gaze was pensive as she looked out the many-paned window onto the meadow below.

His observation lifted to her face, to her elegant jawline, her chin, her cheekbones. She was so beautiful: it never failed to strike him, even when they were together every day. He had not imagined during the war that he would again ever have such luxury as looking his fill, and he savored it.

As he was lost in admiration, he noticed the placement of her hand was unusual and yet somehow familiar. His brow furrowed. He couldn't quite place it. He watched as she lifted her hand to her lips, kissing her fingers and then putting her hand against her waist again.

And then it struck him with force. He stood still for a moment, feeling rather like he had been hit in the head. Straightening, he whispered, "Shannon?"

She turned her head quickly, and she, too, straightened, looking down at her hand. She bit her lip, meeting his eyes as a blush spread across her cheekbones. He crossed the room, not taking his eyes from her.

"John Thomas," she said, a bit nervously.

His eyes flickered over her face, down to her waist, and then back up, questioning.

"I was going to tell you tonight," she said softly. "I was trying to think how best to do so."

"Shannon," he whispered, looking at her in awe. "You're... Oh, my darling!"

"Yes," she said, very flushed now. She swallowed, as though uncertain of his reaction.

"I should have... Why did I—? I never imagined..." He took her face in his hands. "You were so ill with Benjamin. It is too soon—"

"I haven't been ill."

His eyes catalogued her quickly, as though checking that all were in order. "Why didn't you tell me?" he asked breathlessly, his hands trailing down to her waist. "All of this time, and you alone..."

She smiled. "Because I knew my gallant husband would ride like the wind to be at my side," she teased.

Humor lost on him, he said, "Shannon, if you have been as ill as the last time, and managing this house, and Benjamin—"

She shook her head. "I have been far from unwell. Only a bit tired."

"How long, my love?" he whispered, still regarding her intensely.

She blushed again, tipping up to whisper in his ear, "I believe...just before I left Washington." His face softened as his eyes journeyed across her features. She tipped back down. "In truth, I haven't known very long. It didn't occur to me."

"No, it wouldn't. I thought... That is, I suppose I believed—" He flushed hotly, wishing he had bitten his tongue.

"That Benjamin was a miracle designed to unite us?" she whispered.

He met her eyes. "No—yes. Forgive me," he said, looking penitent.

She gave a little laugh. "I thought so, too." She met his eyes. "It would...seem that something has changed."

He studied her closely, and he led her to the bench by the window. Putting his hand on her back as she sat, and sitting next to her, he waited in concern for her to elaborate.

"I...while we were apart—during the war, I mean, my..." She swallowed, flushed. He took her hand, pressing it. "Briefly, when food was very difficult to obtain, my courses ceased," she whispered. His lips parted as he sat, utterly dismayed. "And then, when they returned, they began to grow easier, and the pain I experienced was much less. During our..." She hesitated.

He pressed her hand again to let her know he understood. "Yes?" he whispered.

She moistened her lips. "I have not yet experienced pain. And now..." She continued to look flushed as she peeped up, meeting his eyes. "I can't help but think the two things are related, can you?"

"No, they *must* be," he agreed in wonder, staring at her in awe.

"And now, I believe I must have become one of those tediously fertile women who—"

"Tedious? Oh, no!" he said, remembering the look of fear in her eyes and that he had never reassured her.

"Well, so I always thought them," she said softly.

He looked at her sympathetically, drawing her near, kissing her, his heart beating wildly in his chest from joy. "It is a surprise, but a *most* welcome surprise, Shannon," he whispered.

A month passed, and if Shannon were truthful, it felt as though she were living in a dream. John Thomas was himself, and they lived in a harmonious union. They drove together and read together and talked together until the small hours. He poured affection on Shannon and their son, and polite awkwardness faded to ease, which faded to the assent of two people in love. She could almost believe that the lever she had thought of had been pulled, and that there were at last no impediments. His spirits seemed light; his heart was open to her.

Occasionally, they were disturbed by journalists or a member of the public who wished to glimpse him. But mostly they lived in peace.

On a rainy day, Shannon sat casually in a wing chair, her legs draped over one arm of it, *Antony and Cleopatra* before her. She sighed, closing the tome.

From his desk John Thomas looked up. Standing and walking to her, he smiled, taking her hand and bringing it to his lips. "Shakespeare pleases you not?" he asked softly.

"Shakespeare pleases me not," she agreed.

He took the blue volume from her, looking at its spine, and said, "Little wonder."

"Well, what are *you* doing?"

"I am writing letters to encourage enforcement of the Civil Rights Act," he said with great piety.

"That is very noble, I am sure, and yet I am still bored," she said, eyes twinkling. With a press of his hand, she started to get up. "I must find a different book."

He hastened to stop her. "I'll find something for you, my darling. Don't get up," he said, pressing her hand in return.

She settled back. "A happy chance that the Moores left so much of their library."

"Yes," he agreed, eyeing a top shelf and moving the ladder. She admired him while he climbed.

"And that their collection of Shakespeare was so *very*

thorough," she added, watching him through narrowed eyes.

He looked over his shoulder, his lips tucking as a faint flush rose.

She smiled, her suspicions confirmed. "What are you choosing for me?"

"Something Elizabethan, never fear."

When he retrieved it and climbed down, he handed her a book of excerpts from Spenser's *The Faerie Queene*. "Oh, excellent!"

When she looked up at him with bright eyes, he bent down and kissed her tenderly. "There," he whispered. "Anything else?"

"Yes," she returned, looking up to his eyes.

He lifted his brows.

"Being a weak female," she said playfully, "and in a delicate condition, I should like very much if my husband would read to me."

He smiled, taking the volume and sitting across from her. He opened it not at the beginning, but rather, somewhere in the middle. His rich voice soon filled the room, reading over the old style of English flawlessly. He had turned to the most poignant part, in a poem that was not even his area of particular interest. It was easy, in all of his modesty, to forget how well-read her husband was, and how brilliant. They were well-matched in minds, and that, she knew, was a blessing.

She sat back, listening to the cadence of his voice, watching the way his mouth moved, the subtle movements of his face, the way he glanced at her occasionally.

*"'What though the sea continual doth eat the earth? It is no more at all. Nor is the earth the less, or loseth ought: for whatever from one place doth fall is with the tide unto another brought.'"* His paused for a moment, his eyes lifting slowly to hers. He held them while he finished. *"'For there is nothing lost, that may be found if sought.'"*

John Thomas had just returned from Harmony Grove and given a satisfactory report of Charles. After kissing her and laying his gloves on the desk in the library, he said, "Do you know, Adams told me something most odd while I was there?"

"Oh?" Shannon asked, pausing with her embroidery.

He met her eyes. "He began to tell me of a man from Charleston who was in Boston, wondering if you knew of him, of course."

"Oh?" she said again, brows lifted. "Who?"

"Major Christian, along with his father." Shannon felt him studying her.

She was taken aback and lay her sewing aside. "What on Earth—?"

"Apparently, they have been consorting with that Democratic machine, Mathias Walters." Catching himself, he looked up penitently.

She waved this aside. "Why, do you suppose? I wouldn't have thought the Christians would have the money even to travel!" Her one-time suitor, whose family had once owned the plantation nearest to hers, must have been in similar circumstances as her father and brother.

John Thomas sat down beside her, looking penitent still. "I shouldn't have said that," he said softly, touching her face. "But as to my conjecture... I suppose it would mean there is a conspiracy of some sort afoot." He stroked the skin of her cheekbone before lowering his hand. "The Democrats have been struggling for numbers since... Well, ever since the party split in 1860. They'll want to bring the South back into the fold as soon as possible to change that. There will be back-room deals, I don't doubt, and a bid for power and what little resources are left in the South. And it will all be at the expense of the freedmen. I don't blame Christian for fighting for his state's well-being, but I do blame him for that."

"We both know it isn't in South Carolina's interest to persecute the freedmen. Seymour is a fool if he thinks otherwise." She stroked her thumb over his knuckles.

"Seymour, is it?" he asked.

"Unfortunately. I am given to understand that the war changed him, though I have seen little evidence. I daresay he is bartering for South Carolina's reentry and for the return of Ridgecrest, of course. He'll be in Washington the moment Congress returns to session."

"Hmm. We shall see, I suppose."

Sarah was married to young Mr. Johansen in the parlor of Harmony Grove in early October with all of her family, even Charles, in attendance. The wedding and Charles's better health seemed to lift the Haleys' spirits. Miriam, looking the picture of wealth and style, surveyed across the dancing room with sparkling eyes and told Shannon that she ought to be dancing.

"Well, your brother has not asked me, and I dare not dance with another man," she said, not mentioning her condition.

Miriam looked at her with surprise. "Has my brother grown jealous, then?"

Shannon laughed. "No. But I am under constant scrutiny. Our separation during the war has, unfortunately, given his enemies fodder for claiming his wife is unfaithful. And I would be celibate rather than damage him further."

"Well, John Thomas doesn't want *that* I wager," Miriam said naughtily.

Shannon flushed. "Where is Mr. Winthrop? I must retrieve him to restrain you."

"He wouldn't dare!" she said wildly, eyes bright with perhaps a bit too much of the wine which was being handed out in greater quantity than usual due to the festivities. "Oh, here is Vincent! The busybodies *can't* claim you are having an affair with your own brother-in-law!"

Shannon didn't think she would put it past them, but she went off with the startled Vincent. She soothed him by enquiring while they waltzed about the progression of his term at university. He responded optimistically enough to encourage her that his frame of mind was slowly growing more favorable.

# Chapter Twenty-One

The New Year was kind of hectic with Adrian working late and a thousand little things seeming to fill up Adeline's schedule. Jane was a great help with more than just Jude, but she had a death in the family and had to go back to Statesboro right as the due date drew close.

Adrian was great: always helpful when he got home, taking back over the laundry, and sending her to bed basically when Jude went. Not that she could sleep or anything. Maybe she could once the baby was born. But Adrian always gave a small smile when she suggested that possibility. So, she assumed ever sleeping again was a pipedream.

Adeline found herself alone on his first Thursday night back to teaching at the college. Jude, still on break, was spending another night at his grandparents' house in Statesboro. It was a cold winter's night—or at least, cold for Charleston—and Adeline had lit the fireplace and gotten herself hot chocolate. She was still wearing the black Loft maternity dress she had worn all day and was wavering between *The White Queen* and a sixth re-watch of *Downton Abbey* when she heard a knock on the door.

Lifting her brows, she walked down the hall to the back door. She wasn't really nervous since not much happened on The Battery but was still a little wary. She tip-toed up and looked through the window, opening the door back immediately after catching sight of the figure. "Harris?"

He was standing there, all casual in jeans and a stylish sweater, as if he didn't have work tomorrow in a different city. "Hey!"

"What are you doing here? What's wrong?" she asked, stepping back and letting him in.

"Nothing's wrong. Just thought I'd come to see you." He wasn't really good at bluffing in his personal life.

"Well, that's great, but..." She studied his face, noticing he wasn't making eye contact. "Did Adrian send you to keep an eye on me?"

He winced, brown eyes guilty. "Maybe?"

"Why didn't you say? That's sweet; I don't mind. Come on in." He followed her down the hall. "If you're here to be my babysitter, you're in for a historical drama."

"Sounds good to me."

She got him some hot chocolate, and they settled in. They compromised on a show and watched half an episode of *Parade's End* before stopping it to hash out the moral dilemma. They talked about the character's choices, with never a lull in conversation, and had Cheetos. Adeline got up to start some tea, saying over her shoulder as the conversation came back around, "Yeah, but she cheated on him."

"Oh, come on. It's not that simple," he said, getting up and following her. The hardwood cracked beneath their feet. She was going to assume it was the weather and not structural damage. "He left her in emotional isolation for years."

She tilted her head to the side, considering, almost to the kitchen. "True. And, of course, he knew how she was when he married her."

"Well, he didn't really have much choice in that: she was preg—" he broke off, realizing the infelicitous direction of the conversation as Adeline tossed him a look over her shoulder.

He was still a few feet behind her when she felt a trickle of warmth. Confused, she looked down to see a small puddle at her feet. She stopped, startled, and stared at it for a second. Okay, then. "Um, Harris?"

He looked up from his phone, which had distracted him, coming to a halt himself. "Yeah?"

When she continued to stand there, acting kind of funny, he blinked, understanding dawning. "Oh, my God." He looked startled.

"Um, yeah…" She sidestepped the puddle. Okay, she needed to think. Some yoga or meditation would be good, but…

"What do I need to do?" he said, standing there like a nervous ball of energy. "Oh, my God, why is Adrian never there when you actually need him?"

Her wits starting to return after the initial shock, Adeline said calmly, "Yeah, if you could not freak out that would be good…"

"Sorry. Sorry."

She took a breath. All she had to go on was *Call the Midwife* here. Which had taught her that after your water broke, it could be anywhere from two minutes to three days until you delivered, so… Not helpful. "Okay, I'm going to go up and get my stuff, and then I'll come back down and…clean this up." She looked over at him. He seemed to be newly determined not to lose it, even if he was still inwardly freaking.

"I'll do that," he said, coming forward.

"Yeah, that is *not* something you should have to do for your sister-in-law. Just turn off the lights and put the fire out, if you don't mind." She turned once she was nearly to the stairs, shaking her head to clear it. "And if you could call your brother, too. Gosh. Yeah, that would probably be good, wouldn't it?"

She went up, collected her stuff, and picked up her purse. She was going to be a mom. She wasn't sure she was the woman for the job. She might fail. And that was a biggie.

Harris was waiting for her at the bottom of the stairs. "How are you doing?" he asked, much more composed.

"Good. I'm good."

"I got Adrian. He's on his way to the hospital," he said, taking her bag from her. "He said to call him if you need to."

"Great. Thanks." The water was cleaned up; the fire was out. She was too thankful to care.

They walked outside, and he put her bag in his car while she got in. And then they were heading toward the hospital. She took a deep, shaky breath, somehow not as afraid of childbirth as she was of motherhood. What if she did something wrong? She knew literally nothing about this. "It's getting real, Harris," she said.

He glanced over at her. "I could, you know, offer you a Tylenol, but I don't think it's going to help."

She laughed, needing that. "Thanks."

A silence fell until he looked over at her for a second. "You're going to be a great mom, Adeline," he said softly.

She looked at him. "Think so?"

He met her eyes. "I know so. Literally no doubt."

She drew a long breath. It was just... That wasn't the only thing getting real here.

"Look, Adeline," he said gently, "don't worry about that right now. I mean about you and Adrian. Everything's going to be okay."

It didn't feel like that. It felt like everything was coming to a head and crashing down around her. Hormones, maybe. Hopefully.

Harris was quiet for a minute. Then he opened his mouth and hesitated but finally said, "You're one of the few people I've ever known that Adrian actually likes. I mean, yeah, he's nice to everybody, but..."

She bit her lip. "He must've liked Lauren once upon a time."

"He didn't like Lauren. He loved Lauren. There's a difference."

She dashed away tears, looking out the window. This was all so hard and painful. She hadn't expected that, really, many months ago. How dare Adrian invade her defenses. She tried to pass it off. She couldn't talk about that right now without crying. "You have to admit the mind-reading thing he does with everybody is kind of freaky," she said, attempting a smile.

His brows drew together, and he studied her. "He doesn't do that with everybody, Adeline."

She gulped, eyes flitting up to Harris's face. "He... He doesn't?"

Harris shook his head. "No."

She sighed. So much for steering the conversation away from the deep stuff.

Harris changed the subject soon and tried to keep her mind occupied, which worked fairly well. She was pretty zen by the time they made it to the check-in desk. A Black, middle-aged RN who inspired confidence gave her the paperwork, and she signed some papers and filled out some info.

"Is this dad?"

"I'm her brother-in-law," Harris said, standing beside her still.

The woman in scrubs lifted her brows, thinking she had stepped into the middle of something kinky, and he knew it, too. "Dad is on the way," Adeline said quickly, giving Harris a look. Wow. Contractions. *Okay, just, you know... Breathe.*

"Okay, you can go back with her until he gets here," the RN said.

Harris looked startled, but Adeline dug her fingers into his arm. She wasn't going into that room alone. Hospital staff got everything set up, and Dr. Jay came in, checking screens and asking her if she had ever been to a particular pizza place in Asheville. Her contractions had kicked up a notch, so it was a little hard to concentrate. "Really great pizza. Your labor is progressing pretty quickly. I'm not sure we'll be able to give you an epidural, but we'll see. Good news is, this shouldn't last very long. Yeah, they had good beer, too. A pretty, old historical building."

"Yeah..." Adeline closed her eyes. It was getting kind of excruciating.

Harris bolted with gratitude the moment Adrian stepped through the door. By then, Adeline's contractions were coming pretty steadily, and she was lying on a table/bed that felt much too high off the ground. "Adeline," Adrian said softly, kissing her forehead, his hand tender on the side of her head.

"Adrian," she said, just as her face contorted in pain. "They said it's probably too late to have the meds."

He stroked her hair, eyes concerned. He gave her his hand, and she grasped it; she wasn't sure she would let it go—ever. "You're doing great," he whispered.

Another nurse came in, saying in an oddly cheerful voice, "Yep, it's too late! Things are progressing nicely."

Adrian looked at her with an apology as she gripped his hand. He looked almost as miserable as she. "I'm sorry, honey," he said softly, earnestly, eyes washing over her face.

"That's okay," she said pretty calmly. Maybe it was his presence. "You know I was wavering anyway." She was just surprised things were progressing that quickly, and she knew Adrian was, too, although he didn't say so, of course. She looked up at him, eyes popping open. "I didn't even think to call anybody, Adrian. Mom and Dad, your parents..."

He stroked her hair. "My parents will be here soon, and yours are leaving first thing in the morning." He gave her a gentle, comforting smile, and the tension drained from her slightly. "Do you think he's doing okay?" she whispered.

"There's his heartbeat," he said, nodding toward the monitor at the smaller lines below hers. She turned her head and saw it: evidence of their sweet baby's life. And she had a renewed vigor to meet him.

The next hour was a blur with extreme exertion and random screams from a woman she belatedly realized was her. And then Dr. Jay finally said, "That'll do it!" and took a screaming, feisty mass into his arms.

Adeline covered her mouth and started to cry. Adrian kissed her cheek, lingering there with his face against hers, his eyes closed as she cried. "Adeline," he whispered. And then: "Thank you."

She turned, looking at him, at his dark eyes, her lip quivering. "Thank *you*," she said.

"You can thank each other all night long, but here is the star of the show," the cheerful nurse said, laying the baby on Adeline's chest. "Lord have mercy, look at those eyes."

Adeline blinked away tears, trying to see him. He was petite but probably seven pounds, with a well-defined nose, sweet little mouth, and black hair that covered his whole head. She gave a cry-ey laugh, looking up at Adrian. "He looks just like you."

Adrian didn't even try to deny it. He just laughed softly, which was a lovely accompaniment to his smile and red, misty eyes. He remained close to her, hand on her arm, gently stroking.

The baby gave a coo, and Adeline looked down, amazed. Her child making that noise. Nobody else's could do it just like that. His eyes traveled the room, dark and alert, and stopped on his daddy.

Adrian bent closer, smiled gently, and trailed a hand over his still-goupy hair reverently. "Hey, little man," he whispered. "Recognize me?"

Adeline smiled, chin against her chest so she could see him. "I think he does."

"Definitely you," he said. The baby was gripping her shoulder, lying against her skin calmly, feeling safe. And she knew it was going to be okay in that moment, motherhood. He was hers, and he knew that. All of the rest would fall into place.

It was a rough night. Baby Boy stayed in the room with them and awakened every hour, almost on the hour, hungry, or just generally unhappy. Adeline woke up at one point, realizing she had actually slept through the latest episode. She saw Adrian in the chair next to her (looking like he hadn't slept in about five years) holding the baby and giving him a bottle.

She smiled. "Rusty from disuse?" she asked softly.

He gave a smile in return. "It's all coming back."

She rested her head against the pillow, liking the view. James, Virginia, and Harris had stayed with Jude until they got a glimpse of his little brother in the nursery window, and they had come back briefly to see her. Then they had taken Jude back to Ravenel-Thompson House and were going to bring him in the morning for proper introductions.

Adrian tilted the baby's bottle, apparently so air wouldn't get in it—Lesson One. He watched him for a while. Then he looked up. "Feeling okay?"

"Yeah, just tired."

He smiled drowsily. "You were a trooper."

"It kind of just starts happening and you have no choice," she said. He laughed. He studied the baby's face again, still slightly smiling, totally in love, and her heart seized. "Your mom said you were petite like your boys until you were fourteen, and then you shot up in height. Did you hear her?"

"No, but that's true, I guess. I haven't seen my mom cry in a long time."

Adeline smiled, remembering Jude riding on his grandpa's hip, amusingly telling Adeline about his brother—*Had she seen him yet? He looked like him. Everybody said so.*

"They've been pretty great, Adrian. Harris, all of them."

"Yeah. They're there for me—for us—even if they drive me crazy sometimes."

Adrian got about two hours of sleep that night, but only a real jerk would've complained. Adeline slept peacefully until about seven o'clock when they brought her breakfast and the pediatrician came to check the baby.

They gave her the form for the birth certificate, and she wrote in Emory James Ravenel. Adrian had kind of been holding his breath on the last name, but she apparently hadn't considered hyphenating.

When they got Emory back from his examination, they lay him on his tribal patterned blanket in a soft white outfit, taking a picture to announce his arrival. Then Adeline held him for a couple of hours until Adrian's parents and Jude got there. Jude took his nana's admonitions about being careful seriously while he held the new arrival. The flashes of cameras were blinding for about two minutes.

"Daddy, he's yawning."

"I know, buddy," he said, stroking Jude's hair. "That's because he kept Daddy up all night."

Adeline smiled. "Well, you can't expect him to sleep at *night*. How lame."

"I think he's going to be a handful, just like his big brother."

"No one could be as much of a handful as his uncle, so count your blessings," Adrian's mom said dryly.

"I think he has Adeline's chin," his dad said randomly.

"I didn't think there was anything there, but I see touches of her now."

Adrian looked over at her and saw Adeline's eyes dancing. She met Adrian's eyes briefly before saying, "I was thinking the same thing."

"Well, they're both beautiful," his mother said with simple arrogance. "I honestly feel sorry for other people. Come, Jude. Let's go home. They'll be home in the morning, so we need to have everything prepared."

They were released from the hospital about eight o'clock the next day, and Adrian drove Adeline and Emory home. His mom and dad took Jude out for a few hours so they could get settled, and Adeline's mom went out to buy groceries to make a few meals. When they arrived home, Adrian went to Emory's car door, made sure his blankets were tucked, and got the car seat out. Baby Boy was kind of lost in there, but extremely cute.

He wanted to go to Adeline's door but knew there wasn't much chance she would wait for that. He saw her starting to get out and said, "Honey, your coat. It's thirty degrees." He bit the side of his cheek. That was twice endearments had flown out. He wasn't sure where that registered on the boundaries meter.

"Oh, yeah. Duh." Great. He'd made her feel stupid. He was a jerk.

But she smiled when they met on the sidewalk, and he put his hand on her back, letting her precede him. "Is he doing okay?"

"He's great." He opened the door on Adeline's beautiful house and closed it behind them when they were through.

"Harris and I were having Cheetos," she said once they were walking down the hall. "I didn't think about the mess."

"I think Mom got everything cleaned up," he answered. He put the car seat down. She looked tired. Good, but tired. He absentmindedly swiped some dust on the hall table. "Go on up—I know you were wanting a shower."

She looked at the baby, hesitating. "Can you...bring him up to the bedroom while I shower?"

He smiled. "Of course." He was going to be nearby anyway in case she fainted or something.

She smiled back. "Is that crazy?"

He touched her cheek with the backs of fingers. "Of course not."

She touched his hand, bringing it down and holding it. "Thank you, Adrian. You were wonderful the past two days."

He studied her, smile slipping away. "I'm your husband, Adeline," he said softly.

There was a beat of silence. She bit her lip. Her eyes got a little bit of moisture. "Sorry," she whispered.

He studied her, chest clenching. "Adeline..."

"I'm not upset with you, Adrian. I'm upset with myself." She pulled away and turned to go, going up the stairs without looking back.

# Chapter Twenty-Two

John Thomas was popularly elected in November. With the new Congressional session beginning the third of December, he needed to return to Washington as soon as possible. Because she needed to purchase a few things in Boston and had gotten very much behind in her packing, Shannon sent John Thomas on, telling him she would follow in a week's time with Benjamin. He agreed, kissing her with twinkling eyes that said he expected nothing of the sort.

She had been determined to prove him wrong, and she did, sending him a telegram to expect her on the fourteenth. She alighted from the train to great journalistic interest again. The inevitable flashes of horrid cameras made her glad, first, that she was wearing a very flattering travelling coat and, second, that Benjamin continued to sleep this time. As Rebecca, Jeptha, and the nursemaid emerged from the servants' cars and found her, they all stood together amongst the pushing and shoving of reporters. The employees of the railroad, perfectly aware of her identity, did their best to force the crowds to maintain their distance, and a policeman approached as well.

"Do you see Admiral Haley?" Shannon asked Jeptha, who was shading her eyes and looking across the crowds. As Benjamin awoke, Shannon kept him pressed to her, his cheek against her chest, trying to shield him from the photographers.

"No, ma'am, but I can't see anything in this—"

Jeptha broke off as John Thomas appeared. "Forgive me, I have been here twenty minutes but couldn't break through." He leaned in, kissing Shannon's cheek, holding her arms and whispering seriously, "Give Benjamin to Ginny, and stay behind me, my darling."

As he pulled her through the crowds, she did see, amongst his admirers, a few men who seemed to be taking stock of them. That was when she realized that he had instructed her to hand their son to the nursemaid because she was less likely to be attacked than one of them. Her hand tightened on his, and he pressed it reassuringly, pulling her relentlessly forward.

"Senator Haley! Admiral Haley!" She heard through the din. He would smile and nod politely, not responding to the occasional shouted question or request to shake his hand.

"Your wife is beautiful!"

"Have you forgiven her?"

"Do you want to put the Negros in power across the South?"

"How many Rebs did you kill?"

"His son! There is his little son!"

Nothing had earned a reaction from him before that, but he turned around fiercely, murder on his face, quelling the voice who had said it. He ushered Shannon and Ginny into the carriage, altering his plan to return for Jeptha and Rebecca and helping them in, too.

Shannon looked at her husband during the ride and found him looking over at her. He shook his head slightly, holding her eyes. He covered her gloved hand, and no words were spoken between any of them until the federal style brick house was reached.

When they arrived, Shannon cradled Benjamin, and as soon as John Thomas had ushered them across the threshold, she said, "I will get him settled."

He nodded, and she felt him watch her as she climbed the stairs.

John Thomas found her in her bedchamber in the blue light of the late afternoon. She had taken her hat off and was emptying the contents of a valise she had carried with her. She looked over her shoulder.

He came to her, putting his hands on her waist and kissing her, lingering with his forehead against hers. "I hope you weren't jostled."

Self-conscious, she wondered if he could feel the slight thickening of her figure. He lifted his head, raising his eyebrows in question.

"No, I wasn't," she said, moving against him, bringing his head down for a kiss. She had meant to ask him why there had been danger at the station, how he had occupied himself the past week, and many other things. But she was lost in mere seconds.

"Well, you owe me ten dollars." Shannon walked into John Thomas's study the next day, holding a newspaper.

He looked up from what he was writing, lifting his brows as he stood. He walked toward her, taking her to a chair and saying, "Sit down, my love."

She did so, looking up at him quizzically. "Do you know there are women all over the North and South who work in mills in my condition? And the Gullah women, too, in the fields."

He looked quietly horrified, settling her into the chair, and he admitted, "Yes, I suppose that is true; I had never thought of it. I am sure their husbands wish they could protect them, as I wish to protect you, my darling."

She looked at him tenderly, touching his face briefly before looking away, embarrassed. He caught her hand and smiled. "You are feeling well today?"

"Yes, I'm well," she replied softly.

He kissed her hand. "Now, why do I owe you ten dollars? We have so many bets between us, you and I, that— It can't be that Major Christian *has* come to Washington?"

Her eyes twinkled. "Yes."

He got up, went to a drawer, and removed some bills, which he brought back to her. She tucked them primly into the pocket of her skirt. His eyes twinkled as he sat at her feet. "Who are they staying with?"

"A Senator Del—"

"Delanie. Why did I ask? There is most certainly something afoot."

"I forgot to tell you last night: I saw him a few days ago while I stayed with Adams in Boston. Seymour, I mean."

He lifted his brows. "Did you?"

"Yes, he called on me!"

He blinked, too stunned to speak for a few moments. "That seems rather bold," he said, surveying her.

Bolder than he knew, given the circumstances, but she would spare him the sordid details of *that* dramatic ordeal. "He was cordial. I captured Anna and forced her to sit with us. She was quite taken with him," she said. "He was always rather handsome, and he could be charming."

"Was he? I don't remember," he said, jaw clenching and loosening.

Her eyes danced. "You remember perfectly well."

"And, of course, the war changed him," he added with uncharacteristic sarcasm.

She laughed, bringing his hand to her middle. He looked up at her with such warmth that she resolved to cease teasing him and to think instead of how she would spend the considerable sum of ten dollars.

Elizabeth opened Shannon's seal as she sat at the desk in the library of Ravenel House. Frederick was looking for a book nearby and detailing the rudeness of a man he had encountered in the market.

"Yes, my dear, very bad," she said, eyes amused as she glanced up at him.

Her eyes flew over the words, and she learned that Congress would return to session soon, that little Benjamin was now attempting to toddle, and that Shannon had hosted a political dinner. She gasped, looking up.

Frederick stopped, looking at her. "What is it?" He glanced down at the letter.

She bit her lip, eyes bright. "She is going to have another baby."

"Who?"

"Shannon."

Frederick looked outraged. "Good God! I suppose this is Haley's notion of *polite awkwardness*?"

"Oh, Frederick," she laughed, looking back down at the letter. "We are the only ones they have told. And don't tell your father yet. She fears he will only worry."

"How old is my nephew—four months?" he demanded, unheeding.

"Ten," she returned dryly.

"Well, it makes no difference. Shannon's constitution has always been weak—"

"Has it?"

"—and she seemed to me to have been quite ill the first time."

"All will be well," she said, standing, laying the letter aside.

"How can you know that?" he demanded. "No one can ever know that! Did he never imagine the consequences?"

She looked up and went to stand in front of him, taking a breath and releasing it. She considered him, the slightest affectionate smile in her eyes, but there was, perhaps, also seriousness there. "The truth is, Frederick, that you don't want any of the women in your family to have a baby," she said quietly, but firmly. She lay her hand against his chest tenderly, and she didn't raise her voice. But she did hold his eyes solidly.

His lips parted. He reached up to cover her hand, his brown eyes growing penitent, his beautiful mouth pressing together as he held her eyes.

# Chapter Twenty-Three

Shannon repressed a wave of queasiness. She was at the Executive Mansion for a tea hosted by President Johnson's daughter in lieu of the President's wife, who suffered from consumption and was almost never seen in public.

Despite growing tensions between Johnson and the Radical Republicans over the Reconstruction Act, John Thomas was too great a public figure to be snubbed by the President.

"Military districts, martial law, and Negros with the vote while the white men are banned from the polling places," Mrs. George Rhinebaum said, shaking her head as the ladies sat in a circle. "What has the world come to?"

"This must fall hard upon you, Mrs. Haley," a wife she didn't know with beautiful brown eyes and perfectly parted brown hair, said sympathetically. "Knowing your family will be subjugated in this barbaric fashion."

Shannon sat in acute discomfort. "I do not wish them to suffer," she answered, sipping her tea and hoping her nausea dissipated. "And, of course, I wish for things to heal between the states as quickly as possible."

"I hadn't felt sympathetic to the South," Mrs. Wheeling, a plump woman in middle age, said. "You all know my family's sacrifices during the war. But was *this* what my Johnny died for, I ask you?"

The elderly woman beside Shannon sighed deeply, mumbling, "Tedious."

Shannon looked at her. The woman had perfectly pinned white hair, and she wore a prim lavender gown. But her posture was anything but proper, and she was having her third glass of wine. Encouraged by Shannon's twinkle, she said, "Listen, my child. The ladies and I have discussed it. You must simply not respond to the stories and wait out the storm. It shall pass, and it will be the better for you having not commented upon it."

Shannon narrowed her eyes, studying her, unsure if it was the wine or something else. "Yes, I think so, too," she said carefully.

"It was a Democratic newspaper, of course. I know that publication very well. I'm sure your friends have already discerned that. Whatever you do, do not allow your husband to sue, for I think it would be even more disastrous. I had a scandal or two in my day, and they either pass by or sink you. Either way, you'll know soon."

Shannon was by now feeling quite ill, but she knew that

to show her surprise would be to admit being in the dark. So, she said, "Yes, ma'am. I believe you are right."

Shannon, nearly trembling, gave Rebecca coins as soon as she walked through the door, asking her to purchase every newspaper she could locate. She hadn't asked any questions and had merely agreed with a succinct, "Yes, ma'am."

Now, with numerous publications spread out across John Thomas's desk, Shannon's sharp eyes scanned over them quickly. She threw away the more accredited papers, finding nothing in them. But she found plenty in *The National Intelligencer.*

Her eyes widened as she read the words *Seymour Christian.* Affair—her flight to Charleston... Her mind must concentrate! According to the *Intelligencer*, there had been an affair during the war just before she had returned to John Thomas. The happy occasion of the birth of Mrs. Haley's child had occurred quite quickly after the couple's reconciliation. They were informed that Mrs. Haley had recently seen the gentleman in Boston, and that she now expected the happy event of another blessing.

The door opened, and Shannon looked up, eyes blazing. It was John Thomas. She bolted to her feet. He looked at her seriously as he crossed the room. He reached for the newspaper and tossed it on the fire before turning back to her and touching both of her arms. "Shannon, my darling, you mustn't allow yourself to be upset," he said lowly, urgently.

She took a breath, trembling, and looked at him in fear.

"*Shannon*," he said passionately, "I dismissed it out of hand, every word of it. I promise you. Do *not* be upset." He embraced her, tucking her against him and kissing her hair, then her temple.

Tears streaked down her face. "John Thomas, I—"

"Shh," he said soothingly. "I am as angry as you are, but it is no good, my love."

She broke away, rage and fear and various indescribable emotions coursing through her. Mrs. Rice— Was Shannon's mind fevered to wonder if the woman had something to do with this? And how did the newspaper know about this baby, she wondered, when they had told no one, save Frederick and Elizabeth?

She stopped. There had been a dinner at Senator Hargrove's mansion. They had thought no one was about in the hall between the dining room and sitting room when John Thomas had placed his hand against her waist as they shared a smile. At that moment, Shannon had looked up to see Mrs. Rice. John Thomas retracted his hand, flushing, and whispered an apology to Shannon. She had thought no more of it. But she was thinking of it now.

She broke away and paced back and forth, and he said, "Shannon, you mustn't make yourself ill. Please sit, my darling."

Glaring, she said, "How can I sit?"

"Shannon, the baby," he pleaded with eyes full of pain for her.

She touched her lips, nodding, and slowly sank into a chair. He came to her and knelt beside her. He took both of her hands between his, meeting her eyes firmly. "Your reputation—"

"Is, and has long been, in tatters," she said, looking away.

"—will not suffer once it is seen that I do not heed the stories. No respectable person would pay attention to that newspaper. It has fed its readers for years on salacious gossip."

"Yes, but it is still being circulated, isn't it?"

He kissed her hand. "Shannon," he pressed. "My love, you mustn't heed it."

"Seymour Christian— I shall murder him."

"Perhaps the Christians didn't even contribute to the story. I promise you, the newspaper had only to learn that your family once shared an island with them to start their minds spinning." He framed her hands between his as if he could as easily protect her from the winds of political gossip. He looked away. "This is my fault. I knew what entering politics would entail."

She looked down at him, tears in her eyes, and he appeared to be pierced by them. "They have done this in an attempt to destroy you," she whispered. "I know that full well. To prevent you from having efficacy." Her lip trembled. "I am your weakest part."

"My greatest happiness," he countered passionately. "If God is our strength, how can we have any weakness, my love?"

Her lips parted as his words struck a chord. She held

his eyes, which were growing in the confidence of having won her over. "Yes," she whispered, touching his face. "Yes, you are right."

John Thomas lowered his hat, hoping he wouldn't be recognized and accosted, either by well-wishers or ill. Since he had received multiple and varying threats on his life in the mail, his secretaries had insisted upon accompanying him everywhere he went in public. But he had slipped out today, rather exhausted with being watched like Benjamin in his nursery. He merely wanted to get home to Shannon, who had been nauseated that morning.

"Haley!"

He looked across the street, and after a barrage of horses and carriages had passed, he saw Mr. Christian, the elder. He halted a moment but then crossed the street to the man, who had aged well, his silver hair still thick, his form lean and lithe.

"Mr. Christian. It has been many years, sir."

"Your wedding, I believe. That was back in the days of plenty and security."

"It was in 1859, sir."

"So it was. Well, Senator Haley, I wanted to assure you that neither my son nor I had anything to do with the recent publications."

"You are kind, but I did not imagine that you had. I am untroubled by them, sir. One can't go to pieces every time a newspaperman concocts a rumor," he said kindly.

"That is precisely what I told my son when he expressed his discomfort over all of it. Naturally, it goes too far to be believed. My son feared very much for the reputation of the lady, especially given his part in it. What happened early in the war when passions ran high have no bearing on today, and so I told him. You are right to take it as you do, young man. One has to take the long view of matters."

Shannon helped Benjamin to walk in the nursery. He wasn't quite ready to totter on his own, but he was delighted with his own progress. His blue eyes were full of life, and his expression was characteristically earnest.

"You favor your papa more every day," she laughed, sweeping him up and going to stand at the nursery window. "Do you see the birds?"

Benjamin extended a finger to the window and then looked at her contemplatively, his tubby cheeks eminently kissable, which she did. Looking down, she saw John Thomas walk up the cobblestone path and enter the door below.

The nursery door opened, and the nursemaid came in. "Oh, Ginny. Here is my husband returning. Your timing is excellent, for I must speak with him," she said.

"Yes, ma'am," Ginny replied as she approached to collect Benjamin with a smile for him.

Shannon fingered his little foot and told Ginny to bring him down to the parlor around seven o'clock. Then she went off, her eyes keen with news, for Mrs. Hadden had told her at a breakfast she had attended that Senator Delanie *owned* the *National Intelligencer*. John Thomas couldn't have known that, or he would have mentioned it.

She opened the door of the library, a greeting on her lips, but her words died away when she saw him. He was standing by the window looking out, his expression hollow, his entire being still.

"John Thomas?"

He turned. "Shannon," he said, blinking, seemingly surprised.

"What is the matter? Oh, not Charles?" she breathed.

"No. Oh, no," he said, some awareness seeming to return to his eyes.

She walked more fully into the room, narrowing her eyes, studying him.

"I hope you are feeling better," he said in distracted concern, belatedly remembering himself and walking forward, touching her waist and leaning in to kiss her cheek.

"Oh, yes," she answered. "Never mind that. John Thomas, something has troubled you!"

"No, I assure you. Nothing is the matter." he answered, making a decent show of surprise. He looked ashen to her, however, as he guided her to a chair.

"I don't believe you."

He looked startled. Perhaps he hadn't thought she would challenge him. He had a very short memory if that were the case. He lifted his brows mildly, but he could not formulate a case convincing enough to fob her off. He was utterly distracted.

"Something I wouldn't wish to trouble you with," he admitted in compromise, seeming to think that settled the matter.

Realization dawned upon her. "Something about me."

He looked at her quickly, lips parting.

"Have I displeased you?" she asked softly.

"Of course not," he answered quickly.

"What, then?"

He shook his head, eyes softening as he took in her features. "No, Shannon. I won't say anything to upset you in your condition. It doesn't matter."

"I shall be imagining all sorts of dreadful things if you don't tell me, which is more likely to upset me, you know."

He shook his head. "No," he stated softly.

"Very well, I shall go to my room and make myself ill with dread, and it shall be upon your head."

He sighed and turned away. After a struggle with himself, he drew a hectic hand through his hair. Finally, he said, "I...chanced to see Mr. Christian, the elder, this morning in town. He remembered me." He met her eyes.

Her stomach clenched. It was an instantaneous reaction to the mere name.

He looked away, swallowing. "He made insinuations... Veiled, of course, but I wished heartily to knock his teeth down his throat."

Her face was crimson. "About me?" she asked in dread.

The clock ticked several times, loud in the silence. "Yes,"

he whispered. After a long pause, he added, "During the war."
He drew a breath. "Shannon, if there *is* any truth in them..."

"In *what*?"

"He implied that there had been...an affair," he said,
swiping a hand over his mouth and looking away.

Her color drained. "How *dare* he."

John Thomas said hesitantly, "If there was, Shannon, I
only wanted to tell you that—"

"He is an unconscionable demon!" she exclaimed, gritting
her teeth and coming to her feet. "If you *must* know—and I
had hoped to spare you this, but I can see you are wondering
why a *friend* of my father's would say such a thing—his son
*offered marriage* to me during the war." At his astonished
expression, she added, "Pending the resolution of our..." She
hesitated. "Divorce." His face was so pale that even his lips
seemed to have lost their color. "This offended my father so
much that they nearly came to blows, and they have not
spoken since," she added almost in a whisper.

His eyes swept her face, as though he had just in that
moment realized the severity of all the implications of what
could have happened. He knew how truly endangered their
marriage had been, but perhaps he hadn't allowed himself
to carry those thoughts to their fullest fruition. But he was
doing so now, she didn't doubt. He appeared too shaken to
speak for several minutes.

"You believed that, in truth, I had become his mistress?"
she uttered into the silence finally, studying him.

He shook his head, looking at her apologetically. "I merely

wanted to tell you that if I *had* driven you into another man's arms—"

"How?"

"By my infamous words that night," he whispered, closing his eyes.

The silence grew. Noises from outside were the only sounds floating on the air. The hush was long, but he finally said, "I couldn't help imagining that, with what I had done and said, and the state you must have been in... I wanted you to know that I would've understood, my darling."

She swallowed thickly. "Well, you don't have to," she said. "Because I never invited another man into my bed." She bit her lip; her vision blurred with tears. "I may have said our marriage was at an end in my heart..." she said, closing her eyes against the pain those words invoked.

"Shannon," he whispered, gripping her arms. "Don't, my darling."

"—but I was as a woman dead without you. The thought of another man repulsed me."

He surveyed her with tears in his eyes. "I should be drawn and quartered for—"

"No, it...was a reasonable assumption."

He looked her over wretchedly. "I have exhausted you," he said.

"No. I forced you to speak, as I always do, with my shrewish temperament," she answered, wiping her eyes, striving for normalcy. "I will perhaps go up and take a nap," she declared faintly.

"I'll take you," he said, starting toward the door.

"No, I am perfectly well. I will... I will see you at supper?"

"Of *course*," he said, leaning in to kiss her, as though unsure. She kissed him and turned to go, walking quietly out of the room and closing the door behind her.

She had made it out into the foyer when, suddenly, something occurred to her, and her spine straightened. She paused and then turned on her heel and strode in such a way that one would never know that she had only just attested to weakness. She opened the door and slammed it back.

John Thomas, still standing, looked up at her, alarmed. She demanded, "John Thomas Haley, why *would* that occur to you, that I should be in such a desperate state? Did *you* take another to your bed? You did not reciprocate my answer, and if you say that you did, I shall hunt the female down and rip her from limb to limb!"

He scowled, looking aghast and bewildered. "Is that *likely* while you walk the Earth, Shannon?" he demanded, raising his voice to meet hers.

She stopped, her lips slowly parting, her demeanor changing. After a moment, a smile formed. "It would seem that it isn't," she answered softly.

"It isn't," he confirmed, crossing the room to her without saying anything further and gently taking her into his arms, kissing her desperately, which she reciprocated, and then lifting her to carry her up the stairs.

# Chapter Twenty-Four

I t was when Shannon awoke from a nap late the following evening that it finally occurred to her: Seymour *had* given the *Intelligencer* the story. The man had been very angry since her father had begun to snub the Christians socially. But Mr. Christian had told his sordid tale not just for revenge against her father. Seymour wanted Shannon; he had decided that long ago. And whether it was love, lust, or sheer determination to have his way, he had come north with the break-up of the Haley marriage as his chief aim. It seemed unfathomable, but she had, on occasion, heard of such scandalous elopements involving married ladies.

Seymour meant to have her, as he had once told her. And his father (as Shannon ought to have remembered) had always been equally determined that Seymour should have anything he desired. Neither had calculated into the equation John Thomas's devotion. She supposed also they had heard the rumor that she had returned to him unwillingly, at her father's behest.

And if it were not the Rice woman's infernal gossip that had dropped the hint in Seymour's ear about Benjamin, she would be very much surprised. It had been apparent to Shannon that the man had flirted with Amabel and flattered her at a number of parties. He could be immensely charming, and Amabel Rice had let herself be carried away into confiding her unverified suspicions. Likely, she had poured forth every detail she knew about Shannon since the reconciliation, never dreaming Seymour would use them so publicly.

Shannon supposed the Christians imagined John Thomas would put her out of his house. What she couldn't work out was what they had thought she would do with Benjamin and her unborn child. But that was before it struck her that they more than likely intended for her to give them to John Thomas and never look back.

Perhaps it was that thought which enraged her to the point that she threw back her covers and jumped out of the bed, ripping off her nightgown and throwing it behind her before opening the doors of her wardrobe and digging into the back. There was a ball at the home of a congressman from Pennsylvania, and the Haleys had been invited.

Shannon and her husband had rather reverted to polite awkwardness. Shannon did not blame him. Nor did she think John Thomas doubted her. Only, their reconciliation was too fresh to permit an easy return to normalcy after such a tense discussion. Therefore, Shannon had insisted that they attend the ball, thinking it would be a chance to let the discomfort dissipate, as well as to present a united front. John Thomas planned to meet her there.

She found the dress and pulled it out, surveying it. Then she went to pull the bell. When Rebecca arrived, Shannon told her that she would like to dress, and asked that she lace her corset. Rebecca agreed, of course, but her eyes widened when she saw the dress. She helped Shannon on with her undergarments—pantaloons, stockings, shoes, and crinoline—before helping her to step into the dress. Then she fastened it. It fit snugly due to Shannon's condition. All the better.

She smoothed the bodice and looked up at the mirror, seeing herself in the red gown which had caused, in the winter of 1860, the second-worst argument she and her husband had ever had.

It was entirely possible, of course, that she would enrage him. Perhaps he *would* turn her out of the house for this. To say that it was a gamble was a gross understatement. He had no idea what she intended, and half of the play depended upon him acting his part.

Shannon's coat was primly buttoned, the fashionably cut hem of it naturally showing the skirt, but nothing more. She looked out the window of the carriage at the house, where equipages awaited their inhabitants on the lawn and gas lighting spilled forth from the many-paned windows. The last of the elegant couples strolled through the door.

The stage ought to be set, she thought, her heart pounding. Well, she would have to enter, in any event, for John Thomas would be growing worried.

She gathered her courage, tapping the door. The driver opened it and assisted her down.

She walked to the door of the house, which opened immediately. A footman took her coat. Another came forward, ushering her toward the ballroom where a waltz was winding down.

"Your name?" he asked.

"Mrs. John Thomas Haley," she replied without thinking. It struck her just when the song ended that he intended to announce her, but it was too late. The man pitched his voice so that it carried, proclaiming, "Mrs. John Thomas Haley!"

She had been to a few parties in which that was done in the European way, and any other time, the ladies would have smiled, gentlemen would have inclined their heads, and the music would have started up again. But not when the most talked-about woman in Washington City entered a room. And not when she was wearing such a dress.

Shannon watched as awareness of it struck the other guests. Jaws dropped, gasps sounded softly, and a gentleman choked on his wine. The moment stretched out to uncomfortable lengths, but Shannon tried to appear unconscious of these reactions, merely scanning the room as if looking for her husband. She checked to ensure that Senator Delanie and his houseguests were in attendance. They were. Seymour's gaze raked over her as he held his glass casually among a circle of men, just as though he had not been in open rebellion against the government a year and a half ago. She examined him. He was nothing to John Thomas.

Remembering herself, she looked up and saw John Thomas walk forward as the musicians finally started up again. What he was feeling she could only guess, but he was no fool. He understood his part and strolled forward with an open twinkle in his eyes, taking her hand and kissing it, saying, "May I have this dance, ma'am?"

"Yes," she said faintly, losing heart when she thought of what the repercussions might be. Few men would stand for their wives playing the harlot in public.

He led her out onto the dance floor, a rare occurrence for him. Then he took her into his arms for a waltz. All the while he kept his confident poise, looking down at her with a hint of an amused smile, a knowing glitter in his eyes as though they shared authorship of her plan. Only they couldn't have done so because she had known he would never agree unless he were forced to it. She grasped perfectly well he was ill-pleased, though likely no one else could see it.

Still smiling as the room watched, he said, trying not to move his lips overly much, "I assume my performance is to your standards?"

"Admirably," she said. She glanced up. "The idea was to—"

"I know how your mind works by now, Shannon," he interjected.

She swallowed. "—to make a mockery of their accusations that I am fast."

"Brilliant, and yet terrifying," he murmured. "It fills me with great foreboding that Benjamin is half yours—"

"He is entirely from your side, we have already settled that," she hissed. That was the last they spoke as the dance continued.

The waltz finally ended. Putting one hand on the small of her back and taking her hand with his other, John Thomas walked Shannon past the refreshments and into the small adjoining room where ladies went to rest. Thankfully, the space was empty.

"Shannon, you wretch," he said, drawing a hand through his hair.

She looked up at him penitently. "I was angry. And I had to silence them. They were going to destroy you, and all of your good work."

His face softened. "My darling shrew, where did you dig up this dress?"

"Your mother gave me all of my things that...you had shipped to Boston." She bit her lip. That was hardly a pleasant reflection in this strained moment. "She transported them to Beacon Hill this summer."

He studied her. After a moment he placed his hand on her middle, covering it. "Well, I am uncertain how I feel about my sweet babe appearing in it, love."

She choked on a laugh. "I will burn it, I promise. As soon as we return home."

"You must do as you wish. I only hope you may not have exhausted yourself," he said firmly, moving his hand to her back, leaning to kiss her temple.

"I am a little tired," she admitted.

An anxious look entered his eyes, his hands lowering. "I am taking you home immediately."

"Very well," she returned, eyes twinkling, "I have done all that I came to do."

# Chapter Twenty-Five

A deline sat on the sofa in the living room a week later, Emory in her arms, the house quiet. Her mom had stayed a couple of days to get her settled and to keep Baby Boy occupied at night so they could get a little rest. But she had to return home with Annie after her sister had visited. Her parents' reaction to the baby was everything Adrian had said it would be. All of the awkwardness was gone, and they even seemed to embrace Adrian, accepting the situation.

After her mom had left, Adrian's mom had come to help since he had to go back to work eventually. And the surprising thing was, Adeline actually enjoyed the days with Virginia. She had a lot of good tips on babies and never grew agitated when Emory had a meltdown.

Now Adeline heard the door open and saw down the hall and through the open kitchen door Virginia coming in with paper bags. She had gone out for groceries and dia-pers—Adeline wasn't sure which was more vital.

She came in a few minutes later with Adeline's lunch—a salad from her favorite little deli downtown. "Thanks, Vir-ginia," she said, transferring Emory onto his big gray pillow.

"Is it time for his feeding?"

"No, we still have an hour, and he's pretty content." Con-tent didn't begin to describe the zen look he had while he was asleep. It lowered her blood pressure just watching him.

Virginia sat down across from her, unwrapping her sandwich. "I laid that folder that James found on the kitchen table. More family documents, I think. It must've fallen out of the box."

"Thanks," Adeline said. Emory sucked his legs in and then kicked them out. Amazing. He wiggled for a minute and then settled in, basically in a coma. Adeline bent down, closing her eyes while she kissed his precious little cheek.

Virginia's features softened as they rested on the baby. "How long are you going to keep him in your bedroom?"

Adeline lifted a shoulder. "I'm not sure. It's convenient right now." Adrian did most of the night-time work, giving her a look if she tried to get up and taking the baby out if he got riled. She wasn't sure how he was functioning on about three hours' sleep, but he seemed to be getting through.

Virginia was studying her in that disconcerting way, extremely elegant in a cream drape-sweater thing. "Did you and Adrian have a spat?" she asked calmly.

Adeline lifted her brows. None of her business, but oh,

well. "No, we don't usually...spat. Why do you ask?"

"No reason in particular." She paused. "He's happy, Adeline." She looked away for a moment, and when she looked back her eyes were misty. "I never thought I would see him have that general lightness about him again."

"He's a good dad, Virginia," she said softly. "I never doubted that Emory would add to his...general happiness."

"Only Emory?"

"That's...complicated." *The deal was to get through the pregnancy, and I don't know where to go from here. I think he's happy, but...*

Virginia was still studying her. Now she knew where Adrian got that eagle stare from. "How? Are you thinking that he only wanted to get you through that trying time? You needn't worry. Adrian always does the right thing. And the right thing here is pretty clear."

Adeline studied her, expression arrested. She got a sick feeling in the pit of her stomach. All of the insecurities came crashing in. The way they'd never talked about staying together, never used the L word.

Fear that he didn't want her for *her* made her want to flee toward her office in Charlotte. She'd go before she had to hear it from his lips. Anything would be better than that.

Only he'd never say it, would he? That was on her.

*"It didn't feel right. To divorce the mother of my child."* She was taken, almost forcefully, like time travel, back to the little restaurant at the General Longstreet Inn when he had said that. Suddenly, it all fit together like the pieces

of a puzzle, and the anxiety was all-consuming. She was drowning, and no help was in sight.

"Good job. Now go on up and get your shower." Adrian closed Jude's book, glancing across the room where Adeline was holding Emory. Jude, cute in his cable-knit blue sweater and red tie, stopped by to pet his brother. Jude had been snuggling on the couch in front of the fireplace with Adeline since he'd gotten home, and it had taken almost superhuman effort to get him to do his homework.

"Can I give him his bottle at nine?" Jude asked Adeline softly. Apparently, he had committed feeding schedules to memory.

"Of course," she said, smoothing his hair. Jude preferred that to having his hair ruffled. Her eyes were soft and gentle.

Adrian put papers in folders and signed a field trip release, glancing up at Adeline from time to time. She had been distracted and nervy since he'd gotten home yesterday. His mom said she hadn't noticed anything, so maybe he was just overthinking it.

He glanced at her again. She looked good with a baby. His baby.

"Feeling okay today?"

She looked up. "Oh! Yeah, I'm pretty much recovered, I think."

He got up and walked toward her, sitting on the sofa arm nearest her. "You want to hold him?" she asked. "I don't think you have yet today, unless you count 3:00 a.m. as today."

"I don't," he said, smiling briefly. He drew a hand over her curls. "You keep him." Maybe she wasn't getting to hold him enough. They'd had a lot of visitors.

She held his eyes for a second. Then she bit her lip. She had never felt more remote from him. And he had a feeling it had nothing to do with postpartum emotions. She was pulling away from him. *Why? Why?*

"Adeline—" he started to say, just as she said, "So I—"

"You go first," he said.

"Sorry." She swallowed. "So I've been in correspondence with Janice... She's in over her head in Charlotte. I need to, at some point, make a trip up there to get some things straightened out."

He studied her silently, hearing all she wasn't saying. Finally, he said, "When?"

Another long silence. "I was thinking maybe Emory would be ready to travel when he's a month old..."

The quiet grew until it was deafening. She looked away, down at Emory, rearranging his blanket. "How long, Adeline?" he said quietly.

She looked up. "Just...a few days. A week at most."

He held her eyes for a long time, metaphorically holding her feet to the fire. She looked away first, and then he did, over into the fireplace. When he finally looked at her again, he said after clearing his throat, "I think I will hold him, if you don't mind."

# Chapter Twenty-Six

Shannon rose from her vanity one morning and went downstairs to the warm library, where she found John Thomas already at work returning letters. Massachusetts was bitterly cold in January, something to which she was uncertain she would ever grow accustomed, however little it seemed to trouble her gentlemen. But John Thomas usually kept a fire in the library for her.

He looked up, smiling, and stood immediately, coming to her. "There you are. Were you able to eat your breakfast?"

"Oh, yes, every bite," she affirmed as he embraced her gently, his hand lingering on her growing middle as he pulled away, his eyes loving.

He had brought her to Massachusetts to await her confinement in April amongst his family. They had agreed to it that the family doctor would attend her, along with his mother and sisters, but only after he had offered to take her to Ravenel House if she wished it. But she had wanted their baby to be born at their home. His family was delighted, and they showered attention upon her, coddling her through every little ailment and helping her with her household duties even before she asked.

John Thomas was mostly ensconced at Beacon Hill, although he would make a short trip to Washington for any stray pieces of legislation which required his vote. "You have a great many letters this morning, some of them from South Carolina," he said.

"Oh, excellent!" she said, going to her writing desk, where he always laid them. He went with her, pulling out her chair and helping her to sit. She bit her lip, unable to take her thoughts for long from the thing that had happened the night before...

They had reached, she thought, a state of perfect happiness, and Benjamin had done something to make them laugh so much they cried. But then, right at the end of that tender family scene, she had glimpsed some dread in John Thomas's eyes, some lingering vestige of unhappiness she had seen on the ship in Charleston. It had stolen her breath.

She opened the seal of a letter from South Carolina with trembling hands, trying to put her anxiety about John Thomas out of her mind. She couldn't confront him. It wasn't as though her marriage needed more strife, and with the almost-daily threats to his life, it was all she could do to hold herself together as it was.

And the terrible look she had seen wasn't there most days. She had thought she had witnessed it only once before during a moment of delirious happiness, but she had dismissed it because she hadn't been sure. The only thing that she could liken it to was the dread one experienced after realizing one had been laughing for the first time after the death of a loved one. She knew it well: that creeping, lingering sadness that assaulted fiercely, reminding of something that couldn't be corrected just as one most desired happiness. And that it had to do with her, she did not doubt.

Taking a breath, she settled in to read, her mind slowly growing more ordered until she gasped, causing John Thomas to look over quickly. "What is it, love?"

Shannon touched her heart. "Elizabeth is with child!"

He smiled, standing and walking over. He dropped a hand to her shoulder. "Is she? I suppose she *won't* be coming to us for your confinement."

"No, I don't imagine..." She read on. "She doesn't expect hers until August, but Frederick has expressly forbidden her from all forms of travel. She says that she will defy him if I wish it." She looked up at John Thomas. "But I don't think that is necessary. With your mother and all of your sisters—no, I can't see the necessity in flouting him," she said.

"No, for heaven's sake, let the poor man feel he has some semblance of control, however false that illusion."

She met his eyes, her own smiling.

He smiled but said gently, "This will be very difficult for him, you know."

"Yes, you'll write to him, requesting him not to lock her up?" she asked. "He'll listen to you."

He laughed. "Yes, I will, even though my sympathy is entirely with him," he said lovingly, stroking her cheek. She smiled, her heart piercing, and looked down.

She gasped again, covering her mouth as she reached the end. She looked up with tears in her eyes.

"What is it?" he demanded.

"They have been returned their confiscated lands."

"Oh, that is—"

"But there is more," she said, looking up, lip trembling. "When Frederick and Elizabeth drove out to Santarella... there was a wing left standing. In tolerable condition."

"What?" he breathed. "I thought it was impossible."

She shook her head, accepting his embrace as she laughed softly in joy.

Shannon entered their bedchamber to candlelight. John Thomas was downstairs with one or two gentlemen from Boston discussing a piece of legislation, and Benjamin had long since been put to bed. It was too early for her to go to bed, and the baby was restless besides.

So, she walked around rather aimlessly, a calming hand against her middle, until her eyes landed on the secretary desk. Upon it lay something which John Thomas had been crafting. She walked to it curiously, tilting the folded piece of paper toward the lamp.

Two hours later, she was still sitting at the secretary when the door softly opened, and John Thomas entered quietly. Looking up, he saw her, and he glanced at the desk and the piece of paper. He gave a mild, but slightly reticent smile, and she understood why.

It was a speech he had been preparing to give on the floor of the Senate, and she had been marking all over it. No wife had any business touching her husband's papers, and he would certainly be feeling discomfort based upon her political affiliations. Well, if matters went downhill, she supposed she could always remind him of the baby and escape a reproach.

He walked forward, still smiling in that reserved way. He stopped beside her, picked up the paper, and said softly, cordially, "What have you been doing?"

She waited on tenterhooks while he looked at it and read. Then at the end, he lifted his head. He studied her for a long moment seriously. "Shannon, this... You have a gift."

Her heart leapt. "It was good as it was, I just—"

"Made it into one of the most moving speeches I have ever read," he said, kneeling beside her and reaching for her hand. He made a survey of her, as though finding her unsearchable. "Shannon, what I have just read is an impassioned plea for the rights and safety of the colored man."

Looking into his eyes, she said, "Well, it is what you believe, isn't it?"

"It is, precisely. And I won't ask you if it's what you believe—"

"I want to assist you, John Thomas. And I can, you know."

He kissed both of her hands in turn, not speaking, seemingly moved. Finally, after a time, he said, voice scraping, "Bed?"

"Yes, I'm tired."

He nodded, still studying her. She rose, walking toward the screen to find her nightgown, but stopping and saying over her shoulder, "And it is what I believe, John Thomas."

She went behind the screen, and it was only a matter of moments before he followed her there, as she had known he would. He assisted her and then turned her in his arms, kissing her poignantly.

The end of winter passed pleasantly. The cold lasted longer than in South Carolina, but there had been some glimpses of spring. John Thomas was gone only rarely, and Shannon had constant connection with the Haleys while he was away. Charles had even begun to take his first tentative steps with a cane, and Lizzie, relentless as she was, had begun to break him of his addiction before, they hoped, it had truly begun to damage his vital organs.

Shannon was quite near her lying in, and John Thomas took excellent care of her, treating her with the utmost tenderness. She had requested he play with Benjamin on the lawn since she was not able. She watched them from her window as they played. Their boy was toddling of his own accord. He even attempted a run, though that landed him on his bottom and had his laughing papa dusting him off before kissing his cheek and sending him on his way again.

Shannon, the curtain clenched in her hand, covered her middle and wiped away a tear.

John Thomas entered the house, planning to go up and check on Shannon. He felt she would have awakened from her nap, and he was trying to stay close to her. Something was troubling her, making her sad and, occasionally, he believed, desolate.

It could be her condition, or perhaps she was afraid of the birth. Their doctor hadn't given her any hope that the child she now carried would be smaller than Benjamin had been, but he *had* said that the second was always easier than the first. And she had seemed to take that in her stride in any event.

He knocked on her door softly and then opened it to see her looking out the window, seemingly in a state of despondency. Her posture appeared vulnerable as though she felt entirely alone in the world. His breath hitching, he pondered anew what it could be: the scandal in Washington? But her original method of silencing the gossip had worked beautifully, and that was long behind them. Did she want Elizabeth with her for the birth? Did she have dreadful fears given that it was her second, like Marie?

"Darling," he said, going forward to her chair and

kneeling at her feet. He looked at her in great consternation. "What is it? Why do you look so?"

She hesitated for a moment. He couldn't think why, but her demeanor reminded him of how she had been on the ship. Hesitant, uncertain of her ground with him. He thought she would speak, but she pressed her lips together. Finally, she said, "It is only the baby making me melancholy—my condition, I mean."

"Shannon, my family hasn't..."

She lifted her brows mildly. "No, they have been lovely to me."

"And you know that I adore you."

She smiled. "I have ample proof of that," she answered, touching his face.

He smiled, leaning in to kiss her.

John Thomas took a long ride a few days later. Something was off in his marriage, and the thought sickened him. He racked his brains, thinking and praying, the pastures of his childhood haunts bringing him some degree of comfort.

Finally, just as the sun was starting to fade slightly, he took his horse to the stables, handing his reins off to the groom.

"Do you want me to wash him, sir?"

"Yes, thank you, Jed," he said softly. "I shan't need him again today."

He walked up toward the house, turning the knob and

entering. When he closed the door behind him, he paused for a moment in the foyer before he saw Shannon come out of the library, her hand against her back, the other cradling her middle. "There you are," she said.

He smiled gently at her. "Have you been looking for me, love?"

She sucked in a breath, closing her eyes.

"Shannon!" he exclaimed, crossing the foyer.

Inhaling shakily as she recovered, Shannon looked up at him. "That was what I was going to tell you. Don't worry, your mother and sisters are on their way, and the doctor."

"Why didn't you send for me?" he demanded.

"Because labor takes so long." She smiled up at him. "Or at least...the first one did."

His eyes widening, he took her arms in his hands. "You think it will be soon?"

"Yes," she admitted finally.

He swept her up into his arms, his pulse hammering in his throat. "Rebecca!" he called. "Have you told her yet?"

"No," she admitted again.

"Shannon, you foolish darling!" he said, taking the stairs, trying to retain his senses. "Rebecca!"

She came out into the foyer, and he looked down from the landing. "Mrs. Haley is in labor. Prepare everything, please—quickly!"

Rebecca looked at Shannon, who was closing her eyes in pain. Anxiety entered Shannon's maid's eyes, and she hurried off immediately. John Thomas took Shannon into their bedroom, where he gently lay her on the bed, stroking her arms. "Do you think they will make it in time?"

"Yes, oh, yes, I didn't mean to imply otherwise. I don't believe you will have to deliver your own child today," she said, attempting a smile.

"It makes no difference, my darling. I would if I had to."

"I know you would," she said, closing her eyes as tears seeped out.

"Shannon!" he exclaimed. "Is it very dreadful?" He pressed his fist to his mouth.

"Yes," she whispered. "No. I'm sorry, I...It isn't so bad."

"You may scream enough to bring the rafters down if you choose, my sweet girl," he said, leaning forward to kiss her forehead, fear making his chest pound. How had his father done this eight times? After she had gasped through her next pains, he took her hands in his, pressing them and meeting her eyes, smiling in support. She held his eyes, and then she nodded, leaning to accept his kiss as he heard the door open below and the sound of his mother's voice.

John Thomas held in his arms a feminine copy of Benjamin, with full, fair hair, his own eyes, and a dainty little chin. He looked up at Shannon in the candlelight, shaking his head in wonder, blinking to try to clear his eyes. "My heart is lost anew."

"And mine," she agreed, unable to take her eyes from her.

"Shannon, your children are beautiful," he whispered.

She smiled. "Thank you. I should be flattered were they not precise images of their father."

He looked up. "She might still have the Ravenel temperament. One can never tell."

"Oh, no," she countered, shaking her head. "She hasn't yet demanded anything or been insulted. She will be like her Aunt Lizzie, who delivered her."

He shuddered, shaking his head, eyes soaking Shannon in. "Shannon, when I think that your father would cut me to bits—"

"Because the doctor was waylaid at a cross-birth, and the other doctor nearby had fallen from his horse and broken his own leg?"

"It was agony, Shannon," he croaked. "With every new report."

She smiled at him sleepily, reaching up to tuck their daughter's hand back into her blanket. "We have covered this ground already, my dear sir. Lizzie is perfectly capable."

He nodded. Finally, he dropped a kiss on their daughter's forehead and lay the little bundle back in Shannon's arms. He sat next to her, supporting her weak arms with his beneath and kissing her hair.

"Would you like to name her?" she whispered, pressing her eyes closed. Tears seeped out the corners of her eyes as he lingered in the kiss.

"Oh, no," he rasped. It was almost as though he sensed her distress, heightened as it was, however strangely, by the bliss in her arms. "You have more than earned the right, Shannon."

"Well, I do have a name," she said, biting her lip tentatively.

"Yes? Anything."

She looked back down at the baby's face as she tucked her blanket more securely. She was beautiful to Shannon. A healthy, perfect daughter who made her heart glad—who made her want to sing. "Phoebe Louise."

His lips parted, and he nodded in sweet agreement. "Yes," he whispered, voice breaking. His eyes misted. "I agree entirely."

"That is settled then," Shannon said, looking down at her precious daughter as tears welled in her eyes again.

Phoebe did indeed prove to be of a quiet temperament. Shannon and John Thomas watched her sleep for hours in her little swinging cradle. John Thomas had endured a well-meaning reprimand from their minister, who had heard that he had given his daughter a pagan name. A goddess, or some such thing. One must stay grounded, he warned, whatever one's fame and accomplishments. Happily, John Thomas had remembered that the name had been mentioned in the Bible, a fact which calmed the man's nerves considerably.

When Phoebe was a month old, her papa needed to return to the capital. They agreed that Shannon would bring the children and join him there when Phoebe was three months old. This would be long enough to ensure that she would be stronger, and that she and her mama would be fit for travel.

As he kissed the children in the foyer of Beacon Hill, Shannon feared he was close to emotion, which would, of course, leave her in a puddle. She held Benjamin's hand with Phoebe bundled in her other arm while he catalogued the children's every feature.

"Just two months," she whispered.

"Yes," he agreed, as though fortifying himself. He bent, kissing her forehead and searching her face. "Take care of yourself, my love."

"And you," she said, swallowing with difficulty.

# Chapter Twenty-Seven

Washington City was just as he had left it. Despite the dramatics and intrigues and the fact that he had been elected to one of the most difficult Congresses the nation had ever known, John Thomas enjoyed his new position. And he thought Shannon rather liked hers, too.

Or she had. He sat in his study late one night thinking of her and their children at home, and he was so lonely for his little family that his chest almost physically ached. Since Shannon had returned to him, there had been such a peace about her that, strange as it might sound, and as many as their difficulties, he had never truly feared that she might repeat her actions and leave him. But recently, there had been a general discomfort in the pit of his stomach, some knowledge that he could neither know her fully nor make her happy giving him an inexplicable dread.

Shannon fretfully fanned Phoebe. The day was warm, and the sun bore down hard. She looked for John Thomas, tamping down her frustration. Word of her travel plans seemed always to leak out, and she could scarcely see through the thick flock of reporters and spectators.

"Ginny, do you think he is too warm?" Shannon asked, reaching up to secure the tie of Benjamin's cap more firmly.

"No, ma'am, he's just wanting his dinner."

Shannon finally spied her husband as he emerged through the crowd.

She was taken aback when she saw him, for he looked years older and far thinner. Good heavens, how was this possible in a month! He was also looking cautious where she was concerned. He leaned to kiss her cheek, even though he usually gave the reporters something to speak of by kissing her mouth. "My love," he said, though it was difficult to hear above the spectators. "There is a carriage for the children and servants, and I have brought another for us, if that is agreeable?"

"Yes, I... Yes," she answered, studying him.

He helped the women and children into the carriage and sent them off before taking her to an open phaeton, into which he handed her up. He looked at her lovingly but with sadness. He got in behind her, and she gasped as a thought occurred to her, saying in terror, "You have been taken ill with consumption!"

He looked down at her, brows drawing together. Finally, realization hit, and he said, maneuvering through the street, "I suppose I... Yes, I suppose I have looked better." He looked at her, and then away. "But no, I am well."

"What is it?" she breathed.

"Shannon, I..." His face was ashen. "I can't bear it any longer. Please tell me."

Shannon felt her heart sinking as his words settled around her. Now, it seemed, was the moment of truth, the reckoning. Her memory took her back to that evening when Benjamin had made them laugh. John Thomas's arm around her as they sat in the floor of the parlor. The dread in his eyes. "Do you mean...why I am unhappy?"

He looked at her, as deeply sensitive to her every word, as cautious, as he had been the day she had arrived on the ship. He nodded, her admission of unhappiness seeming to sink him.

"Because *you* are unhappy," she said so softly that he almost didn't hear.

His lips parted. He righted the horses, who had grown jumpy under his startled hands, and he looked at her in confusion. "What on earth—?"

"That night, when Benjamin made the soot fall down on him, and he only wiped it away calmly... The look in your eyes when we finished laughing..." A tear rolled down her cheek. "I shall never recover from it as long as I live."

He stared at her. It took only a moment, it seemed, for comprehension to dawn, and then his eyes flickered with what she could only term as acknowledgement. He looked guilty and then turned his head away.

She shook her head. "You should have married her," she declared.

He looked back at her suddenly. "Who?"

"The Congregationalist wife I always envisioned for you."

"I don't know of whom you are speaking, and I never wanted any Congregationalist wife. Present company excepted, of course."

She swallowed. "Just...tell me, John Thomas. From the myriad of things I have put you through, which is it that your heart can't forgive—though your head has done what is right?"

He looked at her, face more pallid if possible, and he reached quickly to touch her arm. He had opened his mouth to speak when she saw standing on the sidewalk a man in a top hat lifting a pistol and aiming it directly for John Thomas's heart. She did not think. She could not hear; she could not see. There was only blind, instinctual motion, and she heard the report of the gun. She did remember that, though it sounded a thousand miles away.

The next thing she heard was screams, and she felt a thud shaking her whole body. She came to awareness slowly, it seemed, and then reality returned fully, the world in its usual color and noises. She felt that she still had a grasp on John Thomas's coat. Oh, dear God, was this how Mary Lincoln had felt?

"John Thomas!" she screamed, seeing men and women and soldiers racing toward them.

"Shannon, are you all right?" he demanded frantically, gasping for air. The breath had been knocked out of him, but he managed to grasp her head between his hands. "Shannon!"

And that was when she realized: they were on the ground, and her husband wasn't dead. She looked around her, trying to orient herself, and comprehended that she was on top of him, and that she had, somehow, bodily lifted him from the carriage and thrown him to the ground before covering him.

"Shannon?" he demanded, attempting to scramble up.

"I am well. Yes, I am well," she breathed.

His lip trembled. "My darling. Oh, my darling."

"You will defy me in this way?"

Shannon paced their green parlor, her slippers soon to make worn spots on the plush carpet.

"Shannon, for heaven sakes, I am the husband," John Thomas protested feebly, while he sat with eyes following her.

"You intend to stay in Washington despite my *strong desire* for you to leave?"

"Shannon, we are of one mind that there is no question that you and the children must return to Massachusetts. But I cannot lea—"

"Stubbornness. Blatant, blind stubbornness—"

"Shannon, the investigation is still incomplete. They have not apprehended the would-be assassin. I cannot leave."

She stopped, stomping her foot. "You are John Thomas Haley. You may do as you please."

"Very well, I feel that it would be wrong to do so."

"Much comfort your piety will bring us when you are cold in your grave!" she threw at him.

"Shannon. My darling. You cannot truly expect me to give up all of my causes, all of my work. That was what they intended: intimidation or death. Either will cover injustice in silence. Are we to give the country over to such people? What will be left for Benjamin and Phoebe of America if I tuck my tail and run home?" he demanded.

"What will be left of our world if we lose you?" she returned.

"Shannon," he said more gently. "It was one man who is now on the run—"

"It may be a conspiracy. We have yet no notion!"

"Very well then," he responded quietly. "Suppose it is. I have been at war. I am not frightened."

"Well, I *am* frightened."

Crossing the room to her, he touched her thin shoulders, eyes meeting hers earnestly. "My darling, I know. And I *know* this was in response to the speech I gave on the Senate floor last week. Tensions are high just now because of the proposed Amendments, but they won't be forever. The counsel of cooler heads will prevail. I will come to you as soon as possible. And you and our little ones will be able to join me here again soon."

"Do not touch me," she said in disgust, pushing his hands from her. "And do *not* delude yourself that we have reached this agreement together. I will take the children home. But if you stay in Washington, it will be against my will. And if my children are forced to be raised without their father, it will be on your head, and not my own."

Which would be a rather fine way to end things if an assassin's bullet did find him, Shannon reflected as the train bore her and the children north. At least he would have armed guards with him at all times. There was little else to comfort her.

She had demanded a copy of his speech and had just finished reading it. She was stunned at his audacity in confronting the Ku Klux Klan and putting a number on the Negros who had been killed since the war's end. Thousands. She had no notion. He did more than speculate on who made up their members, too. He used direct reports, that calm and peaceful man, who might as well be a wild-eyed zealot.

When she had demanded to know who his source was, he had shaken his head. When she had demanded the fourth time, he had whispered a name in her ear that had stunned her. *Frederick Ravenel.* It seemed that her brother believed that the insurgency would threaten the stability of the South, inviting Federal control in ever-increasing ways. And he was fiercely loyal to John Thomas; there was very little they wouldn't do for one another. She supposed they imagined no one would ever suspect him. Yet, if they did, they would have his head, too.

She took a deep breath, shaking her head, accepting that the men in her life were determined to put her in an early grave from worry. She couldn't have been born among or married into a peaceful family. No! Zealots, the lot of them. Pioneering, crusading fanatics who held so firmly to their causes that nothing would turn them from them. It took her recollecting that she was just the same regarding her own passions for her to forgive them. Only, for once, *finally*, she and John Thomas were in unison of beliefs.

She looked out the window, thinking of their cold parting. Shannon and the children had been forced to leave so quickly, and with the military and police buzzing around their house at all hours, they hadn't been able to speak to each other. Only, he had looked at her occasionally with a certain frantic look. But every time he would open his lips to speak, they had been interrupted.

Shannon awakened on her first night at Beacon Hill, breathing in the cold New England air that was beginning to feel natural. She reached for John Thomas's fob watch and lit her taper to see that it was two o'clock in the morning.

She stood, heart thrumming, certain something had awakened her. Another noise sounded, so she crossed the room and pulled the bell. A nervous feeling she couldn't explain settled in the pit of her stomach.

She looked out but could not see anything in the darkened, frosty night. Then...perhaps she did. At the edge of the field, she may have seen a figure retreating and possibly a torch.

Rebecca came in response to the bell, saying uneasily, "What is it, Miss Shannon?"

"Rebecca, come with me. Perhaps it was nothing, or maybe a tenant, or an animal. But I heard something," she said, drawing on her dressing gown and heading for her chamber door. She and Rebecca took the stairs, going down into the foyer. By then, the butler and the footman had come from their quarters.

"I'll open the door, Mrs. Haley," Simons said. "And we'll see what we can see."

"Yes, all right," she responded, standing with Rebecca, a nervous foreboding filling her. Shannon had known violence all of her life. She could detect the scent of it. And she smelled it now.

They caught a flash of light as they stepped out. And Shannon slowly straightened. Her blood turned to ice as she saw on the lawn of Beacon Hill three massive burning crosses.

"Our coats, Rebecca," Shannon said, voice trembling as she swayed with the crying Phoebe against her shoulder. Ginny held Benjamin, who was sleeping.

In moments, Rebecca hastily put Shannon's coat around her shoulders while Simons and the footmen stood guard outside with John Thomas's hunting rifles.

Jeptha and Rebecca hastened with their own coats. Shannon would need their assistance, and she feared the two of them were not safe here with it being known that this was John Thomas's home. She could not leave them. If the vigilantes had come this far north… She shuddered.

Neither could she leave a note or tell anyone, even the servants for their own safety, where they were going. What they had just witnessed was their first warning—that was what they were termed. The second might be to tie the servants up and burn the house down. And Shannon had no idea how widespread the threat was, but she now knew how serious. She must take the children to safety, and that meant into hiding.

"Senator Haley will be…terrified," Jeptha said, looking like she intended to balk at the plan, This reaction made Rebecca's eyes flit between Shannon and Jeptha apprehensively.

"We have no choice," Shannon said simply. She kissed Phoebe's soft cheek, the surge of love so powerful within her that she could have taken on those men with her bare hands.

"Well, it's not right." Jeptha, having no concept of submission, said these words firmly.

"I cannot risk a note being intercepted," Shannon argued.

"You might leave a note for him here…" she suggested.

Releasing her breath, Shannon said, "Jeptha, do you remember why General Jackson was so successful in his campaigns? Stonewall?" She saw recognition strike a chord in the other woman's eyes and continued. "Absolute secrecy. He told not even his nearest commanders his plans of battle until they were already on the field. Well, this is my campaign.

It may be unnecessary, but I will do anything to protect the children. I do not know if this action tonight was intended only to bring Senator Haley to his knees, or to let us know that his wife and children are not immune from the threat he himself has faced. But I do not intend to wait and find out."

Jeptha nodded, her large, brown eyes holding a rather steely resolve. Excellent woman.

Simons cleared his throat. "Indeed, ma'am. What shall I tell him?" he asked, meeting Shannon's eyes.

Shannon paused, knowing it to be another gamble, especially given their recent troubles. Unresolved feelings, his own unhappiness, and that terrible argument in which her tongue had gotten away from her could so easily toss them again into the abyss. And yet, holding Simon's eyes, she said, feeling as certain as anything in her life, "He will know where I am. And he will come for me."

John Thomas rode onto the grounds of Beacon Hill late in the afternoon just as the light was starting to wane. He handed off his reins and walked up the steps, eager to mend things with Shannon—to tell her that she was right. He was a fool not to have acknowledged it before. He was good to no one dead, especially to his family, whom he supported with his salary.

The little ones would be asleep in their nursery. He could picture them: Benjamin in his crib, his rosy cheek against the pillow, Phoebe lying limply in her cradle, a thatch of her pale hair peeking beneath her little cap. But perhaps Shannon would be awake, reading by the fire in their bedchamber, her lengthening red hair brushed and hanging about her shoulders. His blood quickened, and he smiled to think he had once upon a time felt guilty for such thoughts, although his knowledge that Frederick would once have struck him for them had likely contributed.

He noticed that Simons was reticent when he asked where Mrs. Haley was and, baffled, he turned to Joseph, the footman. "Where is my wife?"

When he couldn't get a straight answer, fear started to grow in the depth of his being, and, abandoning that method, he took the stairs two at a time. Something felt wrong. The house felt too quiet. Their children were always quiet, but surely the servants should be about their activities? His stomach churned with a familiar, unwelcome feeling.

Covering the hall in mere seconds, he opened Shannon's door. The chamber was empty. The fireplace was cold, even though there was a chill in the New England air. Various items of her things were missing.

His blood rushing, he strode down to the nursery, his riding boots making firm, swift thuds. He threw open the door, his breathing becoming more erratic.

Vacant. Entirely empty.

Shannon was gone. And she had taken Benjamin and Phoebe with her.

# Chapter Twenty-Eight

Shannon walked the grounds of Santarella. There wasn't much left, save the gardens, which had grown rather wild. Someone, likely Elizabeth, had recently tried to reclaim them, though, and preparations were well underway for planting in the spring. The flanker was being converted into a house in its own right, and the irrigation systems were being repaired for the rice.

Some of the old slave cabins remained, and the share-croppers (some of whose families had been enslaved at San-tarella for close to two-hundred years) had been living in them. Shannon didn't know how these men and women felt about her family's lands being returned to them. But she would imagine it meant something very different for them than for the Ravenels.

Frederick's son had been born the past week at Santar-ella, and the house was full of Elizabeth's family and their own. And Miss Reed.

Shannon wrapped her shawl around herself more securely, ashamed of her fine clothes when Elizabeth hadn't had a new dress in years. But Elizabeth had something far more precious than riches, as she well knew, in her son. And in Rose Marie.

Shannon's father would scold her for walking alone, but he likely wouldn't have noticed her absence yet, intent as he was upon spoiling his grandchildren.

Her family had been delighted and terrified when she had turned up with no warning. Her recounting of the assassination attempt and subsequent warning seemed to make Frederick wish to seek vengeance. The deadly sparks in her father's and brother's eyes as the three of them had dined together had made her hasten to say that she was certain the perpetrators would be apprehended.

Her father had asked, for clarification purposes, whether she had left her husband? She had not, she answered. Well, that was, he didn't know where she was, but she hadn't left him in the sense he meant. The steady way he regarded her made it plainly obvious that he felt himself cursed as a father.

Perhaps she had been wrong to do it. Doubts assaulted her more with every passing day. She missed John Thomas intensely and worried for him constantly. What if he had been attacked? What if she had been wrong, and he couldn't find her? To say nothing of whether he thought she had abandoned him, a thought which chilled her.

She knew it was terrible to leave him in the dark. But the possibility of her whereabouts being found if she committed them to paper (or her servants being attacked if she had told them) had haunted her. Perhaps she hadn't been thinking rationally. Or perhaps she had. She had only been blindly protecting her children. The thought that they might have a price on their heads still nauseated her and made her deeply grateful for the isolation of Santarella. That was why she had come. She knew of nowhere more difficult to approach than the Sea Islands.

She walked on for a long while. When she finally looked up, a sound breaking her thoughts, she saw a rider. She recognized that posture, those long legs, those boots, and her breath caught. Lifting her hand to her trembling lips, she waited, not taking her eyes from him. A boy ran out, and he handed the reins off to him, giving the child a coin.

She blinked moisture away rapidly and continued looking at him. He spotted her from afar and, pausing for a moment as he looked at her, he started for her among the weeds. Swallowing, she touched her throat and whispered as he grew closer, "I knew. I knew you could not misunderstand."

He stopped before her. "Simons told me," he said. "About the warning." He seemed to shudder inwardly.

"You did not think..."

He still stood a few feet away, long and lean, and not much the worse for his thousand-mile trip, though he was still looking generally haggard. "No," he whispered. "Only for a moment of insanity. And then I remembered that the leaving had been undertaken by the same person who had saved my life, wrestled me from a bullet's clutches with inhuman strength, and I..." His voice quivered, and he looked away. "I decided that I was not wrong to marry her, after all," he said, looking back, smiling tentatively.

She gave a tiny smile in return. "I only meant..." She bit her lip. "That is, the thought of your unhappiness... I would do anything to spare you that, my darling."

"I know," he rasped.

She took a step closer. "And I have been considering the matter while I bided my time here. I realized that, complex as you are, you have a very rare sort of complexity, like the Biblical statement '*God is love*,' which is only difficult in its simplicity. Your heart desired an explanation, and I never gave it to you. Or rather, you would never let me." He swallowed, holding her eyes. "It is the greatest flaw in Yankees that I have yet found. You let things fester until they cause an explosion. You should have demanded an answer of me at once."

He closed his eyes briefly. "I know," he whispered. "But with what had happened to you, and then the baby, and your illness..." His voice trailed away. "The thing is, Shannon... You know I consider it my fault, what happened between us. But I suppose what has always tormented my soul, is..." He met her eyes. "How you could do it," he said gently. "I couldn't have, no matter what tried to drag me away from you. It is simply impossible. You are flesh of my flesh. And when you told me before you left me so long ago...that night we made love," he said, voice lowering, "that it was enough—that *I* was enough... I believed you. And I still do," he whispered in confusion.

She stepped forward, tears in her eyes, and tentatively reached up to touch his fair hair, relishing the very reality of it. He didn't flinch, which she took as a promising sign. "I didn't leave you because I didn't love you enough, my darling," she whispered. "I could tell you things that..." Her voice faltered.

"Tell me," he said, watching her intensely.

She gathered herself. "Yes. But you must promise not to pity me, or grow despondent, or allow yourself to fill with anger." She moistened her lips as he began to look anxious. "The night you...accused me, I...had thought I was with child." His lips parted.

"Shortly after you left, I realized that I wasn't and never had been... Something within me broke," she whispered. "And when I am lectured, I..." She looked up, meeting his eyes bravely. "The school where I was brought up... The disciplinary measures taken were—severe. Never whips—that might've caused bruising, and bruising you cannot hide. But there are other methods. Shaking. Peer-shaming. Starvation. For so long. And they did other things to me, too." He brushed a hand over his mouth, which was set in lines of anguish. "I know to any other woman it might have been just an argument, but they had shattered something within me. I wasn't whole, and you couldn't make me whole, though Heaven knows if anyone could... It required the Father above to do that. And so, when I saw your skepticism and heard your blame, I didn't hear it rationally. To me, it sounded as though you no longer loved me. And that broke me. I was determined to leave you before you left me. That is the plain truth of it. And if you utter the words *forgive me* to me, I *shan't* forgive you for that, for how could you have known? I told you nothing. I didn't even know how to give myself to you. I believe you know that I didn't. Not fully."

"I could have made it possible for you to have told me," he rasped.

"Perhaps the first part. But not the second."

He studied her with tears in his eyes. He didn't appear capable of speaking for several minutes. And then finally he said, "Shannon, if I could convey to you even a tenth of how much I love you..."

And that was what broke her façade of calm; she collapsed against him, saying desperately, "You don't have to convey anything to me. You have done it with every look, every word, every thought since the moment I saw you, whether we were together or separated, in discord or in harmony, at war or in peace."

He kissed her as passionately, every bit as passionately, as he had that night on the balcony of Santarella when he was just her brother's friend, and they had been caught up in the inexplicable tide, the unexpected beauty, of love.

He braced her head between his hands, closing his eyes, savoring her. After a long time, he said, "We'll stay at Santarella until tempers cool. And then we'll stand and fight," he whispered. "Together."

She looked up at him, her eyes swimming with tears. Nothing had ever sounded so beautiful to her ears. She had never imagined this kind of understanding and peace between them. She had never thought, when she had returned to him, nearly quaking, that their rift could be healed. That the broken things could be mended. But in the end, there was nothing lost that might not be found, if sought.

# Chapter Twenty-Nine

The Rav-4 was loaded up and waiting, the car seat sitting in the hall of Ravenel-Thompson House with its precious cargo. Adeline stood outside in her old jeans and a pale blue sweater. She'd already kissed Jude, feeling like her heart was ripping out, and his dad had made him go back inside since there was a cold wind blowing off the bay. She looked around, out to The Battery, where brave sea birds landed, and down the sweeping view of all the grand houses.

Then Adrian came out carrying the car seat, casually dressed since it was Saturday. He turned the little prince backwards and made sure everything was strapped in. He paused a moment to linger on his face and finally, to kiss his little cheek. Adeline's eyes burned.

He turned back, looking at her. "Adeline, are you sure you wouldn't rather leave him here? It's going to be hard, travelling with him."

It was, but he didn't understand. *I'm already having to part from you and Jude.* "I don't think I could bear it, Adrian," she whispered.

He looked very remote, but she saw the layer of vulnerability beneath it that she would've missed not long ago. He was bracing himself.

In things spoken, there was no reason to. But she thought he knew she was trying to figure some stuff out. He also knew that it would be easier to stay in North Carolina once she was actually there.

"I understand that," he said softly.

Of course he did. She was already beating herself up for taking Emory away from him, for however short a time. She swallowed, hands in her back pockets.

He didn't move forward to kiss her or hug her. Maybe he didn't feel like he could.

She needed to go. She was going to have a breakdown. She almost had while she was packing. The smell of his cologne had been lingering in their room. It brought back a lot of memories. Precious memories.

"You need to get on the road if you're going to get there before dark," he said, clearing his throat, taking one last look toward the backseat.

She nodded. "I'll text you when we get there safely."

He nodded, holding her eyes for a long moment. She bit her lip and went to get in the car. He closed the door for her and then stood back, waving once as she drove down the driveway. Away. Leaving him there in Charleston.

Adeline cried all the way into North Carolina. Plus, Emory was a bit...difficult. Adrian had sort of had a look on his face when she had flippantly said, "*I think he'll be ready to travel by one month.*" Now she understood. She texted Adrian and then fell into bed at the hotel room, exhausted physically and emotionally.

She spent the next two days mired in paperwork with Janice. Luckily, her mom drove out and helped with Baby Boy one day. She had a lot of thinking to do and found herself driving out to Asheville that day to look at Carrington Place. To get her bid together. *What am I doing?*

The right thing.

*Nothing is certain yet.*

The place's pull was as strong as ever. It was a dream job. Who knew? She might even get some enthusiasm at some point.

She drove back to Charlotte, met up with her mom and Janice (and Emory, of course) for supper, and then took Emory back to the hotel after her mom left for Asheville.

She got her shower, washed the baby, and curled up on the plush bed. She picked up her phone, and before she knew it, she was dialing Adrian. *What am I doing?* They had texted several times, and she had sent lots of pictures, but she hadn't heard his voice in four days.

He picked up on the third ring. "Hello?"

She released a breath. "Hey."

"Hey." His voice was warm, sleepy.

Adeline adjusted Emory on his blanket where he was kicking in the air, rooting his little blue socks off. "How's it going?"

"It's going. You?"

"Yeah." She looked down at his mini-me. "I bet you would like me to video chat."

He gave a soft laugh. "Yeah."

She hit the button, and when he accepted, she said, "I'll turn it around." He had a full view of Emory then, who could be described more as feisty than zen tonight.

"Hey, buddy," he said. One corner of his mouth slid up. "I love it when you do his hair like that."

It was so long that she sometimes did a mohawk after bath time. "It suits him. His facial structure demands it."

He laughed, eyes roving the screen. She ached inside. He was sitting on his bed in a T-shirt and glasses, leaning against the headboard, looking tired and like he had maybe been reading. And desirable. *Is that what this is about, Adeline?* It had always clouded things so much. But no. Not anymore. Not after everything.

"How's he been doing?"

"Pretty good. He was a little fussy today, but I suppose that's his prerogative. How... How's Jude?"

"Good. He's good," he said. There was something in his voice that indicated he was feeling pretty good about Jude. Maybe he'd met some new milestone. And she wasn't there. "He misses the two of you." A pause. "We both do."

"We miss you, too," she said quietly, throat clogged.

Emory started fussing, saved her right before she made an idiot of herself. "I should…"

"Yeah." He paused. "Take care of yourself, Adeline."

He'd been taking care of her for so long now that she barely knew how. "Yeah. You, too. Night."

"Night."

She hung up and worked for the next fifteen minutes getting the baby settled in his portable bed beside hers. He finally dropped off unwillingly, and she looked around for a distraction. She needed something, anything.

The folder. Hadn't Virginia said something about a folder? Documents—historical documents were always like a cold bucket of water over the head. She got up and pulled the folder out of her bag, going back to the bed and turning the lamp up a notch.

She opened it, flipping through the first few pages, not all that interested in the price of cigars during the years of Grant's presidency or which horse was best to bet on. Then she saw a letter in an odd hand, one she had never seen before. It was beautiful, yet masculine, and she quickly scanned down. It was signed simply, *JT*.

She brushed her thumb over it. What did that kind of intimacy feel like?

She scanned up to the top, but it wasn't dated. She'd have to assume it was some time after the war.

*My Darling Wife,*

*That I regret our separation, even if for two weeks, goes without saying. But I will say it anyway. I miss you with a physical ache. We have been separated so much that it must be against the laws of nature, and I never wished to spend another day parted from you. But so it must be this time, and I hope you are taking care of yourself, my darling.*

*All is well in Washington, and our business should conclude by the 27th, etc.*

*By now you will have seen the enclosed item. I stumbled upon the jeweler's shop I first found when I was a lovesick boy, how young in experience I don't care to remember. And because I know you will ask: I am still lovesick. I hope the necklace is an exact replica of the one we have never been able to find. It brought back a hundred dear memories, and, yes, some painful memories, too. I know we don't often speak of that time, but I thank God that He, in His Providence, gave me a second chance to love you.*

*When you speak of running, you recall fear. Fear that you were not the wife I needed, that you were not making me happy, that I no longer loved you. It often baffles me that you could be afraid of anything*

if you could pass through enemy lines, which no man
I know of has ever survived, except under a flag of
truce. But fear is strange, isn't it? Bravery is only
relative. In running from something which frightened
you, you, with great courage, ran headlong into
something far more dangerous.

It makes me think of when we fell in love. We were
foolish, I suppose, not to see the obstacles ahead.
Or to ignore them. But we were never frightened.
Maybe only youth can capture that kind of laughing
indifference to destiny.

And yet, I was more frightened in the middle of the
fiercest Naval battle known to this country, with a
hundred cannons firing, of the knowledge that you
had left, and that I might never see you again, than
of any of the torture that raged around me.

You are, and have always been, my northernmost
star, Shannon, and my heart points ever toward you.

JT

# Chapter Thirty

Adeline crossed onto the bridge into the Holy City in the afternoon. The sky was overcast, but it was supposed to hold off raining until the evening. She tried to ignore the flightiness of her pulse, attempting to prepare mentally, like a test, for the conversation ahead. But once she'd navigated through the streets of downtown Charleston to The Battery, she found Jane babysitting, unusual since it was Saturday. Apparently, Adrian had gone down to the wharf to do something on Harris's sailboat for him.

She took a shaky breath, afraid she'd lose her nerve. But she deposited Emory with Jane, who was looking at her a certain way. She went back to her car, swallowing her nerves as she got in. And then she headed back toward the wharf. She found it by all of the white sails standing like a fortress against the gray sky.

She scanned the horizon for Harris's boat, not an easy

task, and finally thought she located it. She was walking down the weathered gangplank when a tall, thin figure who carried himself a certain way emerged from one of the boats—one foot on the dock, the other still on the steps.

He stilled. "Adeline." There was surprise in his voice, almost like he was thinking she might be a mirage. Fear flared in his eyes for a second, and she said, hoping her massive vulnerability wasn't too obvious, "It...It's okay. Nothing's wrong."

The fear receded, and, after another second of looking at her, he climbed up onto the dock and stopped a couple of feet from her. This time he was looking at her in a different way. She had really gotten her body back in the past week. He didn't say so, of course. But he noticed all the same.

"Did you just drive in, or..." His hand left the rail.

"Yeah, just now," she said. Her heart was racing again. She kind of felt like she might fall over the side, but no biggie.

He looked down, gaze touching all of her features. He was studying her, trying to read her. "You okay?" he asked softly.

"I..." She tried to think but couldn't with her thoughts in such a swirl. "I...no. I wasn't very, or at least, completely, honest with you when I went to Charlotte. I think you know I needed to think."

There was the slightest nod. "Have you?" he asked softly. Fear was present in his eyes again, a deep kind that he didn't try to hide.

"Yeah." She tucked her hair behind her ear to keep it from hitting her face. "I just... And you may not feel the same, but I think we need to talk."

"I definitely feel the same," he said immediately. His eyes never left her face.

She crossed her arms—protective gesture or normal human response to wind?

He took a step forward, reaching up and cradling her cheek in his hand. He must've seen she was fighting for dear life over here. She looked up, meeting his eyes. "If it's... I mean, there was so much we never talked about, but..." She reached up, covering his hand, looking into his beloved face. "But I want..." Her voice failed her.

"What do you want?" he asked softly.

Her eyes filled. "I want this—you—us."

His hand didn't leave her face. There was a long silence while the wind blew lightly, tousling their hair. He stared at her. With what emotions she couldn't say, but she would've dearly loved to have known. "That's not what I thought you were going to say," he breathed, slipping his eyes closed for a second, almost painfully. The ordeal he had gone through in the past minute was testament to how off-base she had been when she had left. She reached up and touched his face, couldn't keep her hands away, not when he was in emotional turmoil. "Adrian," she whispered, tears streaking down her cheeks.

"I was this close to coming up there and getting you," he said.

"I'm sorry. So sorry," she whispered. "Why didn't you?"

"I wanted the decision to be your own. I could've said some things that would make you stay, but... I wanted you to want to stay."

"Because I love you?" she whispered, barely audibly.

He nodded once, slightly, vulnerably. He stepped up, the look in his eyes passionate, not calm, collected Adrian. He pulled her against him, her head against his chest. "And because you belong with *me*," he said forcefully. "I can't put it into words, how much I love you, Adeline, but I should've tried. I was afraid to scare you. But these last few months have been torture."

She looked up, entirely stunned. She was bereft of words. Not that she hadn't already known he loved her and that he wanted her to stay. She was a fool for letting the voice of doubt tell her otherwise. And she had doubted *herself* more than anything. She was just like Shannon: running from her own happiness, running from the only man who knew how to love her properly.

"What, honey, is that so surprising?" he said, still looking kind of on the edge of emotion. "I've been in love with you ever since that morning—you know the one after we made a baby? A little bit before, but completely then. I'd never seen anyone handle herself with such grace. But that was before I watched you handle the pregnancy, and then slip into motherhood as naturally as if that were what God had designed you for, instead of restoring houses." He bit his lip, his eyes drifting across her face. "And being my wife," he whispered.

Her lip trembled. She couldn't speak, but she could let her eyes wash over his face without suppressing anything, without trying to convince herself she wasn't completely gone. "Oh, Adrian, are you sure? You're not supposed to fall in love under these circumstances."

"Who says?" He was smiling gently, his eyes twinkling through the moisture.

She bit her lip. She had been fascinated with him since the moment she had seen him. But there was no need for him to know that. "I've loved you since..." Oh, how could she describe it, the gradual growing, the spark that ignited and took hold, a thousand little moments and days spent watching, learning, falling? "Since you made me tacos and ate them."

He smiled, looking like he was having a hard time not laughing. She hoped she had conveyed the point, though: that he was absolutely the only one. That he brought every sense she had to life and made her better just by standing beside her. Her smile slipped away, and she had to work to control her emotions.

He got serious, too, studying her. "Did you...go to Carrington Place?"

She nodded. "Yeah. It has amazing potential." She paused. "I called Mr. Thierry." Adrian watched her. "I gave him the number of an excellent preservationist."

His lips parted. "Adeline, no," he protested hotly. "You can't do that. I'll move—whatever it takes—"

"No. Everything I love is in Charleston," she said. "And

I'm not leaving. There's plenty for me to do here. You know, besides being a mom." She smiled.

"To two lucky little boys," he said. He looked moved. He didn't say how much he appreciated the sacrifice, but he conveyed it just the same.

"What have you and Jude been up to?" she asked, voice nearly breaking.

His eyes didn't leave hers, but he seemed deep in thought. "We went to Savannah."

She lifted her brows. "Oh...?"

"Yeah." He swallowed.

Her eyes burned. Maybe leaving wasn't such a massive mistake. Maybe it had been one of those design-things, propelling him to come to terms with all that Savannah represented.

"I'll tell you about it someday," he said.

"Sounds good," she answered.

His eyes dropped to her lips, and her heart fluttered. He looked back up, as if not wanting to mess it up. But a kiss sounded absolutely perfect. She tilted her head, and her eyes fluttered closed as his lips brushed hers, feather soft.

"Adrian," she whispered, almost lost but needing to say this before she was completely overcome by the intoxication of his nearness.

"Yeah?" he asked, kissing her again.

She lost her train of thought but struggled back through the abyss. "Just so you know... When I said that I was in love with you... I probably should've added that all boundaries are off."

That took a second to register, but when it did, he lifted his head, an arrested expression in his eyes. He scanned her face. "All of them?"

"All of them," she affirmed, face flushing.

His lips slowly lifted. A couple of moments passed. "Well. It's going to be an interesting spring."

She bit her lip on a slight smile. "There's still some winter left, too," she said, as his head lowered again.

"Thank goodness."

THE END

# Author's Note

DEAR READER,

I wanted to let you know about a couple of historical liberties that I took in writing *Charleston Tides.* First, while the Year of Jubilee in Charleston happened roughly from February of 1865 through January of 1866 and included multiple festivals of freedom, the one which was actually attended by William Lloyd Garrison was in the spring of 1865 rather than the autumn. He made a speech during the flag-raising ceremony at Fort Sumter on April 14, 1865, the same day President Abraham Lincoln was assassinated. I simply adjusted the months to suit my plot timeline.

In addition, the first few years right after the Civil War would have constituted the Ku Klux Klan's first era, during which an insurgent movement arose to threaten freedmen and resist Reconstruction. During this era, "warnings" typically consisted of barn-burning or the burning of an outbuilding. It wasn't until the second era of the Klan that cross-burning was used. I decided to take historical license and depict a cross-burning because I wanted you to know instantly who had been to Beacon Hill and the message they were trying to send. If Shannon had poked her head out and seen her barn burning, we might have thought the hay had just caught on fire, and that would have been a bit confusing.

The more I learn about the Civil War and Reconstruction Eras, the more I am convinced of how difficult those times were and how deep the emotional stamina called for was.

I hope you have enjoyed Adeline's and Shannon's journeys. I am grateful for each of you who has followed them through to the last page. Your trust in picking up my books is something I never take lightly. Until next time, if you would like to read about the history behind the story of the *Torn Asunder Series*, or if you would like updates on my next project, I encourage you to visit www.TeaAndRebellion.com.

**TARA**

# Many thanks to...

M y sister, Hannah Cowan Jones, for being the plot doctor, who has been on-call 24-7 for a couple of years
now as I navigated the tricky aspects of this series.

My mom, for being able to spot a historical inaccuracy
a mile away.

My dad, for your support and for reading *Northern Fire*
three times.

Dana Womack, for teaching me how to dig deep with revisions.

Beverly Crouch, for your valuable narrative suggestions.

Tara Mayberry, for covers and interior formatting that made
my vision a reality.

I am so grateful to all of the above for your contributions and support. Any errors are entirely my own. This series was so much better because of your talents and knowledge.

Anything good in art is God expressing Himself uniquely through us. None of this would be possible without His inspiration and love.

TARA

# Discussion Questions

These discussion questions were crafted so that book clubs can use them as conversation pieces. Ready, set—discuss!

1. Were you surprised with the history of Charleston right after the war?

2. Why do you think Shannon and John Thomas, loving each other as they do, have such a difficult marriage?

3. What do you think set John Thomas and Shannon on the path to peace?

4. Which storyline did you prefer: modern or historical? Why?

5. What is it about Adrian and Adeline's relationship that makes it work, despite different personalities?

6. Did you have a favorite main character or side character? If so, what attracted you to that particular character?

7. What was your favorite moment from the series?

# Books by Tara Cowan

The Torn Asunder Series
*Southern Rain*
*Northern Fire*
*Charleston Tides*

# About the Author

TARA COWAN is the author of the Torn Asunder Series. A huge lover of all things history, she loves to travel, watch British dramas, read good fiction, and spend time with her family. An attorney, Tara lives in Tennessee and is busy writing her next novel.

Tara holds a Bachelor of Science Degree in Political Science with minors in English and History from Tennessee Tech University and a Doctor of Jurisprudence from the University of Tennessee College of Law.

To connect with Tara, visit her blog at
www.teaandrebellion.com,
follow her on Instagram @teaandrebellion_,
or find her on Facebook or Twitter.